MW00911117

SPIN DRY

Other works by Greg Hollingshead

Famous Players (stories)
White Buick (stories)

SPIN DRY

a novel

Greg Hollingshead

[signature] June 1994

MOSAIC PRESS
Oakville-New York-London

Canadian Cataloguing in Publication Data

Hollingshead, Greg, 1947–
    Spin dry

ISBN 0-88962-518-2 (bound) ISBN 0-88962-517-4 (pbk.)

I. Title.

PS8565.O44S64 1992   C813'.54   C92-093975-9
PR9199.3.H64S64 1992

Published by MOSAIC PRESS, P.O. Box 1032, Oakville, Ontario, L6J 5E9, Canada. Offices and warehouse at 1252 Speers Road, Units # 1&2, Oakville, Ontario, L6L 5N9, Canada.

Mosaic Press acknowledges the assistance of the Canada Council and the Ontario Arts Council in support of its publishing programme.

Copyright © Greg Hollingshead
Typeset by Aztext Electronic Publishing Ltd.

Printed and bound in Canada.

ISBN 0-88962 436-4 CLOTH
ISBN 0-88962 437-2 PAPER

MOSAIC PRESS:

In Canada:
    MOSAIC PRESS, 1252 Speers Road, Units # 1&2, Oakville, Ontario L6J 5N9, Canada. P.O. Box 1032, Oakville, Ontario L6J 5N9

In the United States:
    Distributed to the trade in the United States by: National Book Network Inc., 4720-A Boston Way, MD. 20706, USA.

In the U.K.:
    John Calder (Publishers) Ltd., 9-15 Neal St., London, WCZH 9TU, England.

for David and Rosa

Acknowledgments

I am grateful to the Canada Council and the Ontario Arts Council for financial assistance during the writing of this work.

Parts of this work have appeared in different form in the *Malahat Review* and the *Camrose Review*.

ONE

The address on Forebay Rack Road in the Millpond Industrial Park that Dr. Silver had given Rachel turned out to be concrete block fronted with opaque, tea-coloured glass and divided into number units of varying sizes. *Hodge Moving* was squeezed into No. 3 and *ComputerGrafix* into the phoneboothlike No. 17, but Dr. Silver's Morgan was parked almost at the very end, in front of the comparative sprawl of No. 23: *The Silver Dream Research Centre*.

Rachel parked her Civic right up next to Silver's Morgan, which of course was silver and had licence plates that said DREAM. She was late, almost clipped its rear fender. Back at the house she had got into one of those shock bag-packing states where the packer packs as if in the wake of a blow to the head. Telling her story twice a week in Silver's office over in Village Market Square was one thing. Being given two hours to show up here with her bag packed was another. And also the reason why, though forty-five minutes late, Rachel did not right away get out of her car. Instead sat tracing the bumps on the steering wheel.

Thinking: Nothing quite like no options, is there, to recommend the marginal? If my problem was medical, this would be a voodoo charter to Haiti.

Thinking: Problem? I don't even know whose problem I've got.

Thinking: Her husband gets a little obsessive, and a sane wife will act the moderating influence, right? She doesn't go hog wild too. It's a relationship, marriage, not a mania competition.

Rachel took a deep breath. Listened to it. Attended to the tickle of her armpits dripping like caves. Homed in on that sinking sensation in the pit of her stomach.

Thinking: Was a relationship. Even before he disappeared it *was* a relationship.

Thinking: Great. Terrific. Why don't we have a little cry here in the car? Double over with some racking sobs? Show up with our eyes all red and our face blotched? Do the cliché? Isn't that what we're here to recover?

Thinking: Don't think that.

Took a deep breath. Listened to it.

Checked her make-up in the rearview. Laid hold of her purse and bag.

The opaque glass door of the Dream Centre opened into a narrow corridor in unpainted wallboard. Rachel advanced warily.

"Dr. Silver?"

She had come to a fluorescent room dominated by a machine whose smooth beige surface was a confusion of gauges and blinking lights.

"Dr. Silver?"

No one here. Funny how the most straightforward of arrangements will fail to be predictable. Or had she, in that shock, got the day wrong, and that was why she'd thought she had to be here so fast? Or he had, was here but busy with something completely different, was way too disorganized to be trusted? This was her first sign: small now, but later, as his craziness revealed itself, it would seem to have foretold all, if only she had trusted her own—

Rachel looked to the machine, in its authority. It hummed, gauges softly glowing. At least six red lights on its surface discussed her advance.

Don't be silly.

In the air the smell of cement floor. Perpendicular to one wall, separated by portable screens: three iron cots. White sheets and grey blankets folded and tucked with institutional severity. Directly on Rachel's left, in that same wall, were two doors. One had *Washroom* stencilled on it, the other *Keep Out*. Farther down the opposite wall, the one on her right, a large metal desk, mounded with paper. Bag and purse tight in one fist, she edged towards it, peering. Graph print-outs annotated with pencil jot—

"Oh hi, Rachel— Sorry to startle you."

Dr. Silver was wearing his trademark glasses in scarlet frames but today with matching sneakers. He seemed shorter than ever before, his hair frizzier, and his belly caused that *Born for Therapy* sweatshirt to hang out over his jeans.

"Listen Rachel." He was also chewing gum. "I'll be a couple of minutes. Why don't you take Bed 3, the one on the end, and go right back to the start of this whole thing. What would that be, anyways? *Think fast!*"

"Um— Cam Wilkes?"

"Good enough. The first time you met Wilkes. Take it from there."

"Dr. Silver, could you please tell me what this is all—"

"Rachel? You can quit anytime. But. As I've said before. Until you do, you're going to have to trust me, with an implicit faith. By the way, listen. We're getting to know each other pretty well by now, right? Five sessions? Call me Alex."

"Alex. Tell me it's not going to involve that machine over there."

"First things first. Stretch out and go back to Wilkes."

The *Keep Out* door closed behind Alex Silver with a double click. Rachel set her bag on Bed 3 and sat down next to it. Like a debutante in a motel room, tested the springs. Eyed the machine in its beige humming. Reached out to touch its white roll of paper under a dormant stylus. Tried to understand the pattern of the red blinks. The simpler the more innocuous, right? But it wasn't simple. Not at all. Random, then—? Rivetted to the thing's side, she noticed, were the words *Hewlett Packard*. These meant nothing to her. . . . Computers?

For a while, like a dreamer dreaming she has already got up and is brushing her teeth etc., is fully on the way to the office, Rachel had herself lying down, closing her eyes, and so on, except immediately jolting up like one with a night terror. Finally she really did lie down, close her eyes, lids quivering, stretch, relax all muscles each in turn, from toes to scalp, excluding tongue— she never could do tongue, had always figured she would have no problems ever again if only, just once, she could do tongue— and went back and back, the whole way back, to how it had all started.

One incredibly hot Friday last summer she, Rachel Boseman, was on her way home from grocery shopping at a big new supermall six exits along Highway 303 from Village-on-the-Millpond, one moment rolling along on bearings of pure habit, the next straining into the windshield at identical, alien two- and three-bedroom houses in pastel and aluminum and at street signs she had never seen before (*Arbor* Avenue? *Wheat Berry* Drive? *Sluice* Way?), making another U-turn, hammering her palms on the wheel, turning the radio down lower and lower so she could concentrate, and thinking,

For godsake, I'm lost in my own development.

Finally, after seeing no one— not even, in that heat, a kid ("Get serious, Mum. It's a meltdown out there.")— Rachel noticed a man operating a backhoe in the middle of his front lawn. In streetlit darkness and practically forty-degree heat, digging this big hole. Now, Rachel had lived most of her life in the city, where strange sights were salt and vinegar and sometimes ketchup on the French fries of routine, but here among the lawns and fresh pavement of Village-on-the-Millpond they caused her to theorize. Maybe the job had to be done immediately: a burst pipe. Maybe night was the only chance he got. Maybe he came with the backhoe. Maybe he knew what he was doing.

When he waved she veered in sharp. Immediately he shut off the backhoe and reached for something under the seat. He eased himself to the grass with care. He wore sunglasses, pajamas, slippers, a flesh-coloured workglove on his visible hand. The other hand he held behind him. He approached wearing a soft sad expression, not untheatrical. His stroll was a compendium of compensatory shifts and adjustments, like the sloping float of a camel. His nose was flattened and he was quite chinless; he had a long, forward-canting neck. His hair was wiry and blond, and it stood back far and high off his florid face. He was tall and he was narrow. He was stooped, with a protuberant, forward-thrusting belly. Between the thumb and forefinger of his left hand he held a cigarette, its filter cupped in the upturned palm of the workglove. When he reached the passenger door of the Civic he let those sunglasses slip down his nose to examine her parking: radials bulging over the curb, she just knew. He drew his right hand from behind his back. On it too was a flesh-coloured workglove, but it held a trumpet. This he put to his lips and with muted passion, his body curved like an S, the cigarette in his ear, he played the most haunting, sad, exquisite melody that Rachel had ever heard.

"Thank you," she said when he had finished. Already she'd had to wipe tears from her eyes about three times. "That was really, really beautiful." This was what she said. But there was something more. It was as if that melody was for her.

The man had removed the cigarette from his ear and brought a cupped workglove to his chin for a reflective drag. He squinted through the smoke.

"What is it?" Rachel asked, meaning the melody. She needed a name, something.

The man smiled a melancholy slow smile that kept slipping and replied, "Only a horn rendition of a love that will never die."

"I'm sorry, did you lose your wife?"

At first Rachel thought he turned away then to conceal weeping, but when he maintained this attitude for some time she realized he was gazing at that hole he'd been digging.

Surely it wasn't her gra—? "What are you— ?"

"Trying to find my gas line."

He'd come slowly back around.

"But isn't that dangerous?"

"Can a bus ride change a person's life?"

"Pardon?"

"When the foreseen comes as a big surprise, what's the unforeseen come as?"

Rachel took the Civic out of Park. "Thanks again for playing for me."

"I wasn't playing for you."

Quickly she glanced at his face. Dark glasses to conceal eyes. Probably on medication. "I have to go now."

"Where? You're driving in circles. Normally I'd say, Don't worry about it. Strangers are always getting lost in the Millpond. But you've lived here for two years."

"A year and a half."

"Twenty-one months."

Uh-oh.

"Stood on the sidewalk and watched you and your husband move in," he recalled, watching Rachel again now, over those shades. "Used to make myself go out more in those days. Used to sit and gaze across the waters of the millpond and wonder what it was all about. Used to lie on my patio and stare straight up, watching the evening sky turn navy then black while I waited for Della, my wife, to come home. Heavy dew in the suburbs. Almost caught pneumonia."

"So how do I get there? Just tell me."

"Dell Drive?" Slowly he twisted around, this time to his left and seemed to stare at his driveway. Again he remained in the attitude so long that Rachel felt obliged to follow his gaze. The driveway was simple black asphalt, quite empty. Under the streetlights it had a pleasing sheen, the scuffless look of fresh sealant. As she looked at his driveway, Rachel noticed that the windows of his house were blocked with aluminum foil. One of *those*.

"I used to call that driveway Della's Drive," the man said, coming back around. "I'd tell her, 'Della, there's something wrong here. The part of our little home you know best is the driveway'. That woman was always out. Notice: Dell, Della. What's an *a*? If all you really had to do was *remember*—"

"All I really have to do is get going."

"Yes, I did lose my wife. One day she was out all day, and that evening she called to say she wouldn't be coming back. Della was always considerate. But this is bigger than that."

"What is?"

He bowed his head and touched the toe of his slipper against the door of the Civic. His face came up in a rueful smile. "A little rusty—"

Rachel shrugged. "My husband's unemployed."

Nodding, he drew a long hand from a workglove and laid the glove on the door by his elbow. He reached into the car. "Cam Wilkes."

"Rachel Boseman." Now why did she let him know that?

"Nice to meet you, Rachel. But tell me honestly. Why have you moved to a hazardous place like the Millpond?"

"Mr. Wilkes, I'd love to sit here and talk all night, but—"

"You don't say to yourself it's not hazardous, I hope."

"Everywhere's hazardous for a— Listen. I truly do ha—"

"My card."

His card was printed in tangerine letters on shifting aqua moiré like rumpled rayon. It said:

PAGO* International
    Cam Wilkes, Founding Member and President
    Village-on-the-Millpond Chapter
    *People Afraid to Go Out

"Rachel, do you ever have trouble leaving the house?" His voice had modulated to confidential. He was leaning with both forearms against the car. "That's the first sign. Surprising how many Villagers are afraid to step out that door, ride a bus, or sit under a hair dryer. At PAGO we believe a good twelve percent of our neighbours are agoraphobic, and that's not even counting us! A place like this is at least eight to ten percent above the national average."

"Uh-huh—"

"Guess how many working hours are lost each year in the retail and light-industry sectors of the Millpond due to agoraphobia-related disorders?"

"Two hundred and thirty thousand?"

"Ninety-three thousand. You're just trying to minimize. Last year we absorbed the Shy Persons' Discussion Group. Turned out they weren't shy at all! Just a bunch of misdiagnosed agoraphobiacs! Lately we've been holding discussions with the ultra-feminist group SMILE concerning their work on sexism in the Dick and Jane readers, initially a matter of strictly limited interest to us. But zealotry really is a marvellous stimulus to thought. Those discussions were so intense they sent me straight back to the old readers, and boy, did that ever trigger memories. It turns out Dick and Jane have plenty to say to PAGO. And what a dear, sweet little number that Jane is—"

He seemed to drift off.

"So you're not going to tell me how to get home."

He drifted back. "An umbrella or a cane can be almost as reassuring on an evening walk as a dog, or a spouse. We've just assimilated the VCF— that's Village Cane Fighters—"

"Gotta go." Rachel took the Civic out of Park.

He pointed to his card. It was still in her hand.

"Nice, eh? Evokes the vertigo. Listen. Our new motto. Passed only last week by our International Council. Ready? *Oh, oh, oh!*"

Rachel watched her hand put the Civic back into Park. "From Dick and Jane," she heard her voice say. Ever since Wilkes had mentioned those two, she'd been fighting off a déjà vu, and now it had her. "'Oh, oh, oh,'" she said. "'See funny, funny Sally'?"

Cam Wilkes was amazed. "How did you know that?"

Rachel shrugged.

"I guess they stayed with me."

"But why?"

"I don't know. Haven't they with everybody?"

"But this is *you!* This could be the key to your problem!"

"My problem, Mr. Wilkes, is I'm lost and you won't tell me how to get home."

"You're not alone. Each day as Dick, Jane, and Sally set about their skill-enhancing tasks, what happens? Dick's on roller skates with Spot on a leash, but Spot takes off after Puff. The caption for that one reads, 'Funny, funny Dick,' but Jane and Sally aren't laughing, and Dick sure has nothing to laugh about. It's all danger, surprise, and the constant nervous laughter of fear."

"Right—"

"It's supposed to be a safe, dependable world those kids live in, but that's the last thing it is. Sound familiar?"

"I really do have to go now," dropping the card into her purse.

Cam Wilkes' eyes followed it. "That's OK, Rachel," he said quietly. "I suppose I set it up, talking like a 'One-Track Willie' the way I do. You're not the first to 'have to go', you know."

Before Rachel could respond to this, he threw down his cigarette, stepped back, and played a few notes: defiant, but sad.

Rachel slipped the Civic into Drive.

"You've been lost in here all along, haven't you, Rachel?" He was back at the window. "Whatever you do, don't blame yourself. It happens to people all the time. I see them from my window. Every pass and here they are back at the same old place that little bit worse off. You know, sometimes it seems like they're just ordinary, good-hearted folks doing their best, and really it's the whole place that's—"

"I'm really sorry, but I absolutely have to get going."

He looked at her sadly then off down the street, pointing. "First left, second right should get you onto Glen. Dell has to be around there someplace. Four, maybe five along. There is a certain simple plan. Glen, Dell. You know what I mean? This isn't nature."

"Thanks," Rachel reaching across to wind up the window.

"Here's the main thing we ask ourselves at PAGO." Three hands, one bare, a flesh-coloured workglove on either side of it, were riding up on the glass. Rachel wound slowly to be polite. "What is the reason I am here? What knowledge, what grief, what unutterable emptiness?"

The gap had disappeared; he was crouched to address the glass. "I'm serious, Rachel. Take a hard look in the mirror and ask yourself why. Don't ever pretend moving here just happened. Do that, and in three years a trip to the 7-Eleven will mean a complete change of underwear for you or for someone close to you—"

In the rearview as Rachel accelerated she saw him wave and point at one of those flesh-colored workgloves in a frantic, attention-getting way, then pretend to sob briefly into his hands before curling his body around the trumpet. She wondered if he understood the true meaning of locating your gas line with a backhoe. She wondered if he really had seen her around. She wondered how many apparently humdrum residents of Village-on-the-Millpond were in fact seriously wacked-out crackpots.

"Rachel?" It was Alex Silver, right next to her ear in the Dream Centre. Must have pulled up a chair, or be squatting. "Before you open your eyes. Let me ask you: *Why* when you first met Wilkes? Why not when you and Leon moved to the Millpond? Or when you married Leon? Or long before that, when your father—"

"It was that piece Cam played," replied Rachel, without hesitation. "Nothing's been the same since."

"Nothing?"

A tear gathered at the corner of Rachel's eye and ran swiftly into her ear. "I'm overstating."

"How not the same?"

Rachel thought for awhile. She thought about 201 Dell Drive in that picture on the Mortprop Sales Office wall, a rose-coloured townhouse-type two-and-a-half in Contractor Modern, with optional gun-grey demi-gable roof, lines softened by vague vegetation spilling out of planters and by a tiny childlike person standing out front for no reason at all, holding balloons. She remembered it up there with pictures of clean-jawed smiling men in bulldozers, of intelligent-looking people sitting around a boardroom table gazing serenely at an even more intelligent-looking developer who was pointing at a map, of well-dressed happy people sitting at outdoor cafés, of a mother with a baby carriage staring at a tubular peaked kiosk with schedules of cultural events pinned to it, of two little kids, a boy and a girl, walking hand-in-hand through dappled woods—

And she thought about the first time she had seen 201 Dell in actual brick and aluminum, how it had looked so good, good enough, as Leon put it at the time, to resell immediately, too good to believe that quirky Rachel and scruffy Leon would be allowed to buy it, let alone be able to afford it.

In fact, they could not. Even when Leon was still working they could not.

"Quite an achievement, eh?" he had cried when they first drove through the new development, on boulevards with scored pavement and protruding drainage grates. Landscaping contractors were planting small trees; many windows still had masking tape X-ing them; men were spreading cork chips with rakes. "I mean, your first impulse is to despise it, right? But really, when you get right down to it: *Wow*. Two years ago this was probably just a bunch of broken-down farms."

"Broken-down because the farmers sold out to land speculators."

"Something eating you today, Sweetheart?"

"Bet you any money there's never been a mill or a millpond anywhere within ten miles of here."

"Kind of hard to have a mill without a stream," Leon admitted. "I guess it's just a concept... Gently turning wheel, pastoral setting, swans on the pond. Powerful stuff, really, when you think about it."

Rachel had nodded, knew of course what he meant. Swans, sure. She could go for swans. What was eating her was trying to believe there was not something else about this place that was pulling her. Swans couldn't pack half the promise of all these decisive exclusions made by so much space and simple geometry: Here the man at the wheel would love her forever.

"By the way," he was saying. "Aren't they building this project on a township dump? Didn't I read that someplace?"

"Not in the Mortprop Investments literature you didn't." They had just stopped by the Sales Office, inside the front gates. This was a mobile unit in a frame of giant overlapping cutouts depicting an old gristmill with a cascading water wheel in a lush arcadian setting. Rachel now clutched about a kilo of incredibly slippery brochures on her lap.

"It should be there," Leon said. "None of your soft focus. Dumps are primal stuff. The place has a buried history. Chthonic depth. Beautiful. Rachel, we really should think seriously about moving out here. There's a lot more to this place than meets the eye."

"What's *chthonic* again?"

"Rachel? Rachel?" It was Alex Silver, in the Dream Centre, still at her ear. "Did you hear me?"

But Rachel had forgotten the question. "That time, Alex, I was lost and first met Cam Wilkes? After I finally found No. 201, I sat in the driveway for a long time with the engine off before I noticed that Leon's Subaru was gone. And then I noticed that he'd pounded out the dent he made in the garage with the U-haul the day we moved in and repainted the whole door. What was going on? He'd come out of his depression as Mr. Fix-It? I got out of the car, and the next thing I saw, he'd replaced the heaved brick approach to the front steps with these zig-zag grey cement things, and repainted the front door, and attached a new—

"Wrong house, Alex. I had the wrong house. Right number, wrong Drive. Dill Drive. 201 Dill Drive. Never heard of it.

"I put the groceries back in the car and drove away."

Silver mused. At last he said, "The Millpond stuff is purely symptomatic."

"I know."

"Wilkes knew it too."

"He was trying to get through." Rachel's head came around. "Alex, I'm scared. I don't think I should be here. Why don't I just find Leon and— What exactly are you up to?"

"You're anxious. But first let's focus on Leon a minute. I mean, absent or present he's close to the heart of the actual problem, you'd agree?"

Rachel closed her eyes and settled back. She nodded.

"So tell me about Leon. What happened when you got home after that first time you met Wilkes and heard the melody?"

Twenty minutes after entering the wrong driveway, Rachel was pulling up alongside Leon's Subaru, nosing the Civic against the dent in the garage door. Shopping bags in her arms, she was on the steps leading from the driveway to the front door when she heard a distant, muffled explosion: *Crump.* Dynamiting, she thought vaguely; she was still on that melody. She entered the kitchen calling to Leon that she had got lost on the way home. When there was no answer she put down the groceries and went on into the living room where she found him stretched out on the shag with the headphones on. She flopped over the back of the chesterfield and studied him for a while foreshortened, this person she had married, the soles of his sneakers the biggest thing about him.

The past year had not been kind to Leon. He came back from the unemployment office pale and smelling of smoke and defeat. The cheque he left lying around for Rachel to find, never put it directly into her hand. Except for job interviews and the unemployment office he did not go out much any more, had taken to spending his days on rock and roll odysseys into the past. Now, Rachel had nothing against old, bad rock and roll, but she found something sad about a guy in his late thirties trying to piece himself back together out of it. Sad and a little scary. Same with his practice of sleeping with a pen and pad between himself and his wife, a telling arrangement. Rolling over after each dream to write it down without actually waking up. Freud would have killed to get Leon for a patient. Whereas Rachel was beginning to wonder how not so long ago she might have been ready to do the same to get him for a husband.

In the Dream Centre, Alex Silver cleared his throat. "Did you know or suspect at that time who or what Leon was dreaming about?"

"No."

"Continue."

A few minutes later, the needle eddying in the small grooves, Rachel tried again. "Leon—"

"Whohh*aaahh*!!"

"Sorry."

"Geez, Rachel," pulling the earphones off and coming up on an elbow. "Don't *do* that! Where have you been?"

But for some reason Rachel was not ready to talk about that melody with anyone, even— especially— Leon. "I got lost on the way back," was all she said.

"A distracted driver is a loaded weapon, Rachel."

"Leon," she ventured later, in the dining room, over a pizza they got in. "I don't think the Millpond has turned out exactly as we hoped it would."

But this was heard by Leon as her latest bivouac in an old argument. "Archeologists, Rachel, have traced the suburb back to greater Ur in Mesopotamia. That is thirty centuries B.C."

"Doesn't mean it's what we hoped it would be," Rachel gazing at the joint Leon offered her. "No thanks."

It's just," he continued, toking, not listening, "most of the people who live out here don't appreciate the city. But they don't appreciate the country either. If they did, they would never live out here."

"If the country was all you knew," Rachel replied, "it would be easy not to appreciate the country. Here you might prefer the convenience."

"Your argument is academic. Most suburbanites have moved to where they are from other suburbs. Generation after generation. A breed apart. Like cops. But answer me this. Why don't we ever hear about people in downtown apartments being alienated out of their minds?"

"We do."

Just before they turned out the light, Rachel said, "Leon, what happens if you hit your gas line with a backhoe?"

"Don't worry."

"No, really."

"Kaboom?"

"That's what I thought."

Ten minutes later Rachel shot bolt upright thinking *Crump*. Oh my God! She turned to tell Leon about Cam Wilkes.

But Leon was sunk in buzz-saw respiration.

Next morning Rachel woke exhausted. In the Saturday light her fears of the night seemed lurid and foolish but not to her unconscious. When she got into the Civic for a run to the 7-Eleven to pick up some half and half and a paper for Leon she gave a little scream: a hand was coming for her. But it was one of Cam Wilkes' flesh-coloured workgloves, caught in the window. Must have been what he'd been waving about so frantically. On the way back from the 7-Eleven, that melody nagging at the back of her mind, she thought to check Wilkes' card, but there was no address. A phone number but no address. She didn't want to talk to him, so she decided to drive around a little until she found his house. If it was still standing. She pictured herself tossing the glove at it like the paperboy. Then again, she should probably knock and ask if he understood how dangerous it is to go looking for your gas line with a backhoe.

But she got lost again. This being Saturday morning there were lots of people out on their lawns, but her question about a backhoe caused some pretty strange eyebrow conformations. So Rachel just drove around, searching. She would never forgive herself if she was too late. Or was that just stupid?

Finally she spotted an old guy gripping a cane. The cane reminded her that Wilkes had mentioned the Village Cane Fighters. A sign? She pulled over and asked the old man if on his walk he had noticed anybody digging their lawn with a backhoe.

"You call this a walk?" the old man shouted. "My doctors are considering if I can survive an operation for plastic hip joints, and you call this a walk? How old are you?"

"Twenty-nine," Rachel lied.

He snorted.

"How about fresh-dug earth?" she tried.

"Earth!" he bellowed. "How far do you think I 'walk'? Twenty-thirty blocks? Or is it more like 24.6 miles, the Boston marathon? Well, girlie, I got news for you. Standing where you are you can see every place I was today. Big accomplishment, eh? So you tell me. How much 'earth'?"

Rachel's next question, rattled-aggressive, was, Did he belong to the Village Cane Fighters?

But the old man surprised her by shaking his head in a startled way and saying quietly, "I thought they folded."

"Not what I heard."

He stepped closer, confidential. "You got the number on you?"

"They've been absorbed. How do you feel about going out?"

"Folded, you mean."

"Maybe you're right, but try this." She gave him Wilkes' card.

When Rachel got home Leon was sitting on the front step waiting for his half and half and the paper. She nosed up to the garage, and he came around the Subaru to lean on her passenger door, something the way Cam Wilkes had done. She rolled down the window.

"Nice to see you back. Whose glove?" Cam Wilkes' workglove was lying on the seat beside her.

At that moment a sense of omission, possibly betrayal, about not filling him in— even obliquely— on last night, had Rachel reacting with more rattled aggression. "Leon, why am I the one who runs to the 7-Eleven for your half and half and your paper? And why should you make me feel guilty that I didn't get back faster?"

"Because you're the one who took so long to get home last night the superstore half and half curdled in the heat. Because you've been gone exactly one hour and ten minutes on a fifteen-minute errand. I pictured you bleeding in a ditch somewhere. Think of me, Rachel. Think of me."

"I do, all the time. Maybe that's my problem."

"You stopped off at a garage sale and bought me a workglove. Half price?"

Rachel looked at the workglove. Vaguely she decided to punish Leon by lying. She explained that she had found it and been trying to find the owner.

"Just driving around looking for somebody pushing the mower with one bare hand?"

"That's right."

"I'm going to have to be a little more confrontational than the first time through, Rachel," Alex Silver told her. He was still in that crouch. "That is, talk more. Less like a therapist. More like a friend—"

"A confrontational friend."

"Aren't the best?"

"Shoot."

"Why the hell *not* at least tell Leon about Wilkes? You didn't have to go into the melody stuff!"

"Because I knew I couldn't tell the story well enough for Leon not to think I was telling it because I'd been smitten by Cam Wilkes."

"Ah but," Silver sagely, "wasn't it the fact that you had already fallen out of love with Leon that caused this irrational fear that he'd be jealous?"

"Irrational? What do you mean? He *was* jealous!"

"No wonder! You never told him about Wilkes! You set him up!"

"I did not! I was only trying to spare him the embarrassment of looking like a paranoid!"

Alex Silver placed his face in his hands, nearly lost his balance. "Consideration among the married. Go on. What happens next."

"Leon, Cam, and the explosions."

"Tell it."

After two weeks of that hot spell and two issues of *The Villager* containing no news about anybody blowing up their house with a backhoe, Cam Wilkes' workglove had wormed its way into the front seat crevice of Rachel's Civic, and Cam Wilkes himself had just about faded from memory. Not so the effects of that melody, which had been taking so much energy to repress that Rachel herself had gone into a virtual depression of her own. Everything seemed so second-rate. Always had been, ever would be.

And then it was Friday again, and Rachel was on her way home again from shopping, this time at the local Mortprop Mall, a disappointing, single-level throwback that couldn't touch some of the supermalls opening in other developments. The thermometer was still up there close to forty. Listening to a CFRT MiniReport on the car radio about a rash of ugly explosions that recently had been tearing up the Millpond, Rachel took a wrong turn somewhere past the 7-Eleven and got completely lost. Meanwhile that CFRT MiniReport explained how, as a result of the fact that the Millpond had been built on a former township dumpsite, the pond had chemicals leaching into it that could kill a swan in less than a week. Also, in the extended summer heat, expanding gases inside buried green garbage bags were causing them to explode like land mines. Talk about hazardous waste.

The 'Report had just ended when Rachel spotted five or six people standing around the perimeter of a lawn pointing into a crater a good fifteen feet across. She slowed down to take a look and noticed Leon's Subaru parked in the immaculate driveway. Disoriented now, she got out and checked the back seat for empty beer and Pepsi bottles. It was Leon's car all right. The house was a two-bedroom bungalow with aluminum foil in the windows. Just another Millpond home, and yet who else's could it be? Then again, she'd been wrong before. On her way to the door she paused on the lip of the crater and gazed in. Invariably after these explosions you saw strata of mid-century garbage that made you think of archeology of the future. Not here. Here was just earth and rocks. No twisted ends of gas pipe jutting from the sheer sides, either.

A few seconds later, after recoiling from a pair of bare wires where the doorbell should have been, Rachel knocked, and the door swung open the way doors do in haunted houses. This one, dark because of that aluminum foil, seemed to be filled instead— or also— with large vehicle parts: sections of engine, fenders, hubcaps. He must take in bodywork, Rachel postulated. She remembered how he had placed the toe of his slipper against rust on the Civic.

"Leon," she whispered, stepping forward, staring into pure darkness.

And then she saw him, Leon, right there in the hall, slumped on what appeared to be an old bus seat, his head slowly, like a doll's, rotating in her direction. She did a lot of falling over pieces of vehicle before she was able to drop down next to him, hugging his arm.

Leon tried to speak, could not. He cleared his throat. "Listen," he said, huskily.

She heard it then, the melody that Wilkes had played for her in his pajamas by the backhoe. A melody that seemed to rise from the depths of the earth, its familiarity like a bubble of memory floating up through the still, dark levels of her mind, the melody itself a white ribbon being pulled out of her ear to soar into a shifting blue sky and make restless, changing shapes of unutterable sadness and grace.

"So beautiful," Rachel whispered when it ended, looking to

Leon, who was sprawled white and transfixed, like a man who had just given a gallon of blood.

"That was it," Leon said.

"I know— Was what?"

They made their way stumbling in the dim light amidst leaning tires into a kitchen strewn with more large vehicle parts to a door that seemed likely to lead to the basement. "Anybody home?" Leon called down into the darkness.

"Eee-aw-kee," Cam Wilkes replied conversationally. He added that if they found the kitchen too cluttered they should step out the screen door onto the patio where they would find room to swing a collie.

"Collie?" Leon wondered dazedly as they stood on a patio empty except for withered weeds, a rusty barbecue, a stack of leftover concrete patio squares in faded tangerine and aqua. Many were broken.

"It's Cam Wilkes," Rachel murmured.

"Who?"

Too late to explain. Anxiously they looked about them at pastel two-bedroom bungalows crowding in close at various angles. A moment later Cam Wilkes appeared behind the screen in profile, silvered, a trumpet to his lips. He played *Embraceable You*, segued into *Sophisticated Lady*, and seemed to go away.

Rachel whispered, "Leon, what are you doing here?"

"I freaked out in the 7-Eleven."

And then the screen door slid briefly open, and Cam Wilkes' arm emerged holding a tray containing two beer bottles in foam blankets followed by a cut-glass bowl filled with cheese curds.

What a poser, Rachel thought irritably, taking the tray. She washed down a cheese curd with a swallow of beer.

"Come on out, Cam," she said testily, aware of Leon's baffled eyes soft on the side of her face.

Wilkes declined. "Not after I lost my lawn."

But of course she had seen him on that backhoe. "How *did* you lose your lawn, Cam?"

"Who can say? But I know one thing. This was no garbage bag. Clearly life in the Millpond is even more unpredictable than even we suspected. And that means Dangerous, with a capital D. You folks drop by to join PAGO?"

"PAGO," said Leon, like a man lost in a dream.

Handing out his aqua moiré calling card, Cam Wilkes gave Leon a pitch similar to the one he had given Rachel but with topical emphasis on the escalating danger of going out. He told Leon about PAGO's recent efforts to incorporate the local chapter of Carrot-Top, the red-haired persons' self-esteem raising group, which he described as the "touchiest, most volatile bunch of s.o.b.'s you'd ever want to meet," and added, "With people like that loose, no wonder we're afraid to go out."

Leon kept nodding, mouth open, but his eyes, smarter, were giving Rachel is-this-guy-for-real looks. As soon as Rachel had finished her beer she made leaving motions to Leon, and he was very tractable.

"The only problem with having a friendship through a screen door," Cam Wilkes joked sociably as she hurried Leon off the patio and around the side of the house to their cars, "is, the conversation is strained!"

Leon reached home first because Rachel, the melody back full force, took a wrong turn. He was sitting on the chesterfield with a beer in his hand. There Rachel joined him, and he told her the story of how he had freaked out in the 7-Eleven that afternoon. He was paying for a three-litre Pepsi, reaching, he said, slightly forward across the counter to put the money directly into the girl's hand, when suddenly he was seized by a vision of the Pepsi, himself, the girl, the cash register, the other girl busy making a Slurpee with her back turned, the sallow guy standing behind him with a cellopack of wieners and a bag of barbecue-flavoured corn chips, and the kid with the mauve mohawk by the magazine rack flipping through a *Popular Mechanics*, as all pawns in some pointless game or possibly unknowing components of one vast, pointless Mind. To Leon everything seemed at that moment drained of meaning, and he just wanted to go home and curl up in front of the TV. Abandoning his change and the Pepsi, he stumbled out to the Subaru. After driving for some time around the Millpond in a state of mental blindness, he found himself on Hillock Rise, a flat, curving street of bunga-lows. He pulled over to ask a kid with a bag of Woolco fliers where Dell Drive was; the kid had no idea. It was then that he heard it. That melody, coming from a house with tinfoil in the windows and people staring into a crater in the lawn. The front door must have been open ... He couldn't actually remember. Leon was in a trance, a dream. He staggered in and flopped down on that bus seat, overwhelmed. The melody was so beautiful. He wanted to laugh and cry at the same time. Tears flooded his cheeks and dried and flooded them again. Helplessness came over him. He felt as though a corner of the universe was being lifted to allow him a peek underneath . . . and then Rachel was grabbing at his arm.

Initially moved, Rachel now said, "Gee, you make me sound like a big nuisance."

"You couldn't help it. It's just, there's a difference between experiencing something like that on your own and as half a couple."

"I'm your wife!"

"Exactly."

"*Exactly?*"

"You haven't told me yet how you know this guy."

Sullenly, with trepidation, Rachel described her encounter two weeks earlier with Cam Wilkes. When she finished, Leon did not say anything at first, and then he wondered quietly why she had not told him about this earlier. With lots of recrimination in her voice to compensate for any lameness, Rachel replied, "I didn't think you'd be interested—" And throwing in a self-deprecating little laugh, she added, to avoid a total lie, "—the way I tell a story." Refusing then to be daunted by thin lips on Leon, she stressed her doubts about Cam Wilkes' sanity. She stopped talking when Leon held up his hand.

"Rachel," he said in a voice of high seriousness. "There is something I think you should know." He bowed his head a moment, then turned it to look her straight in the eyes, causing her heart to pound. "You're aware," began Leon, strangely formal, "that I have been writing down my dreams."

"For a year."

"And I take it you don't know what's been happening in them."

"Because you refuse to tell me."

"And you've never peeked into my dream diary? Not even once?"

"Leon, you keep it padlocked."

"OK. What it all boils down to is this." Leon rubbed his face hard with his free hand. "I keep dreaming about the same guy."

"*Guy? Who?*"

"I don't know."

"*Keep* dreaming?"

"Once or twice a night."

"For a *year?*"

"Possibly more. A year is as long as I have kept track."

"And you have no idea who he is."

"Right."

"So what do you think it means?"

"I haven't the faintest idea."

"Well, what do you— do with him in your dreams?"

Here Leon picked a bit of fluff off the sofa and rolled it between his thumb and forefinger. "I'm not ready to get into that right now."

"Why not!?" a little shrilly.

Leon gave her a sharp look. She took a breath, tried to be calm.

"Listen. Rachel. The important thing is this. All I know about him for sure is, he's always accompanied by a tune, sort of a theme song—"

Rachel's immediate thought was *Love in Bloom* when Jack Benny used to stride back onstage after the show in that ascot and dressing gown. And then she cried, "You don't mean— !"

"Uh-huh."

"It couldn't be!"

"Rachel, the shivers are qualitatively identical."

Rachel thought about this for a moment. And then she said, "So what does this mean?"

"I have no idea. But I'm sure as hell going to find out."

In Leon's eyes was a look of focus and clarity that Rachel had been failing to see there for a long time. Even slouched beside her on the sofa his shoulders seemed to square a little.

Later, over Chinese food, Leon suddenly cried, "I've got it! I'll join PAGO! It's bound to be my quickest route to the heart of this thing. Besides, I really should get out more. A man has to be able to handle a 7-Eleven."

In the Dream Centre Alex Silver had pulled up a chair beside Rachel's bed and was sitting in it rubbing the backs of his knees. He looked at his watch. "This is taking longer than I expected."

Rachel's eyes flew open. "You asked me and I'm telling you!"

"It's fascinating. Really. So you were pretty surprised that

Wilkes' melody should have deep significance for both you and
Leon, particularly when there was this dream-guy involved."

"Yes."

"And what did you think?"

"I didn't know what to think."

"How about feel?"

"Scared, baffled, one-upped."

"I see. And you said nothing about any of these feelings to
Leon."

"Right."

"So. We've finally got to what you're here about, namely you
and Leon's dream guy."

"Hal."

"Hal? You never told me his name was Hal!"

"I didn't want to confuse you. When he first had a name it was
Hal."

"OK. So. Better tell it as it happened. How did Wilkes and
PAGO lead both Leon and you to Leon's dream guy who was first
known as Hal."

"If I tell you, will you tell me what you're going to do to me, so
I can leave now if it's too wacko?"

"You won't want to do that. Tell it."

The day after he first heard Cam Wilkes play the melody from
his own dreams, Leon arranged to attend a PAGO meeting, two
nights later.

Afterwards, he woke up Rachel and told her all about it while
pacing the bedroom in a highly excited state.

The meeting had taken place in Cam Wilkes' living room,
which Leon described as looking like the inside of a badly kept bus
after an accident: seats everywhere; bumpers and tires lying around
amidst scattered snack-food litter; windows and fenders leaning
against walls. Altogether, including Leon and Wilkes himself,
there were a dozen people.

One, a short, broad-hipped woman with blue hair and a wan-
ton smile, had to leave early. ("That was Della," Wilkes confided in
a whisper to Leon after seeing her to the door. "My former wife.
She's one of our Honorary Members.") Among those who stayed

were a tall man with a twitch who wore dark glasses and moccasin-style loafers, a middle-aged woman in dark glasses chewing gum and humming incessantly under her breath, an elderly woman asleep behind dark glasses, a nervous teenager with a hawk on his shoulder, a young woman in winged dark glasses that sat cock-eyed on her thin face, a guy of fifty or so wearing a Walkman and nodding to the music, a querulous old man who gripped his cane like a club—

"I met him," Rachel said. "He's from the Village Cane Fighters."

Leon reconsidered. There must have been more than a dozen.

Cam Wilkes, also in dark glasses, leaned against the back of a bus seat, dangling one leg and smoking in his strange, filter-palmed way. From there he chaired the meeting. After the minutes and the treasurer's report, the old man with the cane was intro-duced as a new member and Leon as a special guest.

Then Wilkes got down to the agenda, seven items in all, involving matters such as how negotiations with Carrot-Top, the red-haired persons' self-esteem raising group, were going ("vio-lent and irrational"); the breakdown of talks with SMILE, the ultra feminists (who objected to Wilkes' sexist perception of Jane of Dick and Jane); the purchase of a sign to take full publicity advantage of the hole in Wilkes' front lawn; and the feasibility of setting up a task force to study ways and means of applying for a government grant to provide each PAGO member with a cellular phone. Discussion concerning all business was protracted and at times bitter. Several people tried to introduce motions that would effectively ban smoking at meetings, but Wilkes, lighting up, ruled these out of order. After catcalls when he reported that the subcommittee on venues was still deliberating and therefore the next meeting would as usual be held at his place, everyone adjourned for coffee.

Leon made use of the break to get to know some PAGO members. "Actually they were OK people," he reported. "Not people *we'd* have over for drinks—"

"We don't have anybody over for drinks."

Ignoring this, Leon went on to the "heart of the meeting": members standing up and recounting traumatic agoraphobic expe-riences. Falling to pieces in bank line-ups; running in terror down the median of a Millpond boulevard under an empty sky; and the bottom line: cowering in the front hall too frightened to go out.

"It was sad," Leon commented. "You knew how they felt."
Everyone was extremely warm and supportive. Everyone knew
how they felt.

Soon Wilkes had entertained a motion to adjourn, and Leon
was driving home.

"Why was everybody wearing dark glasses?" Rachel had to
ask.

"I know, I felt so naked. Agoraphobiacs tend to wear dark
glasses."

"I never knew that."

"I did."

"No dream guy insights?" Rachel wondered.

"His name's Hal," Leon replied irritably. "Call him by his
name. Hal."

"Pardon? *Hal*?" She tried to catch Leon's eyes, but he had
started hunting around in the closet for his dressing gown.

Here the phone on the bedtable rang. It was Rachel's mother.
She had read an item in the city paper about those exploding
garbage bags and was calling to express her concern. "Why don't
you both come and stay with me, dear, until they get things under
control out there? You can sleep in my room. I'll be fine on the sofa."

"Thanks, Mother, but I think we can stick it out."

"Why don't I take that cruise. You could have the place to
yourselves, and then I wouldn't have to worry about my plants."

"It's just a few garbage bags, Mother."

"Yes, but they're exploding. Of course, I suppose there's your
job at that insurance company—"

"Millpond Indemnity."

"You'd have to commute— But that wouldn't be a problem for
Leon, would it. Or is he—"

"No, not yet. But any day now. He's looking really hard."

"I was thinking he could look here, and then—"

"Mother, we'll move back to the city when we move back to the
city."

"So you say."

"Mother? Don't worry, OK? We're fine. And I'll call you soon—"

Rachel went down to the kitchen where Leon had gone to tuck
meditatively into a bowl of Harvest Crunch. "So will you go back
to PAGO?" she asked.

"I might.

"Hey, Rachel," he added as she remained standing on the other side of the table. "Let me hit you with a couple of Hal dreams. Give you the flavour of this thing."

"You bet," and Rachel lowered herself into a chair for Leon to tell her a dream about Hal open-air ice-fishing at Buckshot Hole, calmly continuing to fish even after the ice had gone out. As Leon detailed the dream— that miniature school principal Hal was using for bait, the short trek back across open water with the trout snapping at his heels, the chinook feel of the breezes— Rachel thought, he's opening up. For the first time in a year he's in focus, he's on to something. So why do I feel so anxious?

When Leon finished recounting the Buckshot Hole dream, it was as if he found himself at the top of a long motel corridor, doors opening all the way down, a Hal dream behind each one. "Huh," he said, in the tone of a man on the frontier of a few discoveries, and he set off to check out the rooms: Hal with unlit moving cigar stub and green eyeshade dealing blackjack on the QE 2; Hal and Leon flipping a rupee to see who will be the first to jump off of Mount Everest; Hal as Jet Rink in *Giant*, passed out in his consommé . . .

In her mind Rachel scrambled after. But Leon, a real dream and memory hound these days, kept going back and back until she knew that this was not so much time they were moving deeper into as a secret reach of her husband's heart that for some reason he did not care anymore whether she knew about or not, and she got scared.

It didn't stop there. Wired from his evening at PAGO, Leon must have gone on recounting Hal dreams at the kitchen table that night for two or three hours. In the weeks that followed they would flash unexpectedly into Rachel's mind: Hal in flight, hair floating, for home plate; Hal's *Neat, eh?* grin across the popcorn in the fizzy blue air of the Boseman rec room; Hal a hairy coot singing *Heart of Gold* in *joual* on a Paris streetcorner; or else *G-grab hold, Leon!* and here was Windsurfer Hal extending a brotherly hand to his foundering pal. Sometimes Leon would start out describing just such a flash, and the whole dream would come back only gradually, as he talked. When it was all over, when he had told maybe three dozen dreams, Leon could only cluck, shake his head, and murmur, "What a guy, what a guy," in an admiring, wistful voice.

"And still you don't know who he is?" asked Rachel, weary and incredulous.

"Nope."

"But the melody is always there?"

"*Hal's Theme*, uh huh. In the background."

To which Rachel, in a small voice, said, "Leon, why would *you* say you dream about this Hal so much?"

"That's what I'm wondering. It's funny, isn't it?"

"I mean, who is he?"

"Search me. Maybe I need a friend out here."

"Reasonable enough hypothesis." In the Dream Centre Alex Silver had an ankle on his knee and was filing his nails. "What were your feelings?"

"Distress and panic."

"Why?"

"Come on, Alex!" Rachel rose on an elbow. "What did it *mean*? Once or twice a night for a *year*? Who wouldn't be distressed?"

"Yes but don't forget. You'd naturally overreact from all the repressing you were doing around the relationship. Also, look at Leon. Anxiety runs the projector. Worry about last night's dream and you can bet it'll be on again tonight, 'significant' or not. Damn things snowball."

"But why was Leon worried?"

"Put our heads together, we could easily come up with a dozen reasons why Leon was worried, or why he's not around today, and we still wouldn't know a thing. Fortunately what matters here is why you were worried. Why should your husband's dreamlife be such a big deal? In some ways the middle class really is post-Calvinist, you know. People let others, even their spouses, dream anything they like, as long as it doesn't show up in behaviour. Murmur the wrong name at the wrong moment and you could be in trouble. Otherwise, nobody worries too much, except, of course, the dreamer. That much hasn't changed. But anyways. Who did you think Hal was?"

Rachel settled back and closed her eyes. "I'd rather not say."

Alex stopped filing. "Well, lah, dee, dah. Why the hell not?"

"First let me tell you who Leon thought he was, OK? It goes with the Wilkes/PAGO stuff."

Silver rolled his eyes. "OK OK. Tell me, tell me."

Over the next few weeks Leon, though he communicated little, was a new man. His food shopping became competent. Innovative meals were on the table when Rachel got home from work. His dope intake decreased to nil. PAGO, or at least the route to Hal it promised, had given him a new lease on life in the world.

And then one night Rachel came downstairs to find him pacing the living room spinning the dark glasses he now wore. "Leon, what's wrong?" she cried, falling onto the sofa. Still pacing, Leon explained.

At the previous meeting Wilkes had refused to release the names of members of the subcommittee who had recommended that all meetings be held at his house, and so that night's meeting had been boycotted by all members except Leon, who did not think about such things. Consequently he got a chance to talk with Wilkes, face to face. "And boy was he nervous. Over and over he kept coming back to PAGO. That organization is a real crutch for him. But after about an hour, by asking questions, I steered him into a personal area. I didn't find the connection exactly, but I found out something very, very interesting: Why Cam Wilkes is an agoraphobiac."

"Oh really?" Rachel's assumption that Cam Wilkes' agoraphobia was a surface function of deeper craziness had prevented her from ever wondering this.

Nevertheless, Leon told her Wilkes' story.

As a youth with a special talent for the trumpet, Cam Wilkes had once fallen deeply in love with a beautiful girl who happened to ride the same bus that he rode home from his music lessons. Every week for two years he rode that bus with this beautiful girl without being able to muster the courage to speak to her. One day his music teacher, looking a little wan, ended the lesson early. Reaching the bus stop earlier than usual, Wilkes mounted what he thought was his normal bus, but the beautiful girl was not on it. After a few blocks he realized what had happened. Unable to bear the prospect of not seeing her for another whole week, he got off at her stop to wait. As she stepped down from their usual bus, he put the trumpet to his lips and played a melody he had composed while waiting, entitled, *Melody for the Girl on My Bus*. The girl glanced briefly in Wilkes' direction and hurried on. His music teacher sank into a coma that week, Wilkes took a different bus to other lessons, and he never saw the beautiful girl again. He confessed to Leon that his withdrawal from the outside world had begun at that moment of rejection.

"What a terribly sad story," Rachel said. By now they were both slumped at the kitchen table.

"I know. I really sympathize."

"He's still in love with her?"

Leon nodded. "And terrified."

"The poor guy."

"There's something else."

"Oh dear."

"I got him to play *The Melody for the Girl on My Bus*."

"Oh no, Leon. It wasn't the same one he played for us."

"Yup. I know that piece in my bones."

"Leon," Rachel began carefully. "Are you really thinking there might be some connection between Hal and Cam Wilkes himself?"

"Some connection, obviously. This has been established."

"But Leon! He's not at all like the guy in your dreams!"

"You know him that well, eh?"

"Pardon?"

In answer Leon got up and went back into the living room. There Rachel found him on the shag, staring at the ceiling.

This was ridiculous. "Leon, what is going on in your mind? Cam Wilkes is hardly my type!"

"And if he was your type—" Leon inflectionless.

"Leon, what are you accusing me of? I didn't think you'd be interested, that's all! That's why I didn't tell you about him as soon as I got in!" This of course was not true, the way it came out.

There was a long silence. "I said *some connection*," Leon quietly. "Some connection."

"Leon, seriously. What's the matter. Are you projecting?"

"Oh yeah, I forgot. It's all my problem."

"Oh Leon—" Rachel said sadly. A few minutes of silence followed, and then she said, "Leon, I just want us to be happy." She had meant to say *moderate in all things*, but that seemed a little pedantic.

Leon rubbed his face with both hands. For another minute or so he returned to studying the ceiling. When his eyes shifted to meet Rachel's there was hope in them. "You know what I'd like to do, Rachel? Something concrete to help the folks at PAGO."

"Such as?"

"Particularly Cam Wilkes. I'd really like to do something to help Cam Wilkes."

Rachel nodded. After a few seconds she said, "Why him?"

Leon closed his eyes. "I don't know. Maybe because I like the guy. Maybe because he's the one closest to the edge—"

"But not because you think he's Hal."

Leon took a minute to reply to this. "As I said. I'm not ruling out the relevance of Hal to all this, if that's OK with you."

Rachel sighed. "So what will you do?"

Leon hesitated, as if he did not want to say. And then to Rachel's surprise he did say. "I think I'll try to track down the Girl on His Bus for him. At this point it seems as good a place to begin as any."

"But Leon," Rachel said. "Aside from how impossible that'll be, what's it got to do with Hal?"

"Who can say? Hal's the unknown, by definition. But the connection's there. It's got to be. And this at least is something concrete. I've spent too long on barren analysis and introspection. It's time I got back into the world. That's one thing writing down my dreams, and PAGO too, has taught me. There's a little PAGO person in all of us—"

"Yes, but—"

"They're my dreams, remember, Rachel. Mine. I'm the one who gets to decide how I work this through. Nobody else. This is my own business we're talking about here."

From her bed at the Dream Centre Rachel said, "Alex?"

"Mm-hmm?"

"That's when I broke it to Leon who I'd been thinking Hal was: his big hero back at Willmott High. A guy he always used to talk about."

Silver seemed nonplussed. He and Leon had gone to the same high school back in the city. "I never knew Leon had a big hero at Willmott! Who was he? Maybe I'll remem—"

"You."

The skin around Alex Silver's eyes walked back into his hairline and disappeared. "Me," he said, like a man neatly punched in the stomach.

"Alex," Rachel said, watching him. "Does this surprise you?"

"Surprise me? No, no— I mean. Yes. No. Kids have heroes, right? I didn't expect Leon's to be me, that's all. I never really felt like a hero." Silver laughed nervously. "Anybody's hero."

"But you were friends?"

"No. I didn't even think he knew I existed. Leon was a pretty cool guy around Willmott High, you know— So. But. Anyways. What did Leon say? Denied it, I guess, eh?"

Rachel nodded. "He said he never really knew you. You were a grade ahead. In high school, he said, that's like a generation—"

"Yeah—" Silver from the middle distance.

"Later, back in the kitchen," Rachel went on, "I asked him how he could be so sure you weren't Hal, and he looked down at this design he'd been making with some crumbs— a heart I think it was— and with this crooked little smile he said,'Naw. But you know, he really was quite a guy, that Alex. How does Shakespeare put it? "Take him all in all, here was a man"—?'"

Alex Silver squirmed, his face hot red.

"He looked at me," Rachel said, "and at that moment, Alex, I swear, he seemed so keen, so vulnerable, that I just had to go around the table and give him a big hug, but he must have picked up a shift in my muscles or something, because his chair moved closer to the table and his back went into this even more exclusive curve, and I thought, Maybe I should go and lie down.

"And then Leon was looking at me with a dreamy smile on. 'Hey, Rachel?' he said. 'I wonder what's become of old Alex, eh? I mean, I wonder what he's doing *right now*!'"

"Gee," murmured Silver.

Rachel's head came around to scrutinize. "Alex, are you sure you're disinterested enough for me to be telling you all this?"

"Me? Oh sure." Silver shifted in his chair. "Even if it turns out I am part of Leon's problem, our concern here is yours. That's got nothing to do with me. That you should choose to come to me because I'm the big expert around here does, but that's something we can look at later. So. Anyways. You thought Hal was me. What about Leon? Did he think Hal was Cam Wilkes or not?"

But Rachel had folded her arms. "No, Alex. I'm not saying

another word until you tell me why I'm here. You gave me two hours to pack and get over here and you still haven't told me a damn thing."

"You called *me*!"

"I was desperate! My husband's gone!"

"Rachel, the thing is this. I want the events orderly and fresh in your mind before we start."

"Start *what*? That's a legitimate question, Alex, and I'm walking out that door in two minutes if I don't get an answer right now."

"But we haven't got to the dream guy yet, or to why now you're the one looking for him— We don't even know who the Girl on Wilkes' Bus was—"

"And we won't unless you tell me what you've got in mind."

"OK, OK." Silver pushed his glasses up his nose and leaned forward in his seat, explanatory. "Here's what this is about. You sleep here for seven nights or more while this baby—" he reached back to pat the Hewlett Packard— "deprives you of all your dreams. It does this by beeping you awake each time it notices you're sliding into REM sleep. You'll get your sleep. You just won't get your dreams. You know what REM is?"

"I think so—"

"Rapid Eye Movement. It's not the only time you dream, but it's the time that seems to matter for normal functioning. With most people it happens around five times a night, periodicity proportional to body weight. I'd say for you every seventy-four to -six minutes. More often, of course, if you haven't been getting it—" Silver cleared his throat, blushed. "I mean REM. By the seventh day the beeper'll be going every fifteen minutes.

"The first two or three days you won't notice too much difference. A little irritability maybe. After that, you might want to take a few days off work."

"Why? What's going to happen to me?"

"Mild psychosis. People prevented from dreaming tend to dream out loud. Hallucinate, in other words. Same as narcotic and alcohol psychosis, which is simply the result of too little dreaming. That's what the d.t.'s are all about." Silver did a bogeyman. "Jimjams all dat stuff come back tuh haunt yuh!" He turned with satisfaction to the machine, his fingertips caressing the logo. "But anyway, this beauty does the same thing more healthfully and a heck of a lot more efficiently. No liver damage, for a start."

"But why?"

"Why this treatment for you? Because I believe that what you need more than anything at this point, Rachel, is a chance to get into this thing with both feet. Otherwise you're liable to be fiddling around with it all your life. Look at Cam Wilkes. Look at your husband. It's a whole lot easier to deal with material like this if you're conscious when it is."

"But I'll be crazy!"

"Crazy is a relative term. My point is this. Analysis takes fifty years and then some. Who's got time for that any more? This isn't *fin-de-siècle* Vienna, it's Village-on-the-Millpond. Listen to what I'm saying here. In ten days of dream deprivation you'll go farther with this than you would in ten years of twice-a-week analysis. In three days I can break down your Censor. In a week you'll be having coffee with the dream guy in person. Ten days and I guarantee a big dinner party, anywhere in the universe, with all your fears, all your desires— Just kidding—

"A couple of routine side effects you might want to watch out for. Big increase in appetite. Eat, don't worry. You'll burn it off. Also, aggression tends to rise. You might want to keep that in mind. And, oh yeah. Sexual— the, um, sex drive tends to, increase. But you're a big girl. Oh, two things that might encourage you to go ahead. One, you can quit any time. I mean, if it gets too weird. Two, there'll be three of you on the study. All women. So you won't be sleeping in here alone. And you can compare notes. Anyway, I'm in the next room. That's where I'll be sleeping. So what do you say?"

Rachel requested a few minutes to think it over.

"Sure. Take your time." Silver stood up, stretched, and went away through the *Keep Out* door.

Rachel's decision-making process, once she was forced to come down to it, was fairly simple: *This is more than Leon. This is the dream guy, and I have to get to the bottom of the dream guy, not for Leon but for me because if I don't then nothing will change.*

"I can quit when I want to?" she asked when Silver came back sucking his hand. In the other he'd balanced two glasses of soda water, it looked like. He set them down on her bedtable and went over to his desk.

"Sure. Just come back here and fall into bed. You'll dream like hell and be fine."

"OK, I'll do it. What have I got to lose?"

"Your sanity. But only for awhile." Silver bustled back holding out a sheet of paper. "You don't have to read all this. It just says you're responsible."

"Is that responsible, or responsible?"

"You know what you're doing."

"Sure I do." As she signed, Rachel said, "What happened to your hand?" Caught in a stapler? It seemed to be punctured.

"Oh nothing— Join me?" offering one of the glasses.

"Alex, no sedatives."

"Not a sedative—"

"Let me taste it first—*Yuck.*"

"Dexedrine sulphate. Routine in this sort of— Hey. A toast!"

"A toast—?"

"To the dream guy!"

As their glasses touched, Rachel noticed that blood was flowing freely from Silver's hand, down his wrist, and dripping off his Rolex to the floor.

TWO

He was real all right, but he was not here. His limit and ground was the pressure of his absence. Even when his methods were not generalizations, government, public opinion, your husband's obsession, red tape, applause, guest lists, politics, editorials, pecking orders, hard sells— he was never far away. And long after the clamour there he would be, in the shadows at the square's edge, the ghost in the ghost trenchcoat and ghost Wallabees, the trace and residue of everything those gathered voices had strained so hard to assume. Half an abstraction, objective as the clinically insane, grey as cement, he was the monkey wrench more crippling to her heart than anything Rachel had ever known, and for this reason, on a dark night towards the end of November, she allowed herself to be tucked in at the Silver Dream Research Centre with six electrodes glued to her head.

No sign of the other two women on the study until what seemed like the instant Rachel had fallen asleep. Then they entered whispering and giggling, crashing into things. Silver had to come in shushing, reprimand them for fuzzying the first night's results with alcohol, fight off having his pajamas removed, and wire their heads. A few more explosions of cackles and they were snoring like lumberjacks.

Depressed by memories of summer camp, Rachel, now fully awake, lay for a long time and turned over in her mind the events leading to her own, desperate search for the dream guy at that time known to her as Hal.

Two weeks after Leon had announced his intention of tracking down the Girl on Wilkes' Bus, he walked into the kitchen of 201 Dell and announced that he had found her.

"But how?" marveled Rachel, who had been making them a couple of grilled cheeses.

It hadn't been easy. First Leon had cunningly extracted more details— date, which bus, stops involved— from a vague Wilkes. Then, working in secret from his basement study, he had phone-interviewed dozens of people. Gradually the pieces had fallen into place.

"So who is it?" she asked.

"You."

As soon as Leon said this, all details of Cam Wilkes' behaviour crisped into focus for Rachel. The phrases *madly in love* and *fool for love* could be heard in her mind. Oddly, the fact that she had always felt her teenage prettiness to be singularly forgettable did not affect— except maybe inversely— her willingness to believe the contrary.

"Aw, he wouldn't remember me from way back then," she said modestly.

"Don't worry."

"What do you mean?"

"He doesn't realize it's you."

"Then it wasn't! For godsake, it was only a few years ago!"

"Seventeen, to be exact."

"What bus?"

"The Downtown 16 from Madison."

That shut her up.

"So I'm sorry," Leon said.

Or was it the *19*?

"None of us," Leon reassured her, "are what we were. Anyway my point is, he hasn't made the connection. He can't, and that indicates the real problem. He's totally fixated on a dream. In the same proportion the guy is afraid. Rachel? It's the least we can do."

"*We*? *Do*? What are you talking about?"

"Come on."

"You come on."

Leon's disappointed eyes followed her around the kitchen.

"So what are you saying?" Rachel slamming down his grilled cheese. "I should give myself to him?"

"You don't get it yet, do you," Leon said, still watching her face but his eyes less disappointed while he chose his words. "You, Rachel, are the key. Hal has come to me through you. *Hal's Theme* is the same piece that Cam Wilkes played for you at that bus stop seventeen years ago."

"And allowing these assorted unlikely statements to be true?"

"I'll spell it out. Either Cam Wilkes' unconscious mind is broadcasting his old pain to you and I'm picking up the ricochets, or you are broadcasting straight to me because you saw this poor bastard playing his trumpet for you back when you were a knockout, and this was an everyday occurrence for you then. That trumpet solo as far as you were concerned was nothing but a glorified wolf whistle. Things were so all-round easy for you in the love department that you didn't even want to know, and now it's haunting your unconscious, and consequently mine as your husband."

"That's cruel and stupid."

"I knew you'd deny it, just like you've denied the memory itself."

What Leon wanted Rachel to *do* was what he claimed was the least she *could* do: go and quietly tell Cam Wilkes that she was the Girl on His Bus and say she was sorry. Who knew. The apology alone might change everything. But the clincher would be for Wilkes to realize that this perfectly ordinary woman—

("Thanks a lot."

"You know what I mean.")

— was the one of his dreams. By being hit in the face by the discrepancy, Cam Wilkes would see how crazy it is to cling to the past.

"Look who's talking about clinging to the past."

"Let's not get abusive."

"Shock tactics, eh," Rachel muttered.

"You could put it that way."

"And if it wasn't me?"

"But it was, Rachel, it was."

The only person Rachel could remember on her downtown bus from Madison was the driver, whose mucal snuffling worked magic for getting people to move to the back of the bus. No Moondog Wilkes. But Leon was intent. That night he made her a nice canneloni, got her drunk on ten-dollar St. Emilion and stoned on a joint he had bought from the kid with the hawk, and next morning the first thing she remembered was agreeing to do it. *Hal's Theme* certainly had blown her away the first time Wilkes played it for her that night on his lawn, if *Hal's Theme* it was. Or was Wilkes' playing just so incredibly affecting that the melody only seemed familiar? And what about music being the universal language? What if it wasn't familiar but merely true? She longed too and who didn't? Besides, wouldn't Cam Wilkes have cut as odd and unforgettable a figure seventeen years ago as now? These questions, along with disembodied gestures and blurred faces from her years of riding the Downtown bus from Madison, floated through Rachel's mind all that next day until it came time to drop in on the man whose mind and life by one weakness of hers or another it had somehow become the least she could do to acknowledge destroying.

As Rachel and Leon approached Cam Wilkes' house in the Subaru, Rachel saw that thrust into the piled earth around the edge of the crater in the front lawn was a neat but marginless placard of the sort carried by meet-thy-doom and health-food fanatics. "Calling all Villagers!" it read.

HERE WITNESS what going outside can do to you or your lawn. Life does not have to be this way gaping and leaking loneliness like a hole in the brain. Join PAGO and see the World as it was before it blew up in your face, immediate but orderly like a bus transfer in the hand of a beautiful girl.

Cam Wilkes

Founding Member and President

Millpond Chapter, PAGO INTERNATIONAL.

Leon was ringing the doorbell by touching the exposed wires together. The response was a lively trumpet rendition of the Rosemary Clooney favourite, *Come On-a My House*. After a few pleasantries with Wilkes, whom they found lying on a bus seat in the living room, Leon stepped onto the patio, as previously arranged, for a "breath of air," and Rachel sat down on the seat near Wilkes, who had straightened up.

"Cam," she said.

"Yes, Rachel?"

"First, I've been meaning to give you this—" and she handed him his flesh-coloured workglove, which he looked at without recognition. "I'd have let Leon bring it along to a PAGO evening, but—"

"Thanks. I really need one of these."

Wow, Rachel thought. For somebody obsessed by the past he sure has a bad memory.

"No, Cam," she said kindly. "It's yours."

He buried his face in it.

Rachel watched him for a moment. It struck her that he had regressed since she saw him last.

"Cam," she said, "I have something to confess."

"You don't have to say it, Rachel," Wilkes replied, looking up. "Not to me. I understand."

"You do?"

"Yes, and I'm not hurt."

"You're not?"

"No, and I accept your apology immediately, so you don't even have to open your mouth. All is forgiven."

"Thank you, Cam. Thank you very much."

"You're welcome."

Well, thought Rachel, that was easy enough. After a silence she asked, "Did you know from the start, Cam?"

"Yes I did."

"Did you recognize me?"

"I recognize them all, Rachel."

"All— ?"

"That's right. The first law of magic. Like attracts like."

"You lost me."

Wilkes shrugged. "They tend to marry."

"Women—?"

"Often women. The *women* tend to marry men."

"Right—"

"Sex, I suppose. The male and female genitals really do seem made for each other, don't they? And of course, conventional expectations."

Rachel resolved to cut bait and go for a straight confession. Maybe it would sound like a recap, and everything would sort out.

"Reproduction must count for a lot—" Wilkes observed, reflective.

"Cam," Rachel said. "I was the girl on your bus. My parents weren't meant for each other. My father was in another world, and then he was always away. Finally my mother left him. Life was grey at home, like poison fog. I never noticed anything around me. I still don't. I'm sorry. I never intended to hurt you. I didn't realize you were playing your trumpet for me. I don't even remember you, or your trumpet."

In one movement Wilkes swept to the floor some scattered bus tokens and an empty potato chip bag and moved down the seat towards her saying, "You're not telling me you're sorry for not joining PAGO earlier, with Leon, Rachel. You're telling me that you were the Girl on My Bus." He took her hand softly in his. "I suspected it was you from the day I watched you and Leon move to the Millpond—" He bowed his head and paused as if to swallow tears. "I was hurt, terribly. But I accept your apology. Of course I do. And I forgive you from the bottom of my heart."

"Thank you, Cam." Rachel remained silent for several minutes while Wilkes sobbed. She hoped this would be cathartic for him, because the difference between herself then and now had better not have been enough to do the trick.

Finally Wilkes dried his eyes and said, "Rachel."

"Yes, Cam?"

"I also have something to confess. But before I do, I want you to promise you won't tell anyone what I'm going to reveal to you now. Not even Leon."

Assuming Wilkes was about to share a confidence relating to herself, Rachel agreed, uneasily.

Some confidence. A paranoid song and dance was what it was. About how in the years following his disappointment, with money from inherited Chemlawn shares, Wilkes had bought from the township an abandoned bus yard on Highway 303 and there set up house inside the original Downtown 16 from Madison, with plants, propane, water from a shed on the property, and snow when that froze. Before long, however, Mortprop Investments, who wanted the property for building the Millpond, was putting pressure on him to sell: flattening the tires of his buses, hiring a child with an airgun to sit on the shed roof and pick off visiting gulls, etc.

"But why didn't you just accept their offer and get your bus towed someplace else?" Rachel asked impatiently. "They were buying the land, weren't they, not your buses—"

Cam Wilkes stroked his trumpet as he spoke. "I can answer that in one word: agoraphobia. Going anywhere, even towed inside my bus, was inconceivable. By that time I was pretty . . . far gone."

Finally, by paying massive kickbacks to the mayor and council, Mortprop Investments got the township dump site instead, and then the *township* threw Wilkes off his own property for violating zoning laws by living on it. By that time the Millpond had been built and Wilkes had met Della when her car broke down on the 303. He married her, bought this bungalow, and settled down. Unlike Della.

Squinting, Wilkes pointed his cigarette at the near wall. "My bus yard is one and three-quarters mile in that direction as the crow flies. To me it's hallowed ground. Precious memories. When Della left I found I couldn't live without my Downtown 16 from Madison, so after a lot of soul-searching, I had it dismantled and brought here. It's all around you, Rachel. In fact, right now we're sitting on exactly the same seat that you used to sit on when we rode it together."

"Oh really?"

"Do you know why I have that bus with me here today?"

"So you can have my seat?"

"Close. So I can *sniff* your seat."

Rachel jumped up. "That's *gross! Leon!*"

"Love is gross," Cam Wilkes said sadly.

As soon as Leon came back into the room he wanted to find out if Rachel's revelation had worked. Pretending he had just seen something unbelievable outside, he tried to get Wilkes out onto the patio. Wilkes would have none of it. "Lawn yesterday, patio today," was how he put it, shaking his head.

"How'd it go?" Leon whispered to Rachel when Wilkes went to the kitchen for coffee.

"*Go?* Leon, the man is crazy!"

"It might take a little time."

When they got home Rachel tried again, before the light got turned off, in the small pool of time where once they would have made love. "Leon, I've been thinking about Alex Silver, your high school hero."

"Why? You've never even met him."

"Listen to me. Alex-Al, Al-Hal. I'll say it again. Alex-Al, Al-Hal."

"A breathing exercise."

"It doesn't suggest something?"
"Not really."
"Why not?"
"Because I just *call* him Hal."
"Oh, you just *call* him Hal! I see! What's his real name?"
"Rather not say."
"No? Any reason?"
"Rather not say."
"Leon?"
"Yes?"
"I give up."
"Good. You're way more useful to me as a set of—"
"Don't say it."
"Say what? *Ears.* Why do you always assume I'm a sexist jerk?"

In her bed in the Dream Centre, Rachel looked at her watch: 3:05 a.m. This wasn't going to work. How could she be expected to sleep on an iron cot in a strange room with stereo snoring, electrodes attached to her head, and a humming machine keeping track if she did? It just wasn't conducive.

She pulled the electrodes off, felt guilty, got up, had a pee, glued the electrodes back on the way Silver had showed her, and eased back into bed. Funny. He'd assured her he'd be checking all through the night.

Plumped her pillow and lowered her head onto it, uncontrollably to remember further events of that heatwave and what, God help us, followed.

In the continuing summer heat the level of the millpond fell two feet, leaving a stretch of yellow-green, stinking muck bordered by a six-foot band of crushed stone. An unfortunate dog who crossed this foulness for a drink before breakfast one morning died at noon the next day after violent convulsions, and people were advised over loudspeakers mounted on slowly moving cars with *Mortprop Investments* on the doors that if they must go out, under no circumstances to allow their pets off the concrete sidewalks and

Permawood walkways. As the heat, so continued the explosions of garbage bags. For those whose lawns were the heart and soul of their weekend it was a difficult time. Many people stayed inside with the air conditioning turned up high and watched baseball. Quite a few conferred with their lawyers about suing Mortprop Investments for the costs of restoring lawns and driveways. But most who lost a part of their lawn simply called Sod Your World and had the bill sent to Mortprop Investments, who were paying up while publicly acknowledging nothing.

Rachel's mother began to urge her to sell and move back to the city.

"We can't," Rachel told her when she phoned one day. "Leon says it's a buyer's market."

"It's a buyer's market because it's dangerous to live there. By the way, your friend called."

"What friend?"

"You know the one. It's not as if you had—"

"Gretchen Molstad—?"

"That's her. She's looking for you."

"Did you give her my number?"

"I couldn't find my book. I told her you live out in the sticks somewhere. She said she was very disappointed to hear that. Maybe she'll call again. Now there's a girl who always has nice men friends. Of course, she's got spirit."

"So long, Mother."

On Leon the continuing adventure of physical life in the Millpond made little impression, for he had concentrated his attention on getting Cam Wilkes to leave his house. All Leon's jobless energy, all his Hal-haunted loneliness, all his ambitions to make his mark on the life of Cam Wilkes, came to be focussed upon this task. Like a bad psychiatrist, Leon was so intent on returning Wilkes to the world that he was blind to the chaos raging on all sides out there.

"Hey Leon," Rachel pointed out. "The problem is not that Wilkes won't leave the house, the problem is that he is out of his mind."

But Leon was like a man in love, consumed by his object. Sensing this, Wilkes refused to go anywhere. Leon had read that agoraphobiacs feel safe in cars, so he rented a Lincoln Continental at a weekend rate. Saturday morning he pulled into Wilkes' driveway crooning with anticipation. But in the end he had to be satisfied with joining Wilkes in the living room to admire the car through the picture window. They removed a strip of aluminum foil.

"Leon, we can't afford to rent Continentals for the weekend!" Rachel cried when she found out what he had done.

"What was I supposed to do? He sure wasn't going to go for a ride in a Subaru!"

"Buy him a bus pass!"

Rachel should have worried when she saw the lightbulb flash on over Leon's head. The next morning he went to a bus company and rented a bus and driver for eight hours.

It worked. To Leon's joy, no sooner had the bus driver, a taciturn red-haired youth, pulled into Wilkes' driveway than Wilkes came floating out of his house, waving like the Queen to the three or four people gazing blankly into his crater and at his sign. Reaching the bus, he hesitated— that red hair— but after a carefully rehearsed if stilted greeting from the driver and a loud hearty welcome from Leon, he came on board, explaining, "Ninety-five percent of agoraphobiacs are terrified of buses, but thanks to the Girl on My Bus, for me they're counterphobic. Especially empty."

Wilkes and Leon sat together near the back, Wilkes in the window seat, where he looked out upon the world with quiet interest. When, however, Leon casually suggested they head downtown on the 303, Wilkes did not appear to hear him. Later he declined to get out of the bus, even to "stretch his legs," and after an hour asked to be told when they had reached Hillock Rise, because he "had to be getting back." Given x number of years indoors, an hour's bus ride, Leon felt, was a plenty big step for one morning. He told the driver to return to Hillock Rise. But they had trouble finding it, and they were still searching when the bus was pelted by sod from an exploding lawn.

"*Oh oh oh*," Wilkes whispered, sliding down in his seat.

The same afternoon, with a few hours left on the bus and driver, Leon dropped back to take Wilkes for another ride. This time Wilkes refused, arguing that he had already gone for a ride. The next day Leon rented a backhoe for two hours and drove it right up to the edge of Wilkes' patio, but Wilkes just stood behind the screen door smiling and shaking his head. "Watch out for the gas line!" he called. Leon then phoned from a Millpond McDonald's and told Wilkes excitedly that he (Wilkes) had won a free lunch and could he come right over and eat it for the photographers? "Be sure to thank the whole staff," Wilkes told him, "when you convey my regrets."

"He's just being perverse!" Leon shouted at Rachel one night from the tub. "When you first met the guy he was all the way out on his front lawn digging that phony hole, but now he says it's the explosions that are keeping him in!"

Rachel came to the bathroom doorway. "Leon, why are you so obsessed about this?"

Leon sank to his chin. His knees rose hairy through the bubbles. "No use trying to explain," he said, staring straight ahead. "I feel a very real responsibility to get the guy out into reality, it's that simple. This should be a straightforward matter. In a sane world anybody would see immediately that there are some things a person just has to do. There would be no talk of 'obsessed'. So would you lay off, please."

Leon seemed to Rachel at that moment like a lover who has enrolled in a watercolours class in order to be close to his beloved but become so engrossed in his art that when she gets bored and stops showing up he fails to notice. "Leon? One more question? What's this got to do with Hal?"

"Who?"

"Hal. You do remember Hal—"

"I told you what it's got to do with Harry: Nothing. I figured out—"

"Leon, did you say Harry? Hal's name is really *Harry*? Is this true?"

A pause, Leon preparing an offensive, reaching with studied calm for the loofa and soap. "So you see now," he said, slow and teacherly, "why I couldn't let you get hold of it."

"Because Harry was your father's name!"

Leon's father had died of a heart attack about five years before it occurred to Leon that after eighteen years of living in the same house with the man he knew next to nothing about him.

"That's right."

"And you thought I'd assume Hal was the dad you never really knew."

"Superego as good buddy. Just your kind of take on this,

right?"

"And he isn't—?"

"Check, as I knew all along. Harry is your problem, Rachel, and if you can't accept that, then he's your even bigger problem."

"Leon, how do you know he isn't your dad?"

"See? There you go."

"Just tell me why you're so sure."

"Because unlike you I remember my father, and Harry isn't like him at all."

"Is Cam Wilkes?"

"Why should he be? I never knew the guy until the other day! I never rode the Downtown 16 from Madison in my life!"

"Are you still dreaming about Harry?"

"You have to remember, Rachel. All that ever came through strong and clear was the melody. Harry was more confused, as if his personality was just something the melody conjured—"

"Conjured for you, Leon. That's the important thing—"

"Exactly, and for me Harry was like dreaming somebody from their signature—"

"And are you still doing that?"

"Who knows. I'm fed up with remembering my dreams—"

"But how can you know if your theory that Harry connects to Cam Wilkes is right if you don't keep a close watch on your dreams while you spend time with Cam Wilkes? You can't find out about yourself by just always doing what you feel like!"

"Don't get moral with me, Rachel—"

"I'm not getting moral, I'm getting scientific. You're turning your back on crucial evidence!"

"Who's turning their back?" Leon mad now, sitting straight up, bath water sloshing. "Who refuses to believe that Harry is her problem? Who can't accept that her proud and heartless behaviour seventeen years ago is behind all this and the reason she can't is she can't accept that she's not the beauty now she was then! Don't you see? I've moved on. I've finished with being a head person. Now I'm a gut person. I'm way beyond any one-and-one-makes-two understanding now, Rachel, so don't try to reason with me. I'm into something you obviously can't understand. I'm just feeling my way here, like an animal in the dark."

Rachel walked slowly away from the bathroom to turn these statements over quietly in her mind for a long time.

The thing was, Leon's dumping Harry onto her hinted a mad-genius logic that went deeper than either Leon's reasons or his buck passing, and deeper too than her fair intake of Millpondish long-ing. Her husband had moved on, or thought he had, to leave her square in the place that every day now it seemed a little clearer she had more or less always been.

In the shadow of Harry.

And then, just as Hal had become Harry, everything seemed to stay the same but in fact was radically different. For one thing, cooler, wetter weather set in. The pond rose again to meet its white border, and the garbage bags grew quiescent. For another, a whole year after he had forgotten about applying, Leon got accepted to real estate school. For another, about the time of Leon's acceptance, Cam Wilkes not-so-coincidentally, probably, stopped leaving his basement. Nothing Leon said or did could change his mind. PAGO went into extended recess, and Leon stopped wearing dark glasses. For still another, Rachel started her own search for Harry. At first it was the kind that's unbroken only in retrospect, when entire days of absent-mindedness are completely forgotten and all sorts of directionless stumbling get reclassified as dead-ends and nice tries. The actual here and now was not so committed. Other things kept cropping up. And if they didn't really, then her brain circuitry in that area must have kept getting tired and closing down, because Harry kept misting out of priority. When he wasn't right there in the background he didn't seem to be anywhere at all, except in the shape of a faint axiom of emotion deep in her head. Like some old anxiety, or longing. But slowly, as the days passed, he, or his absence, emerged a little more steadily for her, invisible of course, in shadows, watching her, waiting, beyond the sunshine of circum-stance, after the clamour, above the confusion of fumbling imagi-nation . . .

Inspired, Rachel turned to her own dreams, did what she had been wondering for a whole year about Leon for doing. While he dreamt the dreams of a man no longer interested in inner things, his pad in the morning empty, she struggled to get down whatever brainwave had just tossed her onto the beach conscious enough to close strengthless fingers around a pencil. The trick was to write backwards in time, the last dream image evoking the one before, effects triggering causes, and so on back until memory flagged and sleep took over once more. Unfortunately, after an eight-hour day at Millpond Indemnity, memory was too numb not to yield to sleep almost as soon as Rachel's slack fingers touched the old HB Venus Imperial. No signs of Harry dreaming in the anxious little scenarios she did get down.

Meanwhile, busy with real estate classes, Leon at first fell into the habit of leaving Egg McMuffins and Big Macs on the dark stairs to Wilkes' basement. Sometimes on rainy evenings Rachel would tag along to listen to the beautiful, sad music that Wilkes played down there. Wistfully, behind a scrim of tears, she would try to guess which other of those melodies had been written expressly for her. This while Leon, no longer interested in *Hal's* (now *Harry's*) *Theme* a.k.a. *Melody for the Girl on My Bus* and others almost as heart-wrenching, doggedly carried miscellaneous bus parts from Wilkes' kitchen to the den. He wanted the cooking area clear because he had been finding it easier to throw together a fried egg sandwich for Wilkes than to stop by McDonald's or hang around waiting for the Lickin' Chicken Man. The pressure of a crash course in real estate had caused all those hours that had been weighing so heavily on Leon's shoulders to lift off like enormous gulls. The challenge of learning the fine points of real estate and how to earn a living selling it had him taking a voluntary cut in profile from Cam Wilkes' saviour to his keeper.

"Leon," Rachel said one night in Wilkes' kitchen as she watched him make a tuna sandwich for the man in the basement, "if I really was the Girl on His Bus, don't you think Cam would be coming out more now that he knows, instead of retreating like this?"

"Not necessarily," Leon replied, squeezing brine from the tuna can. "Maybe the reality was too much of a blow."

"God, Leon. You sure know how to make a woman feel attractive."

"Still can't get past that part of it, eh Rachel? You know, for somebody keen on looking at things scientifically, you sure do think just like a woman."

"Oh go to hell."

Rachel went out to wait in the car.

There, musing, with the music of Cam Wilkes coming faintly through the basement windows, she could see a familiar pattern emerging. As a Leon enthusiasm crackled across its apportioned synapses, it tended to scar and pit the site of its inspiration so badly that eventually the whole thing died into gloom and darkness, leaving Leon in need of a new charge. Provided this time by a fresh start in real estate. And so Leon's Harry obsession had merged into the Cam Wilkes, and the Cam Wilkes in its turn, as Leon worked his way deeper into the groove of real estate school, had continued to melt on down until it was no more than a puddle of bitter sweat. By now, indeed, Leon was all but completely *into* real estate. "These little pieces of paper, Rachel—" he had cried the other night, shaking a fistful of expired listings in her face— "are gonna make our fortune!"

And that was how Rachel, who could not so easily as the man she married drop everything and rush off in a different direction, came to be left alone to search for the elusive Harry.

A good thing for her she knew the tune.

Early morning at the Silver Dream Research Centre and Rachel is being crowded to an edge of the bed by Alpine snoring. Leon, she thinks. At it again. This time the dreamer's fight for lost mattress takes the form of a struggle up those wet and craggy bluffs, a confused idea that somewhere high above, compassionate in clouds, will be Harry. But foot- and handholds turn out icky and flaccid, this mountain hasn't *gelled* yet, she's not getting anywhere at all, and then Alex Silver swings past on a trapeze . . . disappears . . . swings past . . . disappears . . . swings past . . . talking now: " . . . *you doing dream . . . the whole experi . . . ously machine is mal . . . on! Wake . . . "*

So Rachel woke up, found those snore snags not Leon's but one of those other two women's. Tearful then, she lay in the full wretchedness of the sleep-short failed marriage sufferer until Alex Silver came by to see how she was doing.

"I was dreaming," Rachel told him.

"A sad one." He passed her a Kleenex. His hand was bandaged.

"I'm not supposed to— am I?"

"A waking-up dream, right? A non-REMer, for sure. They're not always just colourful thoughts, you know." Silver stepped back to throw an arm around the Hewlett Packard. "Don't worry. This baby don't make mistakes."

"But I hardly slept at all. And when I did it only woke me up once or twice—"

Silver tore off a print-out and held it in front of Rachel's face. "Five times."

"Oh."

He handed her a non-REM dream report and a pencil. "Here you go— And there's plenty more where that came from."

He wasn't kidding. Before Rachel went to work she had to complete an arithmetic test; a vigilance test (a letter of the alphabet intoned on a tape every 2.5 seconds: press the buzzer when it's Q); the Stroop Colour-Word Test (match 'em up); the Holtzman Ink-blot Test—a nouveau-Rorschach—charting on a seven-point scale the Intensity of her Need; the Reuben Ambiguous Figure Test; and the Nowlis-Green Mood Check List (71 adjectives factor-analyzed into eight scales: Activation-Deactivation, Aggression, Anxiety, Concentration, Depression, Egotism, Pleasantness, and Social Affectation).

She was still on the Reuben Ambiguous Figure Test, sitting up in bed, when one of the other women on the study, small and sallow, stumbled past from the washroom. Oh dear. A sinking feeling told Rachel she knew that profile from somewhere. Somewhere oppressive. As she dressed for work she tried for a peek, but both her colleagues were under their covers, sleeping—not dreaming— it off. Wires emerging.

In her office at Millpond Indemnity that first day of dream deprivation Rachel could already feel the blunt dead fingers of the Nowlis-Green Check List fumbling around in her brain. Otherwise it was a lot like any other Monday.

At eleven her mother phoned, her first question, "How's Leon?"

"Oh— Fine—"

"Is he still looking?"

"Mother, how many times do I have to tell you? Leon's in real estate now! He's been doing it for weeks!"

"On commission."

"Of course."

"Commission selling isn't a job. A man should be in business for himself, like your father was— still is, I'm certain— or on salary."

"I'll tell Leon you said so."

"Things are OK between you?"

"Pretty good—"

"Rachel, if you're not happy you don't have to tell me. Just like you don't have to get blown up by a garbage bag."

"They stopped blowing up when it stopped being hot, in the summer."

"And you're happy."

"Mother, Marg from Road Accidents just came in—"

"Rachel, I know when you're not. All I'm saying is all I've ever said. I'm here when you need me."

Rachel's forehead came to rest on her desk as the receiver came to rest in its cradle. Five minutes later Marg from Road Accidents really did come in. "You just talked to your mother."

Rachel's forehead remained on her desk. "Says she's there when I need her."

"Aw, she's OK. It's hard when you're old."

"She's not old. She's fifty-six."

"She cares about you, Rachel. That's all— Rachel?"

"Uh-huh."

"There isn't by any chance something to tell?"

"Not a thing. I'm fine. Leon's fine. Everything's fine."

"You wouldn't want to look at me when you say that?"

"No. I want to leave my head right here on my desk."

So long did Rachel's head remain on her desk that she began to wonder if she should go back to the Dream Centre at all. Alex Silver was not necessarily the most confidence-inspiring of therapists, was he? And then there was his mother. And Rachel remembered the very first time she had called Silver's office in Village Market Square.

Twice there was no answer. The third time a woman said in a flat voice, "What is it."

"Is this Dr. Silver's office?" Rachel thinking she must have grown careless with dialling so often, and this was one of those wrong-number glimpses into a life you are sorry to know even this much about.

"Did you dial 427-4263?"

"Yes—"

"And so what did you expect to get?"

"I only asked because I tried four times and nobody answered."

"And the fifth time they did. This is what matters. What does not matter is that somebody should step out for a few minutes. Or are the bodily functions of an old woman interesting to you?"

"Sorry. I'd like to make an appointment with Dr. Silver."

"You can't, because this is not his number."

"It's not?"

"You would know this already if you used the correct phone book. Let me tell you what year this is. Do you have a pen?" She told Rachel the year. "Now, you tell me please. What phone book are you using?"

Rachel looked at the phone book in her lap and giggled. Hers was two years out of date.

"Why don't you use the *1910* phone book? Then you would really get a good conversation."

The woman hung up.

Some people. Rachel went down to the living room and found the right phone book, where Silver's number was listed as 427-4275, which she dialled.

"Dr. Silver's office." Funny. Sounded like the same woman. "Hang on a minute."

Rachel hung on for five minutes, drumming her fingers, telling herself the *next* time the second hand came round she would hang up and call again.

"Yes."

"Hello, I'd like—"

"Name."

"Rachel Boseman." Obediently, Rachel waited for the next question. It did not come. "Hello?"

"Hello. Name."

"Rachel Boseman."

Again Rachel waited. Nothing. "Look," she said. "I'd like to make an appointment to see Dr. Silver."

"Just because you had to wait a little, you don't have to act high and mighty. It happens we are getting a lot of crackpot calls on the other line. Are you a client of Dr. Silver's?"

"Didn't I just talk to you?"

"You think that should make you a client?"

"I'm sorry?"

"I am sorry too. You would not believe how sorry I am. But he can see only his own clients."

"How do I become a client? Do I need a referral?"

"A referral? Do you think the man is a headshrinker?"

"Is he booked up?" Rachel tried, still polite. "Should I call back at a certain time?"

"And what time would that be?"

"I don't know!"

"And *I* should?"

"Well, can you put me on a list?"

The woman sighed. "There is no 'list'." And then she seemed to mutter something that sounded like *paranoid*.

"What did you say?"

"I *said*. There is no *list*." And then, as if writing, the woman murmured, more quietly, "Hard, of hear,ing."

"Pardon?"

"*No list*! There is *no list*!"

"This is hopeless."

"You're telling me. An ear doctor you should try."

"Please. Is there a better time I should call?"

"Better for what? For *who*? Me? You? Him? The stars? What is this 'better time'?"

"Listen, I just want to know. Are you going to give me an appointment with Dr. Silver or not?"

A long pause, and the voice, very calm, said, "You should understand. This office does not respond to threats."

"I'm not threatening! I want an appointment!"

Silence. Then, as if resuming an interview, "What other problems do you have?"

"Is this a serious question? I mean, are you screening me?"

"Sar,casm," slowly, half under her breath, a careful speller. "Schiz,oid ten,dencies. Delu,sions." Then, returning to her phone voice: "Looks like we have another problem to add to the list."

"What problem?"

"No appointment with Dr. Silver. Do you think a busy man like him has time for people who are such a mess? Take my advice. Try medication. There are some very good products on the market these days. I am thinking of one of the minor tranquillizers. Some you won't even remember you're on them."

"I don't want medication! And I'm not sick!"

No answer.

"Hello? Hello?"

"Just a little or you wouldn't be calling?"

"Look, I have a straightforward problem—"

"They all do."

"And I want to talk to Dr. Silver about it."

"Maybe you need a lawyer. A good notary. An accountant can solve many of life's problems. You would be surprised."

"I don't need a lawyer!"

"A justice of the peace?"

"No! It's a *psychological* problem!"

The woman snickered.

"Why are you laughing?"

"Don't you people realize there is no such thing as *a* psychological problem? The head is not a filing cabinet. Believe me. It's all one big *mishkebibble* in there." Muttering again: "Naive, poor so,cial skills. Bad, on phone."

"Would you stop that!"

"And what is it exactly you believe I am doing?"

"Making notes about me! Or pretending to!"

"Uh-uh." And as if writing, "Para,noid."

"*I'm not paranoid!*"

"And not, I suppose, violent either?"

Here Rachel slammed down the receiver and threw the phone book across the room.

That was several weeks ago. Eventually Rachel did get through, to his answering machine. And now, this evening after work, reluctant, undecided, she had another session, at his office, on the second floor of a four-storey building in Village Market Square, in an eastern sector of the Millpond. Silver's office was above a post-new-wave vegetarian freshwater restaurant called Chez Pond. As the board in the lobby revealed, the building contained numerous other businesses, including a law office (McQuaig, Quaig, and Quaig), a dentist (Dr. S. Thurm), a hairstyling place (Tease 'n Please), a Fred Hogg dance studio, a talent agency. In the elevator Rachel was joined by a full-dress Clarabell the Clown, every detail perfect, right down to the hornbox.

Fortunately Mrs. Silver had left for the day. Rachel passed with

relief through the waiting room into Silver's office, which was big
and sunny, with minimal furnishing and ankle-deep mulberry
broadloom. Silver himself, reassuring in a blue blazer and flannels,
left a high-back swivel chair to come around a massive cluttered
oak desk with both arms extended. "Hi Rachel! Sit down! So tell
us," squeezing her hands, "how was Day One?"

Rachel shrugged and sat down in a leather chair by a smoked-
glass table with a vase on it containing a giant antherium. Alex fell
into an identical chair across the table, put his Dacks up, and folded
his hands behind his head. "Nothing much yet," she admitted.
"Alex, I've been think—"

"Naw, it's gradual. Listen. I want to hear about the— you
know— gay stuff and about who Harry came to be for you
personally. I want to hear about Nick Sirocco. I want it all and I
want it in order. The more pieces of the puzzle we bring forward
now the more your conscious mind'll have to work with when the
dream deprivation really kicks in."

Rachel sighed. "That all starts with Gretchen Molstad."

"Check."

She took a deep breath.

One Friday in October Rachel was trying to rendez-vous with
Leon at some kind of real estate reception in a banquet room on the
basement level of the Olde Mill. The Olde Mill was a dining and
dancing facility built out of trucked-in stone and old barn timbers,
with a big aluminum water wheel that sent measured ripples out
across the surface of the pond. It was there that Rachel ran into her
old friend Gretchen Molstad. Actually, Gretchen saw Rachel first,
snuck up behind her, and in the voice of a woman who had been
smoking Player's Plain for a long, long time, said, "Found him
yet?" Rachel's reaction was the reaction of a woman who had been
looking for just as long. She jumped a foot.

After that, Gretchen hugged Rachel and pushed her to arm's
length. Over and over. Otherwise shaken by Gretchen's coiffure, jet
black and spiky— used to be a platinum pageboy— Rachel cried,
"Gretchen, how *are* you?" as her brain laboured across the connections from wondering how a familiar-voiced stranger could know
about Harry to wondering how Gretchen Molstad could know

about him. *Leon?* But Leon had never—had he?—forgiven Gretchen
for trying to pass off standing him up one night four years ago as
a surprise blind date with Rachel.

Gretchen went into profile. *"Ted!"* Several feet away a tall,
square-jawed, blond-haired man wearing a bomber jacket, baggy
yellow cords, and duck shoes did an amiable wheel, a braced half-
turn of elaborate surprise. Pretending to spot Gretchen for the first
time ever, he shook his head happily, like a sneezy dog. *"Ted! Get
over here!"*

"Gretchen, where have you been?" Rachel asked as Ted got
over.

"Hi," Ted said to Rachel, pumping her hand and nodding.

"Ted, this is my best friend Rachel Jardine." *Jardine* was Rachel's
maiden name. "Rachel, Ted Eskershack. Ted's in leisure products."

"You bet," Ted said. "Uh huh. That's great."

"Nice to meet you, Ted—"

"Hey, yeah, perfect—" Ted turned to Gretchen, who was
holding a plastic cup in front of her face and making a smile using
only her mouth.

"Ted—?" she said.

"Oh sure, OK. Rachel?"

"No thanks."

Ted went away. Gretchen watched him go, then dragged
Rachel across the room and threw her down on an Olde Mill settee
in earth-coloured Naugahyde. There she seized Rachel's hands,
imploring. "So what do you think."

"About Ted? He seems nice—"

Gretchen dropped Rachel's fingers like hot tongs. "You think
he's dumb."

"Gretchen, I just met him!"

"No, you're right. Like a tuna."

Bitterly Gretchen lit a cigarette. Player's Plain, Rachel marvelled. After all these years. In answer to Rachel's earlier question
Gretchen explained that she had just got back from eighteen
months in the South Pacific dealing blackjack on a Liberian pleasure craft. Too depressed finally by the discrepancy between her
monthly salary and the daily take, she was now working as a
receptionist at a Millpond computer programs company called
Village SoftWorks. "I never thought I'd end up in the suburbs, but
the rents downtown—"

She broke off to go through her purse. "I talked to your mother. She's really disappointed in you living out here—" Gretchen looked up. "Leon likes it?"

"For the sake of argument."

"How is old Bozo?"

"OK. Employed. Coming out of a big depression."

"You look real happy about it."

"We take turns."

Gretchen's hand rose holding a compact like a fat pink oyster.

Ted returned with a drink for Gretchen and was sent away again.

Gretchen and Rachel then sat knee to knee on that Olde Mill settee, Gretchen's eyes roaming freely over Rachel's shoulder as she got caught up on Rachel's news. To be more exact, Gretchen, who knew that with the right kind of pressure even a laconic type, like a good juice orange, can yield a lot, steered Rachel into complaining about Leon. This she did by stifling yawns when Rachel failed to be critical and frowning as if baffled when she failed to be explicit. From experience Rachel knew how Gretchen operated, but as usual reverted to a powerless former age. She'd known Gretchen since they were twelve.

"By the way," Rachel said finally, to change the subject, "have I found who?"

"Don't worry," Gretchen still scanning the real estate crowd. "He's not here." On her face was a look of studied ennui that took a long time to fade. Its last empty lineaments she used to check her eyes in that compact. "Mr. Perfect, remember? For some of us, Rachel, the hunt goes on, despite all evidence that he passed away a complete unknown twenty years ago. Also despite—" tapping the little mirror— "a crumbling lure."

Here an odd sort of conflation happened for Rachel. No sooner had Gretchen mentioned their elusive old high school friend and nemesis Mr. Perfect, than Rachel actually glimpsed, at the edge of her consciousness, in the crowd here, Harry, and if not Harry then a promising candidate. But her distraction by Gretchen at that moment was such that Rachel's unconscious brain recognized the candidate not as Harry but as Mr. Perfect while at the same time *reminding her* of Harry, with the result that instead of dropping her voice and saying *He's here*, she started in on the story of Leon's

Harry dreaming, a complex narrative the marshalling of which served to eclipse for her completely that Harry / Mr. Perfect not ten feet away. She then went on to say a little about her own tentative Harry searching, the connection: Could he be Mr. Perfect, come to haunt her in marriage? But Gretchen, ruthless, cut her off with a snap of that compact. "So that's what it was."

"What what was?"

"I always knew there was something about that guy. Rachel, I can't tell you how much I sympathize. It's a real blow, and I really, really sympathize." Gretchen shrugged. "It's not so much that you and your body have put him off your entire sex, it's that your whole sense of reality is now in question. To be so intimate with someone so long and to be so very, very wrong. It can really shake you up. But remember (though I guess this isn't so relevant in Leon's case): performance itself is no yardstick. Sex is ninety-nine and forty-four one-hundredths percent in the head. Look at me and Karno—"

"Karno."

"This guy on Kiribati. Said he loved me. Why? I just had to know. Bugged him for days to tell me. 'So fair', he finally admits. So of course I immediately—" Here Gretchen grabbed a fistful of that hair. "This is not Helene Curtis, I want you to know. This is an extract from a Kiribati root called blackshank. You do it over and over. Your hair turns orange, green, purple, and finally black. It takes three days of treatments. Dyes the follicles themselves. Lasts forever. Anyway, I hide out from Karno because I want it to be a big surprise. It was. On the third day I do my Big Entrance on old Karno, and he's screwing a beach boy with a complexion like burnished anthracite. My point is, *You never know what the bastards are thinking.*"

"You sound like my mother."

"I sound like every woman from the beginning of time. Rachel, you know me. I never give advice. Life is too variable. People do what they intended from the beginning and hate your guts for meddling. But. Get your evidence. Get a lawyer. Get out. If it's moral support you need, there's a group right here in the Millpond. They'll have you on your feet in a year."

"PAGO?"

"Kiribati. Didn't I say Kiribati? These things take time. So what evidence do you have?"

"None!"

"Rachel, you've got a husband with a year-long obsession about another guy!"

"Gretchen, Leon's *father's* name was Harry!"

"That clinches it, right? And what else. Has he got any close male friends?"

"No."

"Aha!"

"Seriously, Gretchen. You're off the mark. Leon's bent, sure, but if he wasn't he'd be even more repressed."

"How bent?"

Rachel declined to say. She did not want Leon's sexual habits detailed at some dinner party. She assured Gretchen that there was nothing too unusual, really. Herself she assured that everybody went through aberrant phases and that the only thing about Leon's that genuinely worried her was the recent lapsing of them all.

"So who's this Harry?" Gretchen demanded, jumping up to light a cigarette. "If I'm so goddam off the mark."

Rachel just sat there with her head bowed a little and her wrists on her knees.

Gretchen paced for awhile. Then, one eye closed against the smoke of her cigarette, the other narrowed at Rachel, she leaned down and said, "Just thought of something. Rachel, I'm going to say a name to you. I want you to remember it. Alex Silver."

"That was you," Rachel told Alex Silver over his giant antherium. "I gathered."

"It was Gretchen who first told me you had a practice here."

Alex nodded. "Got it. Continue."

Stunned by the name of Leon's high school hero, Rachel looked at Gretchen. Failed to respond.

"I think," Gretchen continued more slowly, peering through smoke at the blank expression on Rachel's face, "you should go and—" She moved closer to Rachel's face— "see him. What's wrong?"

Nothing, Rachel whispered, or may only have mouthed it. Not easy to tell with that blood Niagara in her ears booming *Harry Harry Harry.*

"They love him over at SMILE," Gretchen said, watching. "Very *sympatico—*"

"SMILE—" Hadn't Cam Wilkes mentioned SMILE?

"*Sisters Misused and Ignored Long Enough. Ultra-Fems—. Dr. Alex Silver.* He's a PhD, not a real doctor. Not a pill-pusher. Has his own quiz show on Village TV, *Share That Dream.* Ever watch it?"

Rachel shook her head. At that point, lucky her, she had not even heard of *Share That Dream.*

"Anyway, what you need is an expert to help you come to terms with Leon's problem. So what you do. *First* you check in with SMILE. They run this really supportive little café. *Then* you make an appointment with Silver. *Then* you start getting together your evidence. *Then* you move out. By that time you'll have had a few sessions with Silver, and your life, thanks to me, will be back on the rails. You're a good kid, Rachel. You don't need this." Gretchen paused to grind out her cigarette. "You know the Café Smile? SMILE's doing some work on the curriculum. Sexism in *Dick and Jane.* It's been done, you say? Sometimes these things take a while to reach the newer suburbs. Anyway, they're women, and what you need right now is female support. As you know I flunked Empathy. Oh, and hey Rachel? *Don't forget the bucks.* Sue the jerk into the ground. He's working? How much does he make? Fifty? Ask for thirty, settle for twenty-five. I really should have a talk with Leon. Tear a strip off the son of a bitch. You're not pregnant, are you?"

Rachel's eyes narrowed.

"Too bad. More money."

Here Rachel regressed to adolescence, made as if to throttle her friend.

Gretchen was ready. Deking, however, she inadvertently threw herself into the solar plexus of that Mr. Perfect, who was still there.

"Easy," he said, on the exhale. For some time then the two of them continued to stagger, Gretchen clinging like a drunk at a twenty-five-year reunion while Rachel's attention moved in on the man's face. Despite the blow of a woman to his solar plexus, it was . . . well, glorious. A deep tan (shining with exertion) . . . chiselled features (nose flared from his being so badly winded) . . . perfect, possibly capped, teeth (bared in a wince) . . . brown eyes like dark chocolates, initially bulging sightless but now resting on her own. Expensive, razor-cut hair. One hand then supported Gretchen at the elbow, the other came towards Rachel, who gazed at it, the fine dark hairs that grew on the broad back of it, the tended nails. *A thing of beauty*, she thought as she saw her own unworthy little append-age come up to be taken.

"Believe me," he gasped, a white smile. "I wasn't eavesdrop-ping." But of course he was.

"Gretchen Molstad," Gretchen offering her hand. "This is my friend Mrs. Boseman," she said as it was shaken. "She's here to meet her husband. Are you in real estate, Mr.—?"

"Sirocco. Nick Sirocco. You could say I'm in real estate." His eyes came back to Rachel. "And you—?"

Rachel and Gretchen replied together.

"I work at Village SoftWorks—"

"Rachel."

"Rachel," an oral caress. There was possibly a slight softening along the chinline. A hint of worldly puffiness under the eyes. Late nights, drink, overwork. But he wasn't forty. A thirty-nine-year-old workaholic maybe but not forty. "And where do you—"

"Oh, I, work at Millpond Indemnity. Leon— that's my hus-band— he's just started."

"Started what," from Gretchen.

"Um—" a giggle and glazed glance at her competitive friend— "real estate."

"He's good?" asked Nick Sirocco.

For a second Rachel did not know what he meant, and then she said, "Oh I'm sure he will be, once he gets going. He's just started." She'd said that.

"A real piss-artist is our Leon," was Gretchen's comment.

"Tell him to come and see me," and Nick Sirocco slipped a business card into Rachel's hand. "Of course I can't promise—"

"Thank you," trying to get that card into her purse by feel. "That's very thoughtful of you, Mr. Sirocco. I'll see that Leon—"

"I live right here in the Millpond," Gretchen was saying. "Bolting Reel Manor, Tower Three, Number 1423. It's a cozy little one-bedroom—" Her lashes continued to bat away at Nick Sirocco as if he were a kleig light, even after her actual eyeballs had shifted sideways to fix on something to his immediate left. When Sirocco looked too, so did Rachel.

It was Leon, in his new, power look: short back and sides, three-piece from Holt Renfrew, a fresh pink shave. "Hi. Don't believe we've met. Leon Boseman, Bi-Me Village Realty." Leon shook firm hands with Nick Sirocco. "You in real estate, Nick?" he asked as soon as Rachel had done the introductions.

"You could say that," Sirocco replied.

"Hi, Bozo," Gretchen said. "How are ya?"

That blackshank and gel had apparently rendered Gretchen not immediately recognizable to Leon. He studied her now. "Gretchen Molstad—" he said in nervous amazement.

Gretchen tilted her cheek to be kissed. Hastily Leon responded. Gretchen then tilted the other cheek, but Leon, agitated, ignored that painted surface. "So. Nick. Tell me. Who's your company?"

"Did you say Leon *Boseman*?" Sirocco asked.

Leon blinked. "That's right. You heard of— ?"

"You're the friend of Cam Wilkes?"

Leon's eyes grew anxious. "Friend? I wouldn't say *friend*, Nick—"

"But you have been looking after him—"

"Well, yeah. You know. He's not competent to, uh—"

"Who's Cam Wilkes?" Gretchen wondered. In an instinctive move to protect Cam Wilkes, Rachel had omitted all mention of him when telling Gretchen the Harry story.

"A friend," Rachel said.

"— who you take care of."

"Not *friend* exactly—" Leon shifting in his suit.

"Leon!" Rachel cried. "He is!"

"I'm intrigued," Gretchen said to Rachel. "Tell us more."

"He's just this guy who's afraid to go out of his house," Rachel explained, shrugging.

Sirocco nodded. He turned to Leon. "Come and see me, Leon. It's a cut-throat business. I'd like to give you a hand. Here's my card."

"Thanks Nick," Leon said. "Here's mine."

"We can do business, Leon," Nick Sirocco said, pocketing Leon's card. "Listen Rachel, and—"

"Gretchen. Gretchen Molstad."

Sirocco nodded at Gretchen, and then his eyes moved back to Rachel. "I gotta go. Leon. We'll keep in touch." Briefly he gripped Leon's hand, turned, and walked away.

Gretchen watched him go. "Rachel," she said quietly. "We have to talk."

Leon looked up from Sirocco's business card. "That guy's with Mortprop Investments," he said.

"Cute hunk, eh Leon? Get the lady's coat." Gretchen hooked an arm around Rachel's neck and pulled her through the party until she had put a lot of real estate people between themselves and Leon.

"It's him," she said.

"I know," Rachel soberly.

"A plan. We need a plan."

"I'm crummy at plans."

"He'll make his next move through you. You via Leon. Why's he interested in your friend Wilkes?"

Rachel shrugged.

"A possible way in. He'll offer to help—"

"Gretchen, he seems so efficient. Do we really need a plan?"

"Are you serious? The planless ones wind up with the Leons of this world. This is a man who wears three thousand dollar suits and looks like the young God. We absolutely need a plan."

"Do you think he likes me?"

"Not at all. He was working on me. Anyway, you're happily married, and I'm cresting thirty-five."

Cresting? "But what's Harry got to do with you?"

"Not Harry, Dimbulb. *Mr. Perfect.* Harry is Leon's problem and Leon is your problem. Be fair. It's the least I deserve for the scares I've been getting from the mirror. Rachel, you just have to help me. Especially after what you said about Ted. He's no dumber than you are, you know."

"Gretchen, Ted seemed OK. Honest."

"No, you're right. Let's not start making excuses for stupid Ted." Gretchen peered out through the smoke and din of a hundred people standing nose to nose in pairs and in tight circles holding white plastic cups in their hands, talking, smoking, drinking, laughing. "The walking dead," she observed. She took a step closer to Rachel, hissing. "*See Alex Silver.*"

"Gretchen, I'll think about it. I've never been to a psychologist."

"If you've never been to a psychologist you're not qualified to decide. Rachel, listen. When Ted comes back tell him you don't know where I am. And Rachel— let me know what happens with

Silver. I'm worried about you." And then she broke down sobbing on Rachel's shoulder, refused to talk about it, and ran off into the crowd.

In bed that night Rachel lay beside the new, improved Leon and tried to understand what this transformation in him meant for her. After a while she touched her fingers to his cheek. He grunted and turned away.

"Leon—"

"What."

"Are you sure you want to sell houses?"

"Not at all. I took a real estate course so I could become an investment banker."

"I mean, will you be happy?"

"Happy? How could I ever be as happy as I have been playing idiot nursemaid to Cam Wilkes?"

"Leon, did something happen between you and Cam tonight?" On the way back from the reception they had stopped in to feed him. Rachel waited in the driveway. In three minutes Leon was getting back into the car looking grim. "Did you have a falling out?" she asked now.

"I don't want to talk about it."

Silence.

"So," Leon said. "What would you like me to sell with my new training? Smurfs?"

"You'll go see Nick Sirocco?"

"Sure, I guess so. Why not."

"Sounds like he could help you."

"Molstad landed him?"

"She'll try."

"On second thought, I don't think I will go see Sirocco. With Molstad on the case I won't have a chance. You know how she likes to make trouble for the fun of it."

"Leon, don't be paranoid."

"I'm not big on guys in suits that expensive. I don't trust charmers."

"Harry's a charmer."

"Harry. When are you going to forget about Harry? You really do get stuck in ruts, don't you? Sirocco is no Harry, believe me. Cam Wilkes is the key to that one."

"But he could help you."

"Sure. Like I could help Cam Wilkes. He could also screw me over and steal my wife. I saw the way he was looking at you."

"Oh, Leon."

"Oh Rachel. Try to see past the aluminum siding for once. These guys in the expensive suits are birds of prey. Vultures. Cormorants. They don't do favours out of the goodness of their hearts. They don't have hearts. If Gretchen Molstad doesn't do me in, there's bound to be an ugly catch, like suddenly I'll owe a favour to some Mafioso in Tonawanda. No, I think I'll take a pass on this Nick Sirocco. Let's just say I don't like the cut of his jib."

Rachel did not have to keep on at Leon to see Nick Sirocco because Sirocco dropped in that Sunday afternoon. Leon was out on the back deck doing steaks on the propane barbecue he had bought himself to celebrate passing real estate school and getting a job at Bi-Me Village Realty. "Hey Rachel! Look at this!" When Rachel came out onto the deck what she saw settling down on the rhomboid of grass beyond the back yard was a shining black helicopter. Dogs and kids from all over the neighbourhood were pelting towards it. "Feel that?" Leon murmured, in awe. He meant the breeze from the propellors. The noise, ricocheting inside a perimeter of townhouses, was deafening. "What's it say on the tail?" Though near-sighted, Leon refused to wear glasses.

"6544T3."

"Huh."

The propellors were individually discernible now, the engines quieter. The *whut whut whut* of those big blades, the barking dogs, the happily screaming kids, were the dominant sounds. A door opened on the far side of the cockpit. A slight delay, and a crouching man in a dark suit sprinted out from under the blades.

"It's Nick Sirocco," Rachel said as a thrill muscled through her stomach and up into her chest. "He's coming this way. The house is a mess—" *My hair is filthy.*

"You've got 45 seconds to tidy up. The kids are slowing him."

Nick Sirocco waved. Leon waved back. "Want a beer, Nick?" he shouted.

Rachel plumped a few cushions and floated down to open the back door.

And Nick Sirocco was right there. Smiling. White teeth, brilliant in sunshine. Could this really be Harry? Broad daylight was certainly not as hard on him as Rachel had hoped. He was definitely still a member of the class of All Slightly Dissipated Men Who Look Like God. The reason of course Rachel was hungry to find physical flaws was that it did not feel right to be desired by so attractive a being. Too disproportionate a level of outward beauty would indicate scales balanced on his part by inner flaws discrediting to his taste in women. Nick Sirocco kissed Rachel's cheek, right next to the ear. A shiver passed down her body. He confessed that he had come to take her husband for a ride. "Hey, I'd really like to ask you along," he murmured, "but I can't. It's confidential. I'm sorry. I'm going to have to tell Leon not to talk about it to anybody."

Disappointed, Rachel nodded. And then she found herself standing next to Nick Sirocco and calling up to Leon, "Hey Leon! Mr. Sirocco wants to take you for a ride!"

"Me!?" Leon pantomimed against the sky, forefingers pointing at his chest. "Great!" Already he was fumbling with his apron. "Just let me do something about these steaks here—"

As hissing and smoke hid Leon from view, Nick Sirocco said, "Hey, what's this *Mr. Sirocco*. Call me Nick. Didn't you tell me you work at Millpond Indemnity? In the Village Green?"

"Yes—?"

"I'm with Mortprop Investments. Same complex. How about lunch Wednesday. Timbers 'n Spokes. Twelve-thirty, by the elevators."

"Gee, I don't think I should—"

"Come on. Just a little lunch—"

"Well, OK."

"Terrific."

They stood and gazed at each other until Leon was there looking foolishly, heartbreakingly keen. "All set, Nick!" he cried.

Ten minutes later, amidst a cheering, barking crowd of Millpond residents buffeted by the wind from those enormous blades, Rachel watched the pilot manipulate a stick and the plexiglas bubble lift off. She waved, but Leon was too engrossed in talking to Nick Sirocco to notice.

Rachel walked back to the house depressed. *Divide and conquer.* Wasn't it an Italian who said that?

Rachel sighed and got out the vacuum cleaner. Five minutes later, as she was changing the attachment to do the parquet in the front hall, it came to her that Nick Sirocco had no deal for Leon. He was working on her. A promise of something for Leon to make her grateful enough, long enough, for him to make his move. An extension of that feigned interest in Cam Wilkes. Either that or there really was a deal, but the only reason he'd chosen Leon was her. Sleep with me baby or your husband is not handed this sweetheart contract.

Unless of course the picture was even bigger and nastier. The 'copter would not return. She would never see Leon again, her willingness to eat lunch with Nick Sirocco, directly, in some sickening, hard-line, bad-novel way, responsible.

Gawd, Rachel thought as she wriggled the vacuum nozzle around under the little hall table, accept one lousy lunch date and I'm losing my mind. Did I always think the world was this sleazy? Or am I the big sleaze around here? I mean, was I always such a pushover? Whole days before I've been pushed?

Vacuuming the stairs, she thought, Who am I kidding. Do I really believe a hunkerama like Nick Sirocco would be interested in a Plain Jane like me? Here Rachel's knees grew weak, and she had to sit down on a stair.

Alex Silver was looking at his watch. "Whups, we're over the hour. Better resume this tomorrow. OK, Rachel. Go home, have something to eat, relax— no napping— and be back at the Dream Centre by ten o'clock tonight. No sign of Leon?"

"No sign."

"Maybe he's there now."

"I don't think so. Alex? I want to quit the study."

"Three days, Rachel? Just three, and then decide? For the study? For science? For me? So you can tell yourself you gave it a chance, you tested the waters? So you won't feel like a complete shit?"

"C'mon, Alex—"

"Please?"

"All right. Three days."

Leon wasn't home. Rachel was wandering through the darkness of 201 Dell, too sad to turn on the lights, when the phone rang. Cam Wilkes? Hadn't heard from him in a few days. Nor from Gretchen, but that was hardly surprising. Rachel took it in the streetlit living room.

Her mother. "How are you?"

"I'm OK. Mother, what is it?"

"I'm sorry if I tire you."

"You don't tire me."

"Your tone says otherwise. Anyway, it's not you I want to speak to. Please put Leon on."

"He's not in."

"Out with the boys, I suppose."

"Leon has no friends. He's at work." Rachel wished.

"Excuse me while I pick myself up off the floor. Leon is *at work*? Why didn't you tell me? Not management, I hope. The man couldn't organize a one-float parade."

"I have told you. Over and over. He's been selling real estate since the summer, practically."

"Oh. In that case I do have to talk to him. There's a real job opening up, with Vera Hedstrom's cousin Jerry. Stock control."

"Leon wouldn't be interested. He likes selling houses."

"You don't have to put up with it, you know. I didn't. If you're unhappy, Rachel—"

"I'm fine, Mother. I'm also hanging up!"

"Get him to call me. As soon as—"

That night Rachel spent at the Dream Centre with Alex Silver and her fellow guinea pigs, who turned out to be two women she had met with Gretchen one evening at the Café Smile: Babs Goreau and Frankie DeSoto. Babs was a tall, strong-boned woman resembling Sophia Loren's deranged cousin. Frankie, a head and a half shorter than her friend, was a sallow, ratlike person with oily hair and a small aggrieved face. Babs chaired, and Frankie sat on, the SMILE SIS (Sexism in the Schools) Committee currently engaged in a study of the Dick and Jane readers. That night at the Dream Centre, Rachel wondering why Babs and Frankie were being dream deprived, the three of them were sitting around sipping dexedrine sulphate with Alex Silver, when Babs opened a Dick and Jane reader called *We Work and Play* to a picture of Dick and Jane on a teeter-totter, Dick *up*, all smiles; Jane *down*, her back turned.

"Notice anything funny about this picture?" Babs asked.

Rachel studied it. There was Dick: familiar, forgettable, as ever; the back of Jane's head. Alex Silver studied the picture too, leaning forward with his hands on his knees. Being on SIS, Frankie already had her opinion. She smoked a cigarette in her cheesed-off way.

"Why's Dick *up* if he's heavier?" Silver murmured.

"Exactly," said Babs.

After Rachel had checked that Dick wasn't closer to the fulcrum, she said, "Wouldn't Dick's legs be longer and stronger, and so, I mean, what's wrong with realism?"

"Of course Dick's *winning*," Babs said. "But it's beyond *realism*, isn't it. The kid is definitely *just hanging up there*. He is violating gravity."

"Maybe the artist couldn't do movement," Rachel offered. "So he did them right at the moment between teeter and totter."

"The artist was a woman," Frankie said. "Eleanor Campbell. She could do movement all right."

"How's this," Silver said. "Here's this winsome little thing, but on the inside Jane's a fatty. The flip side of *sweet helplessness* is *big drag*. Weight. Load. Of course she's heavier."

Babs levelled a look full of sabres at Silver. "So it's all Jane's fault."

"Could just be," Alex replied mildly. "Most real thinnies are fatties."

"*Bullshit*." From the sternum.

"Next page please," Rachel gaily.

On the next page Spot grabs Dick's shoelace in his teeth and pulls Dick down level with Jane.

"Wow," from Rachel.

And on the page after that, Dick's shoe comes off and he flies up.

"Proving that Jane is fat inside," Silver concluded.

"Or," Babs glaring at him, then looking around significantly at the others, "not only does Dick have to be better at everything than Jane, he has to be *higher in the frame*. Even when Spot pulls him 'level' with Jane, he is still *higher in the frame*. Literally, he is *above her*. The law of gravity has just been repealed. We are talking about an apparently ordinary little boy who in fact is portrayed as a *higher being*—"

While Babs elaborated her point, Rachel slipped into that reader. Dick and Jane, who were those kids anyway? Once when the world had been elemental as earth, real as her father's shoes, her mother's Tabu, as love, she thought she knew. But now—?

Baby Sally, a yellow-haired coquette stepping out against an enormous black umbrella, the sweet smile of a bimbo.

Jane, vaguely pretty, strapping on roller skates, eyes downcast, curiously self-involved, possibly ill.

And Dick, fists deep in his pockets, feet in high-lace leather running shoes planted wide apart. Cowlicked brown hair, high forehead, wide eyes that did not quite meet hers, pug nose, long upper lip, teeth bared in a grin. Foursquare. Absurd. Sphinx . . .

Harry, in short pants?

"Rachel?"

"Huh?"

It was Babs. "Gretchen mentioned something about you having problems around Leon's sexual identity. Frankie and I were wondering if you'd like to come to the Wednesday night discussion group at SMILE and share your feelings."

"Um, I'd like to, Babs, but I really don't have any 'feelings' worth sharing—" Rachel's low-key irony here backfiring to replicate textbook low-self-esteem.

Babs looked at Frankie and Frankie looked at Babs and they both looked at Alex Silver, who pushed his scarlet glasses up his nose and cleared his throat.

"I mean," Rachel doggedly digging herself in deeper, "he doesn't *mistreat* me or anything—"

"Just remember this, Rachel," Babs laying a remarkably unwelcome hand on Rachel's arm. "There are more colours in the rainbow of marital abuse than black and blue."

A half hour later, in bed, her head wired, Rachel thought, "Hey gee, maybe you're right, Babs. Let's see— There's chartreuse, magenta, nile green, puce, vermilion, ochre—"

THREE

Numero Uno Question about Harry: Was he the guy responsible for the incredible tackiness of the behaviour around here, the general dumpiness to the quality of life in these parts, this contagion of mediocrity— or was he the guy who kindly arrives by dogsled, 400 SL, chariot of fire, to lift the veils? Was Harry an unnatural by-product of some haywire reflex of neurotic dissatisfaction— or the Touchstone of Touchstones? What happened if you said, Hey Harry, I think I love you? Seriously Harry, I'm head over heels. I mean, your will is my will. You are the only theatre I will ever need. Let's shack up and make a world. What happened then? Would this be redemption? Or one of the more predictable mistakes of a minor life?

The second and third nights at the Dream Centre were one long beep from the Hewlett Packard. The third morning dawned edgy, the place less and less familiar instead of the usual more. The path is a wild and rocky one, it seems, when there is no nightly healing. Speaking of healing, when Silver removed the electrodes from her head, Rachel noticed that his whole left forearm was now bandaged. Half asleep, she asked what had happened.

"This? Oh, just a scratch."

Even un-dream-deprived, Rachel would have found such evasiveness on the part of her therapist cause for concern.

And then she looked at her watch and shot out of bed. Twenty minutes to get to work! Babs and Frankie were still unconscious, so there was no waiting for the washroom.

Rachel was on her way out of that cubicle when she heard something like a child's cry, or scream, from the next room. She tried the handle. Locked. "Alex!" she called in an urgent whisper. "Alex! Is everything all right?"

A muffled sound, possibly a curse, followed by something more like a snarl.

"Alex! Let me in! What's wrong?"

Suddenly Silver was right there, on the other side of the door. "You're off to work then, Rachel?"

"Alex, what's going on in there?"

"Nothing— You did your non-REM, Vigilance, Stroop, Arithmetic, Holzman, Reuben, and Nowlis-Green?"

"I'll have to do them at work. I'm late— Alex, I—"

Behind the door a digital watch alarm sounded. "Gotta go, Rachel. Tonight, my office, six o'clock, OK?"

After work Rachel drove over to Silver's office to resume her story of the search for Harry and the loss of Leon. Silver kept his now heavily bandaged hands under the table with the giant antherium on it, but the table was glass.

"Alex, I'm not going on with this until you tell me what's going on in that other room at the Dream Centre."

"I can't do that.

"I'm serious, Alex."

Silver studied her face. "Rachel, I'll take this request under advisement, I promise. I'll consider it. Very seriously. Honest I will. OK?"

"OK—" dubious.

"Good. So talk."

Rachel sighed. "Where was I?"

"Sirocco and Leon, up in the helicopter."

Soon the helicopter deposited Leon, and five minutes after that he was back in the living room with an irritating glow on. When Rachel asked how the flight went he said, "It was great, just great. But it was also business. I'd love to tell you all about it, but I can't. I promised Nick I wouldn't say a word, even to you. All I can say is, this could be really, really big. I mean *really* big."

"What could be really big?"

"Uh uh *uh!*" wagging a finger. "No you don't!"

"How was Nick Sirocco?"

"Nick? A nice guy. A fabulous guy. Very smart. Very focussed."
For a moment Leon mused, a look of admiration lighting his face
sickeningly like the one he once had for Harry. When he saw Rachel
looking at him, it went away. "Hey, how about those steaks," Leon
said and returned to the deck. But Rachel stayed in the kitchen, did
not pursue him, and Leon had never been in a helicopter before, so
he kept coming in from the deck and telling her more and more.

While gripping the seat as the machine did a swift diagonal
climb into the blue autumn sky, he had shouted to Sirocco that this
was his first helicopter ride. "It's a wonderful development!" Leon
shouted next.

Sirocco nodded. "Want to show you something," he said.
"When we're higher."

Leon was right at the window. He pressed his forehead against
the glass and gazed down at the toy-neat boxes and tried to
understand that real lives, just like his own, were being lived inside
them.

"Not many aerials!" Leon shouted. "Thought I'd see aerials!"

"That's like looking for vacuum tubes when you take the back
off the new radio," Sirocco replied. "Seventy-eight percent of the
Millpond's on cable. It's a plugged-in community. But real grass-
loving. Look at the green. Over there you can see the millpond,
completely man-made, and our new drive-in church. People like to
be on their way. Mortprop Mall, biggest single-level shopping
centre in the area. Over there our light industrial park; more than
a billion cubic feet of indoor space, a model of its kind: fire
sprinklers, compressed air and gas, thirty-five foot ceilings, cranes
with twenty-seven-foot overhead clearance. We're still adding.
And four years ago all this was farmland."

"I thought it was a dumpsite—" Leon shouted.

"Only a small fraction. Reporters are assholes. They blow
everything out of proportion. Look." What Sirocco was pointing to,
Leon might perhaps have forgotten he had promised not to say. But
at that moment the phone rang, and he went out to turn the steaks.

It was Gretchen, checking to make sure that Rachel had called
Alex Silver.

"Gretchen, stop pushing me. I'm not ready to go to a psychologist over this."

"Nick called, didn't he. Rachel, tell me or I'll have you shot."

"No, Nick did not call," Rachel sticking to the letter.

"So you're just trying to convince yourself that Leon's obsession with his new career means he's back in the closet."

"Gretchen, be honest. Isn't all you're really thinking about—" Rachel had to drop her voice in case Leon heard— "Nick Sirocco?"

"*Who?*"

"*Nick Sirocco.*"

"Pardon?" Leon said, coming into the living room, reaching. "Nick? For me? He's got a cellular?"

"No," cupping the mouthpiece. "I'm telling Gretchen about him—"

"Oh God—" eyes to the ceiling. "I knew this would happen." Leon went into a ferocious whisper. "Don't tell her *anything*! It was strictly a *joy ride*, OK? And while you're at it tell her he's way too good for her."

"Relax, Leon."

"What's Leon saying?" Gretchen asked. "Too good for who?"

"I can't stand this," Leon muttered and went back out to the deck.

"*What* are you telling me about Nick Sirocco?" Gretchen wanted to know.

Rachel explained about Nick's taking Leon for a helicopter ride.

"So he didn't call."

Rachel did not reply.

"How did he know where you live?"

Rachel had not thought of this. She called to Leon to ask how Nick Sirocco knew where they lived. Leon appeared in the doorway a moment, thinking, then shrugged and walked back to the barbecue.

"Phoned Leon's office at Bi-Me Realty, I guess," Rachel said, thinking he could not have phoned *her* office because they had met on a Friday night.

"The question's dumb, tell her," said Leon, reentering the living room. "These guys can find out anything they need to know. That's why they're in charge of hundred million dollar deals. It's all initiative and networking. Sniffing out the hungry new talent. It's all seeing what new directions are possible when everybody else is just window-dressing the old bullshit—"

"He doesn't know," Rachel told Gretchen.

Leon returned to the steaks.

Gretchen wanted Rachel to meet her after work tomorrow at the Café Smile. She had found out a few things about Nick Sirocco but couldn't talk on the phone. "Knowing what I now know about the guy, he's probably got me tapped."

"Steaks ready," said Leon, standing in the doorway.

So it was that at 5:30 the next day Rachel pulled into the parking lot of a small plaza somewhere in the midwest of the Millpond, an area level and treeless as a developed beaver meadow, its northern vistas abbreviated by the twenty-foot corrugated steel fence that enabled Mortprop Investments to build up-market homes thirty feet from a six-lane highway, its western prospect a giant berm like a barrow for genocide. When Rachel, generally edgy and spooked since accepting that luncheon date with Nick Sirocco, climbed from the Civic, squinting to see if she had the right place, a hard autumn wind, practising for winter, flattened her skirt against her legs and sent her coat flapping against the side of the car like something possessed. With heroic effort she wrestled the Civic's door shut, except on her coat, which meant an ugly, stitch-rending jolt when she tried to walk away.

"Shit," she said, the magic word. Instantly a man in a brown suit, one hand clamping to his head a '50s fedora, came from nowhere to lean past her and open the car door, freeing her coat.

Next he offered his arm. Disoriented—the arm had a cast on it, and a white cocker spaniel was somehow there too: big black patches on a white ground— Rachel accepted. It was a long time since she had been offered a man's arm, even a broken one. Together, amidst pelting debris, they headed for the plaza, the wind a firm hand against the smalls of their backs. Meanwhile the spaniel worked deftly with his mouth to wrap Rachel's coat tighter.

As the three of them reached the curb, Rachel noticed two things: One, the faces of three women pressed against the inside of the Café Smile window, watching. Two, approaching along the front of the little plaza, one of those mini-tornadoes that are always blowing up in parking lots: dust, leaves, candy wrappers, empty potato chip bags, all whipping in a hostile funnel. "Thank you very much!" Rachel bellowed to the man, intending to duck inside fast, but this is not what happened. Instead the watching women were obscured from Rachel's view by revolving grit and litter as Rachel, the man, and the dog continued for a long, long moment frozen in the eye of that little tornado. The man was gazing down at the dog with a look of abstraction, thinking perhaps of something to say. Suddenly the dog shot sideways, into the whirling dust. When he ducked back out of it his tail was wagging his entire body, and he was looking now at the man and now at Rachel in the eager silly way that dogs have. In his teeth he held a bright, red apple.

"See funny funny—" the man said, anxiously, his words cancelled by the roar of the wind; that tornado had shifted again.

Rachel laughed politely, at the reference. "Thanks!" she shouted then, dust like needles in her eyes, causing them to water and her to lean into the café door, a blurred and skittering image on her retina of the man tipping his fedora, a hat and gesture out of a 1950 *Saturday Evening Post*, except for the hair blowing wildly under it.

"... any chance know ... ?" she thought she heard as he glanced at the Café Smile while repositioning the hat carefully, squarely, on his head.

"No—" shaking her head, waiting for more. Though not really able to see, her subsequent memory of his face was pinned to that moment of confused anticipation. It was a homely, boyish face, a high forehead, the nose short, a long upper lip. A big smile, square teeth showing. He seemed about sixty years old, maybe more. There was something remarkably familiar about him, some tremendous *promise*— "Do I know you?" Rachel whispered. But he was gone. Her eyes cleared. The wind had dropped. Still on the sidewalk she looked around. Twenty metres along, the spaniel, forelegs stiff and splayed, was down on one haunch, twisting around to go after a flea near his rear end with amazingly white, humanlike teeth. Had the man gone into a store?

Wondering, Rachel became aware of a rapping on the inside of the Café Smile window. When she stepped away from the door to look, the nearest of the three women who were pressed to the glass glared in the man's direction and gave him the finger. Shocked, Rachel looked away, towards the dog, his jaw now at rest on his paw. Suddenly the man came striding out of a store with a giant rolled newspaper under his arm. The dog was on his feet, dashing behind and around the man. But he must have clipped the backs of the man's knees, because the newspaper and the cast rose together as the man's legs buckled under him and he crumpled to the sidewalk. Immediately the dog, after deftly catching the paper in his teeth, let it drop to tug at the padded shoulder of the man's jacket, pulling him up. His master seemed to be all right, shaken, but recovered enough to brush himself off and carry on. Limping a little, the newspaper back under his arm, the dog in step, he continued towards Rachel, who had started in his direction as soon as she saw him go down. Their return encounter was even more awkward. The wind was blasting again. Gaily, like an idiot, Rachel cried, "Still here!" at the exact moment that he said something like, "... see jay ... ?" And then he was standing before her in that high wind, brown shoes planted, one fist against his waist, fedora pushed back, doing a slow, Norman Rockwell headscratch. The dog just wagged, though he seemed puzzled too.

"Pardon?" Rachel said, and then, "Are you OK?"

In answer, the man, who could not have heard her, leaned smiling past her, hat in hand now, hair wildly blowing, to open the Café Smile door.

"Thanks," Rachel said and ducked inside.

"— welcome," she heard.

The dog had ducked in too. He circled the foyer in a blur, yapping wildly. He clamped onto her coat and tried to spin her like a top. Rachel fell against the outside door, it opened, and he rocketed out. The last thing she saw before the door closed was the dog flying excitedly for the man's chest, the man's good hand flung up in surprise, his mouth an O, the newspaper cartwheeling into the grey sky.

As Rachel entered the Café Smile from the foyer the group at the window was already scattering. Cowards. To one who was leaving, she said, "Who was that man?"

"Does it really matter?" the woman replied, bending to gather parcels from a chair by the coatrack. She had a long auburn crewcut like a dyed hearth brush.

"Sure it matters!" Rachel cried. "He was very nice!"

Immediately the woman's face was six inches from Rachel's, her dire, caffeine breath in Rachel's nostrils, a plum red nail making jabs in the direction of Rachel's collarbone. "It's when women can't open their own doors that the nice guys take over." The woman stepped into the foyer and pushed against the outside door with one hand. "See?" she said with a smile. "Not difficult."

"Bitch," Rachel said to her back as the woman left, and then wondered if men were this hard on each other.

Gretchen was late. Not committed to being here, Rachel took a table close to the entrance and looked around. To the eye it didn't seem such a bad little place, really. Soothing earth colours, booths down one wall, the wall opposite hung with lots of interesting antiques. What a great idea: A café by and for women. No male in sight. (Correction: A waiter. "Hi there, I'm José." Rachel ordered a cappuccino.) Everybody was smoking heavily, elbows on the table, leaning forward to confide. Eyes floated over to check out Rachel, slid away, returned, remained fixed a moment while heads nodded to indicate. Other heads turned then, new eyes came scanning, and Rachel found herself doing little pretend-absorption gazes, semi-poses, not at all knowing where to look . . .

After a few minutes Rachel's own attention had settled on a large-breasted blonde, somewhere in her fifties, sitting, like Rachel, alone, drinking a coffee. The woman was a non-starter in the correct-fashion stakes going on in here, and Rachel liked her for that. She was dressed in a worn brown sweater-dress that gave her the look of a discarded teddy bear. Her face was broad, sympathetic. A little puffy. She seemed tired. Worried. She also seemed familiar. Or was everybody going to look familiar this evening?

When the interest in herself had died down and Rachel had stared so long at the blonde woman that she got a smile, still Gretchen did not arrive. Bored, Rachel turned to those antiques. Maybe she could pick up a few decorating hints. A small part of her still believed that if she could somehow get the decor of 201 Dell exactly right, things would improve between her and Leon. Anyway, there was something about the warmth that burnished copper and cracked, sunbleached wood could bring to drywall. Let's see . . . There was, huh, a black and pitted old ball and chain, looked like a whipping post, and down the wall a ways a . . . ducking stool. Hmm. A chastity belt, a rack, a stake for burning, a thumbscrew, an iron boot, a pillory . . . Sort of a leg-iron-is-worth-a-thousand-words history of the better half, here.

"Guess why I'm incognito." Gretchen Molstad was wearing a flop-brimmed hat, dark glasses, and a trenchcoat. She was pointing at Rachel's cappuccino and mouthing *I'll have one of those* to José as she flopped down.

"You're disguised as a food critic for better service."

"No. Because I can't take the chance of men seeing me come here. They'll think I'm hostile."

"What do they know."

"The jerks," looking around.

"So what did you find out about Nick Sirocco?"

"Rachel, please! Give me a chance to catch my— Oh hi, Babs— Frankie!"

Babs Goreau, the tall one, was the woman who had given the nice man the finger. Frankie DeSoto had been the third woman at the window. This was the first time Rachel met them. In a voice of feigned warmth, Gretchen invited them to sit down, but they couldn't, were on their way to a SIS meeting in back.

Watching them go, Rachel said, "Now. Sirocco."

But Gretchen was lighting her five billionth Player's Plain while gazing around more widely. "Hi, Sally!" Sally was the woman with the look of a discarded teddy bear. "Join us!"

Sally carried her coffee over and was introduced to Rachel.

"You just met my brother," Sally told her.

"The guy in the fedora!?"

Sally nodded.

"Babs and her friends didn't like him holding the door for me."

"Yeah, he's a mannerly guy."

"How's your sister?" Gretchen asked.

"Not great." To Rachel Sally said, "Flume Fields." Flume Fields was the psychiatric wing of the Millpond General. "Depression. Her cat disappeared."

"I'm sorry," Rachel said.

"So am I." Sally lifted some strands of grey out of her eyes. "The doctors want to give her shock, and our big brother, the one in the fedora, thinks it's a terrific idea. I'm trying not to murder him in his sleep."

"That's terrible!"

"I don't know how people can believe in scientific miracles when they don't even believe in brain tissue."

"Have you talked to him?"

"I'm staying with him, over on Smutter Circle. Looking after him while she's out of commission. He's kind of accident prone. When she's not there, he and the dog takes spills for the three of them. I do this for her. About the shock, we always have the same conversation. I say, 'Look. We can't let them do something like that to our own sister', and he gets this concerned look on his face and says, 'Sally, I've been giving the matter some thought, and you know, Dr. Hodgson's electrotherapy idea just might be the ticket for poor Sis. Medical science can get people out of some pretty bad mental scrapes nowadays. I don't think we should sell it short'. He's a wall. 'Poor Sis' is right. And the damn thing is, she wants it. For awhile there, fifteen or twenty years ago, I was sure she was going to make it. She was working, she was looking great. Taking the bus by herself. Scared, but happy. And then— But anyway. It's not your—"

Sally looked at Gretchen, who was gaping at her watch. Gretchen turned to Rachel. In an unmodulated voice she said, "If he wants a threesome, remember two words: High. Risk."

Immediately all eyes from adjacent tables locked on Rachel, who had steam coming out of her ears.

"Anyway, the bastard." Gretchen was gathering her things. "It's tragic, really tragic." She stood up. "Hey guys. I've got to go. Rachel, call me." And Gretchen was gone.

For a few minutes Rachel and Sally marvelled at Gretchen together like old friends, and then there was an awkward silence, Sally sitting with her head on a tilt twisting a strand of tangled hair between her thumb and forefinger, looking old, a faraway smile, and Rachel smiling politely back about to say, Sorry, but she guessed she probably also should—

"Rachel?" Sally said. "Don't screw Nick Sirocco." When Rachel, who was too surprised, did not say anything, Sally added, "Gretchen told me."

Damn Gretchen. She had done this to Rachel all her life. Told other people more than she let on to Rachel she had even heard. "Why not?"

"Cause he ain't no Harry."

"No? And so who is he?" Rachel's anger rising.

"Just a guy. Not a nice guy. I— this, friend of mine used to go out with him. He broke her—"

"I know. Heart."

"Arm."

"So who's Harry?" quickly.

"Wish I knew. I'd get out my bazooka right away."

They looked at each other until Rachel said, "Gretchen put you up to this."

"Nope," shaking her head.

"Yeah, right—" Rachel reached for her coat.

"She didn't—"

On her way out, Rachel looked back just once. Sally was sitting with her elbows on the table, her face in her hands.

Rachel arrived home murderous. Guilt sufferers can do without public reminders. She was still debriefing herself on that broken arm when she came upon Leon hunched at the dining room table. Working late, in order to become a big success at real estate. Going all out. Giving it his best. Rachel's heart swelled. Tears filled her eyes. How could she even consider— Oh shame, shame!

Softly she spoke his name.

Like those of a man shot in the back, Leon's arms flew into the air. "*Whhaaaghh!!*"

"Sorry—"

"Why do you always have to pussyfoot around?" He was slumped across the table. "One of these days you're going to give me a coronary."

"Leon—"

"What is it." Leon's upper body came off the table. "I'm busy here."

"I have something to tell you."

"Don't bother." Straightening papers. "I know all about it. Have fun."

"Leon—!"

"I'm not a *complete* fool, you know."

"Leon, I want you to know there's nothing to it—" Yet—

"Nothing covers a lot of ground, Rachel."

"It's just lunch."

"No no. Be my guest. Take breakfast and dinner too."

"Pardon?"

"Rachel, thanks. But it's a little late for me to appreciate it. I'm sure he does."

"Too late—?"

"Right. I've stopped."

"Stopped what?"

"What are we talking about? Feeding Wilkes—"

"You've stopped feeding Cam Wilkes? Since when?"

"Saturday."

"Saturday? Leon, he'll be hungry!" Rachel thought of stocking your birdhouse all November and then spending the winter in Florida. *What about the birds?*

"I'm sure lunch'll do him."

"Leon, are you ducking out on Cam Wilkes the way you ducked out on Harry?"

As soon as this question had sunk in, Leon's eyes swelled with rancour. "Once and for all, Rachel. Harry was never really my problem, was he. And if I was fool enough to think Cam Wilkes was mine, I learned better Friday night."

It then came out that after that real estate reception on Friday, Leon had found Wilkes in the kitchen eating a Baskin and Robbins Mud Pie, right out of the foil.

"Baskin and Robbins don't deliver, do they," Rachel murmured.

At the time Leon had been so angry he could only slam down a Burger King double cheeseburger and a large Coke and stalk out. But last night, thinking that if there had been a misunderstanding he had punished Wilkes enough by not feeding him for two days, Leon went back with a Wendy's fishburger and asked him point-blank where he had got that Mud Pie. Here Leon paused to glower at Rachel until she cried,

"*Me?* Leon, I didn't take him any pie! You saw me. I was at the reception with you!"

"So what have you just been telling me? Who's the Girl on His Bus? Listen, Rachel. If you want to take over the feeding and general maintenance of this hypocritical I'm-too-damaged-to-come-out-of-my-basement bullshit, then go right ahead. I'm fed up with playing Ronald McDonald to that dingbat. It's time he joined the outside world."

"Leon—"

"Rachel, I'm saying I'm done with that guy. *Finito tuto.*"

So Rachel got back into the car and drove over to see Cam Wilkes. On the way she picked up a McDonald's L.T., fries, and a coffee. Like Leon, she did not bother to ring. The key was under the mat. She switched on the hall light, aware of dismantled bus parts looming from the dark of the dining room as she made her way down the hall towards the kitchen. There she sighed with a great weariness because Leon, his mind more with real estate than with

Cam Wilkes lately, had been letting things slide: dishes were piled high on the counter, a dozen green garbage bags stank at the door to the patio.

Rachel crossed to the cellar door and called, "Cam! Dinner!" down into the darkness, listening until she heard a kind of scrabbling. At her feet was the Wendy's fishburger. Untouched. "Cam!" she called again, scared now. "Are you all right?" No answer. She replaced the fishburger with the L.T., fries, and coffee on a styrofoam tray but could not bear to close the door on it the way she had seen Leon do so often. She worked on dishes for awhile, checking every few minutes. Then she did close the door and worked for a long interval on dishes and on carrying the garbage out to the garage. When she came back into the kitchen the basement door was open and Cam Wilkes was standing on the top step holding the tray of food. "Cam!" she cried. "It's so nice to see you!" He was gaunt and wispy-haired but carefully groomed. His pajamas, though bottle green, had pleats.

"I saw her," he replied, holding out the tray.

"Who did you see, Cam?" Rachel asked, automatically stepping forward to take it.

Cam Wilkes' teeth bared in a wolfish grin. "No need for this," he whispered.

"Come sit down and we'll talk," Rachel tried, setting the tray on the kitchen table. "I haven't seen you for weeks, Cam. Why don't you have something to eat, and we can chat."

The smile dissolved. He remained where he was. "You're not her, Rachel. It's that simple."

"You mean I'm not the Girl on Your Bus."

"Right," nodding.

If Rachel was disappointed to be displaced, she was more afraid for Cam. Like Leon, like Gretchen, like herself, like probably the whole world, he was slipping, wasn't he?

"Oh, Cam!" she cried, stepping forward, reaching to grasp his hands as if she would pull him back to sanity.

But his hands were not available to her. "She came to see me," he said.

Oh, you poor, unhappy man!

"She heard me playing the *Melody for the Girl on My Bus,* and she remembered, Rachel. She heard it from another bus, the one that stops across the street. My basement window was open. She heard and got off and came to find me. She came straight down into the basement where I was playing, behind the furnace. She touched my shoulder and said seven simple words. Words I will never forget: 'You were the Man on My Bus'. In my heart I knew right away it was her. But amazement made me stubborn. I insisted that *you* were the Girl on My Bus, Rachel. A frightened lie. She knew it was. And she went away."

"Oh no!" Rachel did not know if it was sadder to have an imaginary visitor or for your imaginary visitor to go away.

"That was Thursday," Wilkes continued. "On Friday she brought me a Mud Pie. We talked and talked. There was so much to say. So many years of cloven longing. And she'll come again. Perhaps one day you'll meet her, Rachel. She's someone you'll recognize—"

"Who!?"

"You'll see—" Wilkes was half-turned to go back downstairs.

"Cam!"

He paused. "Rachel, thank you both for everything. And please thank the people at McDonald's for getting it all to taste the same, not just from day to day but as everything else. There's a lot to be said for old-fashioned reliability in today's uncertain world. Except, I don't need that kind of assurance now. I found her."

He went back down into the blackness. A minute later there came floating up those dark stairs an ineffable melody of sadness and grace.

Fearing it had come time to call a social agency, Rachel finished cleaning up Wilkes' kitchen and drove home. Leon was still at the dining room table.

"Leon, he says he got the Mud Pie from the Girl on His Bus, and he insists that she's not me."

"I thought you looked shaken."

"He's refusing to eat. He says he's in love with the real Girl on His Bus and he doesn't need food."

"Makes sense."

"He says she came to him in his basement."

"That was bold. Maybe from our failing hands she'll catch the torch."

"He says it's somebody I'll recognize."

"In the mirror."

"He needs help, Leon."

"To that I say, from now on let's just help these two folks right here, OK?"

Rachel sat down in a chair at the end of the table. "Leon, why are you being so callous?"

"Because I believe our Mr. Wilkes is perfectly able to take care of himself. He tried that no-need-for-food stuff on me too. All it means is he wants out of being fed by me, because he knows I've seen through him and I'm breaking it off anyway. He's sly, but he's got his pride. With you it doesn't matter. He knows you're so smitten by being the Girl on His Bus that there's nothing he can do that will shame him in your eyes."

"What are you talking about?"

"I'll tell you what I'm talking about. He's making you jealous by pretending he's found the 'true' Girl on His Bus, because he knows that in your eagerness to reclaim that title, you'll do anything he wants, such as continue to feed him and whatever else you two have worked out—"

"Leon, don't be a creep. What if he really is so deluded? What if it's you deserting him that's made him crack? Don't you think you just might have come to mean a lot to him?"

"What if it's all my fault, you're asking me? Is that it? The old story for you, eh Rachel?"

"Please don't get defensive. I'm worried about Cam, that's all."

"Well, don't be. He's playing love games, and that's strictly your business. I've got more important things on my mind."

"Like what?"

"Like tomorrow I'm having lunch with Nick Sirocco, and I have to be up on my homework. Tomorrow he breaks the details of the deal."

"He didn't break them in the helicopter?"

"Not everything. Tomorrow it's him and me across the table."

"You'll do fine."

"I intend to. I'm holding out for 12%"

"Instead of what?"

"Ten, probably."

"Leon, that's *crazy!*"

"Thanks for the immediate, gut support."

"Leon, why risk it? You could make some money here—"

"A lot of money."

"And you intend to hold out for two lousy percent?"

"Look at it objectively. I'm new at this game. If I wasn't the only possible one for the job, why would he pick a fledgling? Obviously I've got something he needs."

"Leon, it sounds like you don't really know what this is about yet. You're just feeling anxious and trying to find some way to screw up because that's what you're used to doing."

"Whew. Thanks, Rachel. But, unbelievable as it may sound to you, I don't need this. Pep talks with a knife can start to get a guy down after awhile. I mean, didn't bloodletting go out around a hundred years before bobbysocks?"

"Leon, don't worry about tomorrow. Listen to what the deal is and then respond as intelligently as you can. That's all you can hope to—"

"*As intelligently as I can?* Thanks again, Rachel. You sure know how to mete out the insecurity. I guess I had to be feeling confident again to see how good at it you are."

"It's not true, Leon. You're just upset—"

Leon threw down his pencil. *"Stop telling me what I just fucking am!"*

Leon's bellow was still echoing from the living room when the phone rang.

Shaking, Rachel took the call upstairs. It was Gretchen, with advice for dealing with Nick Sirocco. "It's simple. If he happens to call you first, make the date, and I'll go instead."

"Sounds familiar."

"Right— Hey, are you OK? You don't sound so great."

"I'm fine."

"And didn't it work? Please, Rachel. All I have to be is more surprised than he is. You can't afford to get involved at a time like this. The guilty party is Leon, remember? You'd be risking a major income supplement. Sirocco's a businessman. He'll understand. You thought better of it but didn't want the poor guy to spend an evening alone— these business dynamos get so lonely— and thought of your best friend. Had to trick me of course or I'd never do it. I'm practically engaged to Ted, after all. Sirocco's so smooth he probably won't even let on."

"I won't do this for you, Gretchen."

Gretchen blew smoke past the mouthpiece. "Leon comes out of the closet and immediately you have to reassure yourself you're still a woman. Rachel, you've got more on the ball than that."

"Goodbye, Gretchen."

"He's already called, hasn't he."

"I have to go. Leon and I are having a fight."

"Is it Harry?"

As Rachel put down the receiver it occurred to her that if Gretchen was not up to something very different from what she appeared to be, then age had dulled her cunning. It was not like her to beg. What was the Molstad family motto, again?

The phone rang. "*Numquam desperare,*" Gretchen said. "The female Molstad is not an animal."

"Right."

"Just remember that."

"I was trying."

"Good. Carry on."

When Rachel came back downstairs, Leon had descended to his basement study beside the garage, to signify that he was not to be disturbed.

"Rachel," said Alex Silver, slumped in his chair across that smoked glass table with the giant antherium on it in his office in Village Market Square. "My first question. Were you afraid for Leon or for yourself? After all, he *was* getting himself together—"

"Himself, yes. Our relationship, no."

"But why undermine him? What if he needed a little success in business before he could feel confident enough to work on his personal life?"

"I wasn't undermining him. I was trying to prepare him for—"

"Failure?"

"Disappointment!"

"Same diff! Surely you already knew that any fooling on your part with Nick Sirocco would jeopardize Leon's chances? Could this be one of the reasons you were so attracted to a punk like—"

"Dammit, Alex. Are you suggest—"

"No, I want to leave these questions with you and go one step further. I want you to tell me what, exactly, you thought at that point about Harry. One guy by definition, you'll notice, not a failure. You've got three minutes."

Rachel objected for at least that long to Silver's insinuations, and then she considered Harry. "It wasn't all that coherent, really. Sometimes I blamed him for the big moral slide I was on, and sometimes I thought of him as the guy who turns up and fixes everything, but like a proper saviour first he shows you just how bad things really are. Other times I told myself Leon hadn't left Harry and me behind at all. The reason he was so volatile and impatient was not his old insecurity but the knowledge, in his heart, that he was getting into something he didn't really want to be getting into. Harry was still alive for Leon too, only he didn't want to know it—"

"And Sirocco?"

"I said not coherent. Because if it was true, then obviously Sirocco was no more my Harry than Leon's. Or the worst kind of Harry. My only hope was that Sirocco could give me more than a tacky little affair and Leon more than a tacky little sweetheart deal.

"And I thought, hey, maybe Harry goes deeper than an idea; he's a habit. Ticking over whether the thoughts about him are pro or con. It's all grist. So Sally could warn me this Nick Sirocco thing was an irresponsible aside, but what if it *fed in* to Harry, like a crucial step in some kind of spiral progression? Sirocco would be an *experience*, and the experience would *feed in to* Harry. That was it. It would feed in. Somehow. Like studying Latin to raise your consciousness."

"A Latin."

"Aha ha. Otherwise I was too busy stonewalling Gretchen to think about it much."

"Did you want to think about it?"

"And all this cold and hostile behaviour from Leon," ignoring the question, "was great for easing the guilt. But just to make sure, I stopped off at a Millpond fish place after work. In celebration, or consolation, after his meeting with Sirocco, Leon was going to get an intimate shrimp meal by candlelight if I had to ram it down his throat— But you know what the funniest thing was, Alex?"

"No, what?"

"That I could go from intending to sleep with Sirocco to intending not to sleep with Sirocco and back again without even noticing."

"It's not so funny, believe me."

On her return to the Dream Centre after her session with Silver,

Rachel stopped by 201 Dell for a shower and something to eat. She sure had been hungry the last couple of days. Sighing, she ate straight from the fridge, squatting in its puddle of light. Cleaned it right out.

An hour and a half later she was back at the Dream Centre, where she found Alex Silver at his desk in the big room going through print-outs. Babs and Frankie were not around.

"What did you decide about the other room, Alex?"

Silver glanced up looking helpless. "Rachel, I can't."

Rachel turned on her heel and went straight to the *Keep Out* door.

"*No!*" Silver screamed.

But the door was unlocked, and Rachel walked right in. What she saw first was Alex's bed, neatly made. Second, a chickenwire cage. Third, a large, glass-sided water tank on legs. In the middle of this tank, rising head and shoulders above the sides, was a sitting cat, moving towards her. The creature was white and orange, and it fixed her with a mad, red-eyed stare.

Alex Silver's hands gripped Rachel's shoulders. "This," he said with monumental restraint, "is Puff. Puff— Rachel."

Rachel stepped closer, Silver right behind.

Puff was approaching on a moving belt that ran along the surface of the water. As Rachel reached the tank, the belt under Puff's front paws was about to loop under and throw her into the water, so Puff twisted to hop to the high end of the belt and start another approach, still sitting upright but this time dozing.

"Puff's taking part in our experiment too," Silver explained quietly.

"How long has she been on that thing?"

"Eight hundred hours. Over the past 48 days. She's not always on the belt." Silver indicated a small fiberglass perch rising an inch or so above the surface of the water. "Sometimes she dozes on that. When she slips into REM the tonus leaves her neck muscles and her head drops—"

"Into the water!"

"Waking her up. And so on."

"*And so on*! Alex—"

"She's like you. She's getting her sleep. She's just not getting her dreams."

"But this is cat torture!"

Here Silver rotated Rachel by the shoulders to examine her face. "I'll be honest with you, Rachel. You're looking at a man of science plus ambition. It wasn't guilt that had me not wanting you to meet Puff. It was fear that seeing her this way would freak you out and you'd quit the study."

"I am freaked out!"

"I know. But listen to me. For an animal like Puff, this is just another life experience. When the experiment is over, she sleeps and dreams, wakes up fine and goes back to her owners."

"What kind of people would—"

"The cat is not in physical pain."

Puff leapt to the top of her moving belt and started again, licking her paws.

"But already I know a little how she feels," Rachel said, "and it isn't terrific!"

"That's only because neither of you can dream, and that means you can't learn. A brain filling up with information it can't *fix* is a brain *in extremis*, and how. But think what both of you'll have learned by the time it's over!"

"That you're a madman!"

"That's only what you think now! Rachel, look at it this way. You can be Puff's friend, her mentor, in all this. She's been at it longer, but you're smarter. She needs your help."

"I'll help her right out of that tank."

"Then you better put on a cat-proof suit."

"Alex, I don't like this at all. How long will you go on doing this to her?"

"Another week. In a week you too'll be ready to catch up on your REM. You can celebrate together."

"How? By clawing each other's face off?"

Puff sprang to the top end of her belt. This time she came towards Rachel and Silver with her eyes moving from side to side like a tennis spectator. "She's hallucinating a little," murmured Silver after a glance at Rachel's dismay.

"Alex—"

"Help me take care of Puff, please, Rachel? She's getting to be quite a handful." Silver held up his bandaged limbs. One of them pressed a key into Rachel's palm. "Keep an eye for yourself on how she's coming along. And you can still quit anytime. Only one thing. Don't tell Babs and Frankie. Things'll just get complicated."

"More than not telling them? Hey, who's the psychologist around here? Let me sleep on it."

"Won't do you a bit of good. When you don't dream, nothing gets worked out."

"Anyway, I'll tell you tomorrow. I can't think right now."

"That's what I'm saying. Tomorrow's going to be worse."

Puff scrambled to the top of the belt and rode towards Rachel and Alex ducking imaginary tennis balls.

Next morning— Babs and Frankie still asleep— Rachel, hearing distressed sounds she now knew to be cat, let herself into the next room in time to see Silver, wearing elbow-length leather gloves— "I finally learned"— lower Puff through a hole in the top of a chickenwire cage. "Rachel, could you help me with this? Shut the door as soon as I get my arms out?"

Getting his arms out was not easy, Puff digging her claws into those gloves with no intention of letting go. At last Silver got the creature shaken off and his arms pulled free. Rachel slammed the lid. "And lock it," Silver advised. "Like this." He fastened the latch.

Inside, Puff was busy hallucinating another cat. Stalking circles around it, clawing at its face. Silver lit three sparklers, stuck them in a plate of cat food, slid the plate into the cage. Puff swept aside the sparklers and devoured her meal in 17.32 seconds. In 3.13 more she had licked the plate clean and returned to pacing.

Rachel knelt with her face close to the chickenwire. Puff hissed and bared claws, but Rachel did not pull away. For what seemed a very long time she and the creature just looked at each other. Just? Had any human being in history been gazed at so intently, so searchingly, by a cat? Divine Grace was a pat on the bum compared to this. Released, finally, by those eyes when they looked to a last flare from a sparkler, Rachel straightened and knew that she could not walk away now. Not after an experience like that.

"Alex? I've decided to stick around. But it doesn't mean I approve."

"Great. Of course not. I knew you'd be reasonable about this."

Resolved then but edgy, definitely edgy, Rachel drove to work where the marble polish and disinfectant smell of the Village Green lobby worked to soothe her, inserted her back into the daily present, the snug Birkenstock of habit, even as she stepped onto the elevator with fifteen others, aware of firm young male asses under the Fortrel, headed for the twenty-third floor, stepped off saying Hi to all the familiar, irritating, not-unlikable faces as she wove her way through the open-floor, larger office to her own, one of the partitioned ones, lucky her, with her white walls and cork memo board, her plants, her metal desk, her IN and OUT baskets, her new computer terminal that had only lately stopped making her palms sweat, her privacy from prying eyes. In fact, so private was Rachel's office that it had no window. That came six promotions from now, when she would be too old to be a worried fool about men, or too old a fool not to be. But anyway. It probably said something even more damning about her than last month's eagerness to lock genitals with a dark stranger, but she did find her little work rituals comforting, especially, on bad mornings like this, the settling in: hanging up her coat, checking her make-up, her IN basket, her terminal, priorizing the hundred small tasks of the day.

These things Rachel did now.

And when she was ready to start work, she paused a moment to consider how lucky she was to have this clerical side to her brain, this cut-and-dried desk job here, to be able to put the entirety of what at this moment, at *most* moments these days, was the total disaster of her personal and emotional life. This morning, for example, as she went speedily about a dull, accomplishable series of almost completely pointless tasks, she did not have to wonder who Harry was. She did not have to think about where Leon was or what his Harry night dreams had meant about their relationship. Neither did she have to think about what her Nick Sirocco daydreams had meant about their relationship. She did not have to wonder what had become of a man that she and her mother had left over a quarter of a century ago, or why Cam Wilkes hadn't been in touch (she had given him the Dream Centre number). And she did not—

The phone rang.

"Millpond Indemnity. Rachel Boseman."

"Leon never called me. I told Vera Hedstrom he'd talk to Jerry right away. He doesn't want a job, obviously. He came home last night? You gave him my message? What real estate firm? I can't stand a procrastinator."

"Uh, mother? Leon's— out of town."

"Where out of town? For how long? Doing what?"

"A deal. Bi-Me's—national. Anyway, he's not interested. So far he seems to like real estate— Mother, I have to go. There's somebody on the other—"

"Bi-Me Real Estate, eh?"

"He's happy, Mother." The bastard. "You don't have to—"

Her mother had hung up.

Trouble. But Rachel was hot. Already a good two months into her backlog file, firing into her computer the most incisive letters in the insurance business, and why stop now to worry? By noon, however, common office features— waxed floor, swivel chair, corkboard, fluorescent lights— were looming and glaring, just a little bit resentful. Could this be dream deprivation? In the washroom before taking the elevator down to lunch with Marg from Road Accidents, Rachel redid her make-up— needed tons for the eyes— and noticed herself in the mirror: pin-stripe grey skirt suit, white blouse, heels. Hmm. Went into a cubicle, put the seat down, sat on it, crossed her legs, leaned into them, rotated her hips ever so slightly around an axis of labia. And came. Just like that. This dream deprivation was really something.

After work that night, Rachel drove straight to Silver's office at Village Market Square for another session. Silver told her to pick up the thread from the candlelight shrimp dinner following Leon's first big meeting with Nick Sirocco. "I want to hear exactly how this triangle developed."

"Triangle? How about parallelogram? There was Gretchen, remember, and—"

"Tell it, tell it."

Rachel was still fine-chopping green onions for their candlelight meal, Leon not home yet, when Gretchen called with fresh "news" on Nick Sirocco. "I was right. Danger. Trouble. Stay away."

"Explain."

"Leon seen him again?"

"What's your news, Gretchen?"

"Maybe you should call him. Nice women are more aggressive these days. You want to go out with a guy, you ask him out."

"I call him and you show up."

"Do you really think it's a good idea? You're nice but unpredictable. I'm not nice but right there."

"What did you find out?"

"He's already called and you're lying to me, Rachel."

Pause. Bluff: "What did you find out?"

"Rachel, I just want you to know that I am not telling you a single thing about Nick Sirocco until you come clean about this. You are the lousiest liar I ever knew in my life."

Ten more minutes of mendacity concluding with a whopper about Leon coming through the door, and Rachel put down the phone to sit depressed at the kitchen table, the vegetable knife slack in her fingers.

And then she did hear the Subaru and could tell by the percussive slam of the car door and the way Leon took the front steps bounding that the meeting with Nick Sirocco had gone well.

"Yay!" Leon said into the bowl of giant shrimps after making a *ta-dah*! entrance in his good blue suit. "Aw, that's so nice, Rach'," kissing her shoulder.

"How'd it go?"

"Fabulous."

"No hitch?"

"Hitch? Not really. Leon Boseman is no dark horse. He is— as I predicted— the only man for the job. Did you feed Cam?"

"No," surprised at the question, "but I thought I'd take something over after we—"

Leon was looking at his watch. "It's six," he said. "I usually try to feed him by 5:30."

"I thought he could wait until—"

"Hold everything! How many shrimps did you buy?"

"Eighteen," apologetic. "If I told you how much—"

"Perfect. That's six each. We'll transport the whole deal. A candlelight meal! If he won't come up, we'll eat down there with him."

"But Leon—"

"Come on. We'll do the actual cooking on his stove. What pots do we need?"

In the car on the way, Rachel tried to get Leon to say why this sudden change of heart about Cam Wilkes, but he refused to acknowledge it as anything of the sort. "Why can't I extend our little celebration to include my old millstone if I want to?"

"What exactly are we celebrating, again?"

"Sorry, Rachel. You know what eighty percent of the game is? Professionalism. This is something I'm beginning to learn from Nick. You move fast and you move discreet. It's all in the moves. Timing, precision, style. This is the key to success in the real world. I used to think the important thing was the ideas you had. It didn't matter how slow they came or if you ever gave them any form— I mean beyond letting them filter down until you're living and breathing them— or how good your grooming was while you mulled them over. But, let's face it, that's a pretty unrealistic way to go through life. Unless you're, say, a professor of philosophy with no career ambitions beyond tenure at a second-rate university. Life in the real world is moves, you know? Yours and anticipating the other guy's. I've always said it's a wasteland out there, but boy, wastelands sure groom some stylish and effective predators."

"Did you get the 12%?"

"Not quite."

"What did you get?"

"Nick was great. He laid it all out right off the bat. Monday the upstairs boys told him it had to be eight, and after he spent two days fighting it up to nine, how could I—Stop nagging me about a few lousy percent, would you?"

Rachel turned her face to the glass and watched the picture windows move past like little dioramas in the Millpond night.

Cam Wilkes' house was dark. Right at home, Leon kneed open the door and went straight in with his pile of pots. Rachel followed.

"Cam!" Leon called, "We're here!" and passed on to the kitchen.

To Rachel's surprise, Wilkes was in the darkness of the living room, among the bus parts. He seemed to be on the phone. "Darling—" she heard, "Tomorrow—" and a receiver being replaced.

"Cam!" Rachel cried, approaching him with her armful of dinner supplies. "Was that her?"

In the darkness Wilkes' face was invisible. "Yes."

"*I* know!" Rachel cried, stumbling forward into the dark room. "Where does she live? Why don't you invite her over? We'll have a nice meal. The four of us—" thinking, She can have my shrimps.

"Oh— I don't think—"

"Cam! Buddy!" It was Leon, crashing in from the dining room, catching his foot on something immobile and sprawling onto the floor at the feet of Wilkes, who placed his trumpet at his lips and played a few bars of *They Can't Take That Away From Me.* "Beautiful, beautiful," Leon murmured, still prone when Wilkes had finished. "Like a white wine, Cam?"

"No thanks."

"Rosé?" Leon rising to his knees. "Liquor store's still—"

"No, honest. I should be getting back to the basement."

"Cam!" Leon seized Wilkes by the shoulders. "We'll come with you! Got a little table down there?"

"Not really—"

"We'll squat! Shrimp-in-a-basket, by candlelight! Like Bedouin!"

"Thanks Leon, but I don't think—"

Rachel took Leon aside. "Leon, did it ever occur to you we might be imposing here?"

"Nonsense. He's just being cagey."

"I thought you were finished with feeding Cam."

"Tonight I resumed."

"Why?"

But Leon had pulled away. "Hey Cam. We'll eat in the kitchen. A big informal spread. Just the three of us. Like old times."

"I want to thank you both for everything you've done over the past few weeks," Wilkes said, stroking his trumpet. "You've got me through a hard time. A very hard time."

Rachel turned to Leon. "I suggested to Cam he invite the Girl on His Bus to join us for dinner."

"And what'd he say? What'd you say, Cam?"

"Some other time. But thanks. She's not up to it just now, I'm afraid."

Cam you poor guy, Rachel thought. "I'm sorry to hear that, Cam. Nothing serious—?"

"Chronic, Rachel, but not serious— yet."

"I'm sorry—"

"I'd tell her you were asking, but she's a little jealous—"

"Jealous? Why?"

"Get off it, Rachel," from Leon.

"Cam," with daggers for Leon, "won't you join us in the kitchen? A nice meal? We could talk?"

"Thanks but no. I think I'll just go back downstairs now. But please— make yourselves at home." And Wilkes sloped from the room and down the basement stairs playing tender, upbeat phrases from the *Melody for the Girl on My Bus*.

Rachel and Leon remained a moment in a frieze of frustration. And then Leon said, "Let's get out of here," and headed for the kitchen to gather pots. Rachel followed, but first, her eyes now used to the dark, she located the phone. A live line, at least.

Back home Leon lowered himself thoughtfully into a kitchen chair while Rachel resumed work on the candlelight meal. "I must remember to take Wilkes' garbage out," he reflected.

"So what was Nick like this time?" Rachel asked.

"A great guy. A terrific guy. One of the few who's really going to leave his mark. A mover. Razor-sharp. Mind like a steel trap. So efficient he's a nice guy, because he understands that niceness is the perfect lubricant."

"Sounds like Harry."

"Don't start."

"What's the deal?"

"Can't say."

The phone rang. Rachel picked it up in the living room. It was Gretchen. "Why don't you answer? If you're having another fight about Harry just tell me and then I'll know."

"We're not having a fight about anybody. We went to feed Wilkes. And now we're going to eat."

"Rachel? Keep in touch, OK? Lie yourself blue. But keep in touch."

To Leon Rachel said when she came into the kitchen, "OK, what about Sirocco. Who is he?"

"You met him!"

"Well, is he married?"

Leon threw up his hands. "I don't know! We didn't get into personal narratives. We're not a couple of women, we're business-men! We talked business, pure and simple."

"Leon, is this deal moral?"

"*Moral*? Are you kidding? Moral is a meaningless concept in business, Rachel. You'll have to get used to that. Legal/illegal— or, more exactly, their appearance— applies. Moral/immoral does not."

"OK. Is it legal?"

"Fairly."

"Is it likely to go through?"

"You mean, is it a sure thing? In business, Rachel, nothing is a sure thing until the deal is completed, and even then you never know. The guy could come back and sue you, tie up everything for years. It's all just part of the game. When you're a player you're a player, it's that simple. If you played only to win you'd retire after your first few million, and what's the point of that? You play to win but more than that you play to play again. When you play with the big boys it's not a means and end kind of a thing. That's what I was saying about style. Your means is your end. You see, Rachel—"

Leon went on like this throughout their intimate shrimp meal by candlelight. He was still talking twenty minutes after they had got into bed and Rachel had turned out the light.

"— it's like the song says. There is no success like failure, and a failure is no success at all. In business it's as if you have no mammalian brain, so you never really experience failure as such. You try this, it doesn't work, you try that. There's no scarring, no dreaming necessary to assimilate the error. There is no error. You're like a fish or a reptile. A protoplasm. A total psychopath. It's a very straight-ahead kind of a life. Sort of morally streamlined. No, *morally* isn't the word, is it. More like—"

"Goodnight, Leon." Rachel pulled a pillow over her ear.

Leon's ardent chatter degenerated into a broken-down mumble shortly before it lapsed entirely to be replaced by fortissimo snoring.

At noon the next day Nick Sirocco was crossing the concourse of Village Green towards Rachel Boseman, smiling tan above a pale yellow suit. As they spotted each other through the lunch hour throng it might have been the cue for one of those weightless sprints toward mouth-crushing union, but Rachel was too busy dreading an occasion on which every word she spoke would be hers only in the characteristic way that it failed to be what she had intended to say. And if she tried to explain, it would be more of the same but worse, the explanation all in knots from her knowledge of being on dubious ground just being here. She was hopeless on dubious ground. Why couldn't she ever remember that? Her unconscious mind, sadistic orchestrator of the cruelest humiliations, was merciless. Her heels crossing that lobby were leaden and skittery.

Shaven, fragrant, Adonic, Sirocco murmured something, kissed her cheek, steered her through the lunch hour crowds, a revolving door, and down the stairs into Timbers 'n Spokes. Rachel's mouth was too dry for speech. Her lips kept sticking to her teeth. Fortunately there was little need to speak before the hostess had led them to one of the private tables at the back.

There, staring into her eyes, Sirocco began. "I talked to your husband yesterday. I like him. He's an oddball, but he's fresh, he's an entity. And I like that he should have tried to do something for Wilkes."

"Uh huh."

"It's rare you find a man who'd do so much for a basketcase. A burden on society."

"I think Leon did it for complicated reasons."

"What reasons."

"Oh, boredom. Loneliness—"

"The thing is, he did it. Don't forget that. You're used to him. You've got him all figured out, your way. If Christ had a wife, to her He'd be just another guy. It takes others to see what's special."

Pause. "You mean like, the *disciples*?"

The waiter was there. Rachel ordered a seafood salad, Nick Sirocco the veal, two glasses of red wine. They both watched the waiter walk away, and then Sirocco said, "Rachel, it's a beautiful name."

"Thank you."

"Listen. I want you to do something for me, Rachel. I want you to tell me everything about yourself. Everything. I want to know it all."

"Everything?"

"OK. Start with what's most on your mind these days, what's grabbing your heart and guts. Tell me all about it."

"I'm afraid there's nothing—"

"So tell me about Wilkes. The guy fascinates me. I understand you met him first."

Haltingly, in dismay, Rachel told Sirocco about meeting Cam Wilkes and about some of the good work she had heard from Leon that PAGO was doing. As she spoke, Sirocco's expression remained sober and attentive, although a certain ... hardness, was it? in his eyes suggested an unfriendly interest in Wilkes. Jealousy? Like Leon? It was a relief when her salad came and she could pretend to be too interested in uncovering its contents to be able to continue.

"I hear he used to live in a bus," Sirocco said.

Eager to defend Wilkes but not wanting to go into the Girl on His Bus business, Rachel confirmed the bus story in such as way as to imply that it was the attempts to hound him out of his bus that had pushed him into serious agoraphobia.

"This phobia shit," Sirocco replied, slicing his veal, "it's all in the head. You're bound to get a certain amount of riff-raff when you aim mid-market. If he don't like the place he should move out. But he won't. You know why? Because he's a flake, and ninety-nine percent of flakes are born troublemakers. I'll tell you something else," pointing his fork at Rachel's face. "Ninety-nine percent of the times a troublemaker has an accident it's no accident."

"Cam Wilkes doesn't mean any harm."

"He's telling you we tried to harass him out of his stupid bus. I call this slander. We're a respectable company. Don't tell me he don't mean harm."

"He made me promise not to tell."

"Yeah, right. Tell that to a woman it's like taking out a full page ad. Hell, you just told *me*, and I can have his legs broken."

"*Pardon?*"

"A little joke. You should laugh."

When Sirocco's plate was empty he looked at it briefly then lifted his eyes. "Anyways, you're a beautiful woman, Rachel."

"It's the lighting."

"Don't be modest. The first time I saw you, I couldn't take my eyes off. You're a knockout. A tiger. A queen. When you talk, we communicate. Something resonates inside. Your words are champagne for my heart. It's like I know you from a long time ago. It's like we were lovers in another life or something." His hand closed over hers. Rachel looked at it. A strong hand. Little dark hairs lying in parallel. "So what do you say. You and me. I'm crazy about you." The waiter was standing by the table looking at Sirocco, who checked his tie knot. "Bring us two coffees." The waiter went away. Sirocco leaned closer, squeezing Rachel's hand. "Listen, Rachel. I want to hear you say you know what I'm talking about. This is real what I'm feeling, right? I mean, you're not going to tell me I'm making it all up."

"I wouldn't do that, but you don't know me, Nick."

"That's what I'm saying. What is there to know. I'm a man, you're a woman. The magic is there. You know what came to me as you were just talking? Love is magic, it's not somebody's life history, their stupid opinions. Love is cosmic. You could be life to me, Baby. Everything I ever wanted. Don't let me down. Don't say I'm wrong. Don't tell me I'm losing my mind."

"It's not that, Nick."

"Oh yeah?" skin tightening around his eyes. "So what is it."

"It's just that, well," intending a mood-lightening little quip here, "when you've got a mind that's basically deluded, it must be really easy to lose!"

Oh dear.

"I mean—" A nervous giggle. "That didn't exactly come out the way I, um—"

Sirocco was absorbing Rachel's witticism with fortitude. Afterwards she might have remembered his eyes going completely dead while he did this had not one of them begun to tic so savagely.

Sirocco leaned towards her. "I get it. It's a joke."

"That's right—"

"Hey, you should have told me you were a joker. When you said OK to lunch maybe you should have said, 'Listen, Mr. Sirocco. I should tell you. I'm a real joker'."

"Look, I'm really—"

"You always joke like this?"

"Sometimes—"

"Only when a man is opening his heart, right?"

"I really am—"

"You joke like a real flake, Rachel. You do this with everybody?"

Here Rachel made no reply.

"What's the matter? You won't talk to me now? I thought I asked you a question."

When Rachel started to get up, Sirocco caught hold of her forearm and lowered it, slowly, the rest of her following, to the table.

"Let go of me."

"Mistake Number Two. You don't leave this table. I leave this table."

She watched his other hand take out his wallet and flick a fifty dollar bill into her face. The next three bills she batted away with her free hand. Without letting go of her arm, Sirocco stood up, leaned across the table, and said, "Now, Rachel. You be careful. Three mistakes and a girl could have some kind of accident. Like to her face."

With these words, Nick Sirocco let go of Rachel's arm and walked out of Timbers 'n Spokes.

She was still rubbing it when the waiter set down her coffee. "Say the wrong thing to Mr. Sirocco, Miss?"

Rachel nodded. "I guess he's insecure about his mind."

"Hey, who isn't?"

"Right. Here, why don't you take one of these for yourself." Her hand shook as she passed him the fifty.

"Sirocco, I take it," Alex Silver said from the floor of his office, where he had been doing pelvic tilts for the past fifteen minutes of Rachel's session, "was no Harry."

Rachel nodded. "I'm not that sick."

"So Sally was right."

"Yes, she was. Alex?"

"Mmm-hmm?"

"Why don't we face it? This is going nowhere. Harry was Leon's problem. He's not mine, really, is he, except that he was around for the screw-up of my marriage. I mean, I'm obsessed just because I need somebody to blame, right?"

"Maybe. But also maybe Leon was half right about the ricochet thing. Harry was you broadcasting some more original problem that Leon was picking up, and I don't mean Cam Wilkes. Like what if Harry was Leon's internalization of your ideal of how he, Leon, should have been. What if Harry was a name for the distance that Leon fell short of measuring up. So Harry, as a piece of imagination, was feeding off Leon's dissatisfaction with himself *and* off your dissatisfaction with Leon, which obviously would channel in."

Rachel had not thought of it exactly this way. "Sounds like I *should* find Harry," she said quietly when she had done so.

"Yeah, maybe you should."

That same evening, after her session with Silver, Rachel hung around 201 Dell Drive with the lights off, reluctant as a PAGO person to go out, wandering like a ghost through the streetlit ruins of her dream of a perfect home with Leon, bound not so much by memory as by melancholy. Melancholy tempered by rage and lust. Mostly lust. It was something of a sleep of desire that Rachel was wandering through 201 Dell in when the phone rang.

Her mother. "Bi-Me says Leon hasn't been in for days, and they're not national. Rachel, you're lying to me. He's moved out. Admit it."

"I admit it."

"How many times did I tell you, you should have left him like we left your father? Beat the bastards to the punch. Didn't I drill that into your head?"

"Mother, why? You've missed dad for almost thirty years!"

"Not as much as when I lived with him, believe me. You think *I'm* afraid of closeness? You know how in movies women are always telling men, 'You make me feel so dirty', meaning whatever it is they mean? Well, he made me feel dirty. Not low dirty or filth dirty. Sex is not a problem for me. Mess dirty. Like I was always messing up his space. I'm not talking literally here. The fact that I was not born to clean some goddam house is strictly by the way."

"And then he started to get jobs— he designed, you know—"

"Buildings. You've told me."

"Of course, once he became successful he was never home. I've missed your father since the day I first laid eyes on the willful bastard. Why stop now? I liked him. He had his problems, but I liked him. He was an original. And he loved animals. Except cats."

"You always said he was bad news!"

"Only because he made me feel like bad news. You remember him."

"No!"

"It's just as well. Also, he couldn't handle uncertainty. I gave him a lot of that. Besides youth and a terrific body, what else did I have?"

"Mother, you're excited."

"You're damned right I'm excited. I'll strangle the bastard. I knew when he started selling on commission. It's no life for a man. Didn't I tell you that? At least now there's nothing to keep you out in that godforsaken— Change all the locks. You can stay with me."

"No, Mother. I'm trying to work this out on my own. There's more to it than—"

"The tilt-up tits on some Bi-Me secretary? Face reality. Two weeks back in the world and he's fallen for a twenty-year-old piece!"

"Mother, you're raving. You don't know anything—"

"Thanks to you I don't know anything. Until it's too late. Oh, why couldn't you have learned from what your father did to me—"

"I don't remember him, Mother!" Rachel sing-song. "Bye now!"

The phone rang again immediately, but Rachel was already moving out the door, heading back to the Dream Centre and another night of serious deprivation.

FOUR

As a kid Rachel did what she was told, at least figured she ought to. It was superstition, really. Little girls always washed their face and hands at bedtime, always did their homework without complaint if not in actual happiness, never talked with their mouth full or sang at the table. Just as there was a definition, there was a rule for everything, and these rules, like the common will of her mother and teachers that they sprang from, made things real, but they also threw them in shadow, the shadow of that greater reality where nobody sings at the table. Sometimes it was not much fun living in the shadow, but the alternative, bare-faced defiance, blew open too many doors to damnation.

And then Rachel got older, and the rules seemed more unimpressive but just as binding. Why else spend your teens kicking against everything in sight? Damnation by that time was looking pretty tasty, and so were broad shoulders and 3-D pectorals, but somehow sooner or later it always came back to the shadow. Same more lately, and cruelly, with love and marriage in the Millpond. Except this time the shadow came with a melody and a name, and Rachel was tracking the bastard— the real one this time, no more Siroccos—and when she found him she would check him out, and depending on how that went she would either take him to her heart and never let him go, or else she would bundle him into the Civic for a nice long ride, way out beyond the suburbs, to where the guys who never sing at the table belong: the dump. With the bulldozers, the gulls, and the ruined bears.

On the fourth morning of dream deprivation (felt like the fourth month) Rachel woke up feeling exactly the way the last couple days' Nowlis-Green Mood Check List had said she was feeling: Anxious, Irritable, Aggressive. And speedy. She was noticing a lot more, fielding more details, her subliminal identification scores radically improving, her drawings beginning, incredibly, to resemble those hundredth-second exposures that constitute the Reuben Ambiguous Figure Test. So like lightning were Rachel's reflexes, in fact, with her slipping into REM onset so fast, that Silver had begun to worry she might be getting too little non-REM sleep not to muddy the experiment with debilitation and fatigue symptoms. That was why he had upped her dose of dexedrine sulphate. He said.

Also paranoid. Looking either Babs or Frankie straight in the eye was now out of the question— she just knew they were trying to find out what Leon was up to or else were fully informed. Liked to watch her twitch. And then on that fourth morning a remark by Babs about somebody leaving hair in the sink in the little washroom elicited from deep in Rachel's throat an authentic animal snarl that touched off another from Babs. Silver too was beginning to bug Rachel, though intellectually she knew that as Type-A personality psychologists went, he was not such a bad egg. Aside from appearing more agitated each passing day— projection, right?— tormenting an innocent cat, having endless mama's-boy phone conversations with his mother, beeping Rachel awake all night with his infernal machine, rustling the print-outs on his desk in the morning when Rachel "woke up," and hounding her every hour at the Dream Centre with his goddam tests, what had he done?

Quiet moments at the Centre were spent with the unfortunate Puff, whose ordeal on the belt and waterbound platform Rachel had taken, mornings and evenings, to accompanying with soothing sounds of comfort and inspiration. Occasionally Puff hissed and promised to gouge Rachel's eyes, but Rachel had no trouble sympathizing with that. Mostly Puff dozed while Rachel talked, hummed, sang. It calmed them both. Secretly Rachel was waiting for another Moment of Creaturely Communion, but in her tank Puff now seemed too zonked or pissed off for that, and in her cage she was either gobbling down food or sunk in combat hallucinations. Still, anything could happen.

No sign, so far, of Harry. Not in the non-REM dreams that Rachel managed to remember to write down for Silver. And not in the course of her ever edgier days at Millpond Indemnity.

After work on that fourth day, a Friday, Rachel's session with Alex Silver in his office at Market Village Square began with the question of Rachel's father. She had told Silver about her mother's latest call. "So what do you remember about him?" Silver asked.

"Two things."

"That's all?"

"Alex, I was four! First, a photograph. Black and white. He's standing on a jail roof looking down at the camera. He's in a white suit."

"Big black stripes?"

"He designed the building, my mother says. His first commission."

"What did he look like? Have you got the picture?"

"No, but it'll be somewhere at her place. Unfindable. She cleans up by filling drawers. He had a long face. Maybe it was the light or the angle, but in the picture his nose looks pressed in at the top, as if somebody took their thumb and—" Rachel took her thumb and pressed it into the air. "His eyes were sunken too. Unreadable. In the picture. A thin mouth. Like mine."

"You don't have a thin mouth."

"Sure I do."

"And Memory Number Two?"

Rachel laughed. "His closet. Giant shoes. Dozens of them. When he was away— he was always away—I'd crawl in there and go to sleep. I— *Oh God!*"

Silver jolted forward in his chair. "*What is it?*"

"*I'm smelling it*—!"

"Great!" Silver scrambled for his notepad. "An olfactory hallucination! Describe it!"

"Um, shoe polish, shoe leather, feet. Real, chemical, animal certainty."

"Got it."

"That was amazing!"

"Uhh-huh—" writing.

"Anyway, sleeping in his closet meant I didn't know when he was actually gone for good. My mother always took his stuff when we moved."

"Ah— but she left him—"

"That's right."

"Your mother was conflicted."

"Is. I used to imagine him catching up one day, with a sole flapping, and thank us for having all those shoes waiting." Rachel paused. "I just remembered something. Once from one of his trips he brought me my own pair of saddleshoes, in red and white. Not pair. Two lefts, in different sizes, a mix-up at the shoe store. I guess his mind was on something else. Just as well. They were too beautiful to wear. I displayed them on top of my dresser, like polished souvenirs of a world beyond ordinary symmetry—mother, father; left, right—where feet grew like that." Again Rachel paused. "Gee, Alex, you don't think Harry—"

"Could be."

Silver was drumming his fingers on the smoked-glass table jiggling that antherium. To do this he had to slump down in his chair until he was practically horizontal. "Anyways," he said. "What happened with Leon after your bad-move lunch with Sirocco?"

What happened was, Rachel worked the rest of the afternoon at Millpond Indemnity with her brain doing reruns of that Lunch in Hell.

She was not home long when Gretchen called, wanting to know if Rachel thought she should ask Nick Sirocco to lunch.

"Gretchen, don't," was Rachel's immediate advice. And then she had to explain that she herself had just eaten that meal with him, to say how it had gone, and to pretend to be offended that Gretchen should refuse to believe her when she said that Sirocco had called her at work only that morning.

"So anyway," Gretchen interrupting, "you will see him again."

"Don't want to."

"Rachel, lip means spirit. It was a *good* thing you did."

"I'm saying we were over-eager on old Nick, Gretchen. He's nothing but a little bully. An arm-breaker. An acid-tosser—"

"Rachel, you're under-selling yourself again." Gretchen exhaled smoke. "So should I call him or not."

"Call him, call him."

Gretchen said she probably wouldn't bother, she was too deeply in love with Ted.

And then Leon was home. He went straight upstairs to change. When he came down he said, "Let's go to that restaurant in the Olde Mill tonight, The Buhrstone. Nick says they're doing fabulous ribs these days."

The Buhrstone was a restaurant with a revolving floor. It had two curving walls, one of glass, for the view— the millpond, and a greater sea beyond of townhouses— and a wall papered in a blown-up daguerrotype of a flour mill, for atmosphere. It was the kind of place that at noon on formica tables offered a daily special or club sandwich and at night on checkered cloths with candles in fishnet containers served ribs, baked potatoes with sour cream and ersatz bacon bits, salads with roquefort dressing, desserts from a wagon. Besides that old mill mural the distinctive thing about The Buhrstone was its floor, which was meant to depict the actual grinding surface of a giant, revolving millstone. In a real mill, of course, it's the upper stone that revolves. Not here. The floor was poured concrete, grooved like a millstone, and scattered with genuine grains of wheat. The ceiling was the upper stone, probably only styrofoam but still menacing. The main problem— or, if you were a kid, virtue— of The Buhrstone, however, was that it rotated so fast it was not always easy to keep your footing. Somebody must have installed the wrong gauge sprocket. Dinnerware at The Buhrstone millimetred centrifugally, and occasionally a novice diner would stagger pale down one of the spokelike aisles towards the washrooms. Kids, who recognized it as the Rotor version of a Chicken Chalet, loved the place. It was always busy. And since even old hands could take only so much, the turnover was a fast-food marketer's dream. "Nick tells me," Leon commented as he finished his shrimp cocktail, "Mortprop's making a fortune out of this place." Maybe that wrong sprocket was inspired.

Rachel, not hungry, the lights of the Millpond showing up relentless every few minutes out the long curve of window, poked at her baked potato. She was still in a state of nervous distraction from that disastrous lunch. When the mural came around, she studied it for swans. What she saw was an old mill rising a featureless two storeys of stone to the far right of a dark expanse of water. No swans. To the far left, a blasted dun landscape of stumps. To the immediate left, shadows in the dark of bushes, a half dozen unwashed, moustached men of uncertain age in cloth caps, high boots, poorly fitting jackets. The labourers, probably, who had built the place. In the foreground, on the near side of the water, the miller, a fat man on short legs in Sunday black, a broad-brimmed hat. Stiffly posing, vain about his mill. A pace away his rail-thin wife huddled with three small children, squinting out at The Buhrstone diners, the children peering from under their bonnets like dazzled midgets.

No swans.

Rachel dropped her eyes to Leon, who was eating fast and enormously, the way he did when he was keyed up. "When are you seeing Sirocco again?" she asked.

"Monday," chewing. "I've got some things to do on the weekend first."

"Like what."

"Can't say."

After awhile Rachel became aware that each time their table came around to the window, Leon would pointedly peer into the darkness beyond the floodlit rectangle of cork chips against which in warmer days pansies spelled out *Village-on-the-Millpond: A Nice Place for Nice People.*

The twentieth or so time this happened, Rachel asked Leon what he was doing.

"Nothing."

They ate in silence. From invisible speakers Rachel could hear orchestrated Beatles, and she remembered the spring that she and Leon had first moved to the Millpond, when he still had his old speech-writing job, had not yet started writing down his dreams, when they used to make love for hours on summer evenings with the windows wide open, summer laughter and conversation, catches of Cole Porter, the Dorseys, Beatles, wafting all the way from the Olde Mill balcony: Muzak, really, but snuggled in Leon's loving arms and with the melodies coming and going on the night breezes, those old standards sounded just fine. More than fine. Tender, Aching, Magnificent, and True.

Rachel wiped her eyes.

When Leon had finished his ribs, he pushed his plate away with a greasy thumb and sat back, whistling between his teeth. After a while he mentioned that Mortprop Investments was planning to build a new mall in the Millpond.

"That's good," Rachel said. "The Mortrop Mall doesn't make it. Where?"

Leon pointed out over the illuminated cork chips. "It'll be really something. If Nick has his way, a super-regional theme mall with a million square metres of leasable space and another quarter million for condos."

"Really?"

"Right now Nick's in a power struggle with the architect about the details. The guy sounds like a classic prima donna. Anything to leave his stamp. Ego like a hot air balloon. Nick's being more reasonable. Why fool with success? He wants a world-class super-regional. Four stretch-dumbbells in an octagon. Magnet stores pulling pedestrian traffic along eight spokes— Natural lighting used sparingly, for dramatic effect. Otherwise it swamps the store lights—"

"What does the architect want?"

"Are you ready? A park with shopping walks, basically, under glass. He's talking about a return to the grand Victorian arcade, with vegetation. The only thing between you and the sky is the minimal steel framework and the glazing—"

"Doesn't sound so bad—"

"Not *per se*, maybe. But he's just showing off. These guys are like barbers. Compelled to make every customer a walking ad for a haircut. People don't like that. The architect gets famous, but if nobody shops there Mortprop is out a lot of money. That's Nick's point. So he and this guy are really locking horns. Nick doesn't like to be stopped. The guy could end up in cement."

"*Cement?*"

"Joke. Anyway, whatever the final details, we're talking about a major mall. A truly major mall."

"And you're helping to put together the land for Sirocco?"

"Business. Can't say."

"Where?"

"Northeast corner. South side of the 303."

"What's the theme?"

"Nuclear Winterland." This from the waitress, who had come by for their dessert orders.

Leon gave her a dirty look. "Two coffees." She went away. To Rachel Leon said, "Arcadia Centre."

"Sounds more appropriate for the architect's mall than Sirocco's."

"Whose side are you on? The irony of it is, most of these old-time Syndicate guys are still living in the fifties. They wouldn't know a super-regional from a postmodern hole in the—"

"*Syndicate* guys?"

"Yeah, aside from not arguing with success, who controls the brick and cement business? That's Nick's other point. Glass can get expensive. So what if when they built the Millpond they broke every greenspace statute on the books? They pay off the town council one by one, maybe throw in a new library, and that's the end of that problem. Why go to a lot of trouble putting a park under glass when it's not even either necessary or to the point? Anyway, a park is basically dogs and Frisbees and dirty diapers in the trashcans polluting the ponds. And yet these old guys are just as likely to listen to this big-wheel architect as to Nick. The power of a name, eh?"

Rachel reached for Leon's free hand, but it had moved sideways for a piece of garlic bread. "Leon, let's move back to the city, OK? This place is really closing in."

Leon was stunned. "Are you serious? Just when I'm getting my teeth into something gigantic?"

"You'll hate selling real estate!"

"So? Want to hear what a one-bedroom condo downtown costs these days?"

"Leon, this won't be good for us. Only last night you said business was for psychopaths and protoplasms—"

"Why do you always quote me out of context? Think what a North American drawing card like this could do for prices in the Millpond! Think what a house right up against the West Edmonton Mall would be selling for right now if the oil market wasn't up and down like a toilet seat!"

"Leon, please!"

He shrugged. "You just told me the Mortprop Mall doesn't make it. So what are you saying. Rachel, listen to me. Adaptation is what life is all about. Anything that can convert gills into lungs and crawl out of the sea can adapt just fine." Leon thought for a moment. "They'll probably put up a good fence."

"Leon, the Syndicate."

"The Syndicate's everywhere, as everybody and his kid

knows. Nick's a civilized guy. This isn't black shirts and white ties. It's just where the financing happens to come from. Who else would have the kind of money for a project like this?"

Leon waxed philosophical. "You know, Rachel. Looking down from that helicopter Sunday, I could see so clearly that PAGO hasn't quite got it right. It isn't that there are scary things out there. What's scary is that the out there itself doesn't really exist, except to separate you from the next guy. Or to drive your car through. It's not a place to *be*. It's not a 'place' at all. This is the real reason agoraphobiacs are afraid of being crushed by open space. The point about the Millpond is not that the houses are jammed too close together with no parks, the point is that everything is perfectly convenient by car and that there is exactly enough space between you and your neighbour to guarantee you both the freedom to do exactly what you want. He can fire up the barbecue behind his seven-foot fence and you can go in and watch dirty videos. You're both happy. If everybody's got a TV and you're far enough from the next guy that you can handle the backbeat from his stereo after eleven with a set of earplugs, what's the problem? It's like front lawns. They're not there to be on, except with the lawn mower. They're a frame. To separate the house from the sidewalk."

Their coffees came. The waitress gave Leon a look of good-natured contempt. She went away.

"Mental space," Rachel suggested.

Leon nodded, sipping. He was on to his next point. "And you know what the other side of the coin is?"

"Fear?"

"No, the *other* side of the coin. Home. The *idea* of home. Modern Man doesn't need physical space and physical home, he needs mental space and mental home—"

"Mental home is right."

Leon sighed. "So what a place like the Millpond offers is these two illusions, home and space, in perfect symbiosis—"

"What's symbiosis? I keep forgetting."

"The meaning of home—sanctuary—" speaking slowly, as for a group of note-taking underachievers— "grows out of the scary nothing of space, and the meaning of space—freedom—grows out of the frustrating constrictions of home—"

"Is that how you feel about our home, Leon?"

"Why do women always personalize everything?"

"But Leon, there has to be more to life than fear and frustration."

"Right. There is one way to transcend this symbiosis of illusion. Know what it is?"

"Love?"

"Late Twentieth Century, remember. Stick to the late Twentieth Century."

"Relationship?"

"That's just jargon for love. I'm talking about present-day *reality*."

"I give up."

"Spending. Spending affirms the freedom of the outside. At the same time as it asserts control. Unfortunately, where freedom *actually* occurs, such as it occurs, is in the home. At home you can spend your time, energy, seed, just about any way you want."

"Your seed."

"But you can't spend money at home."

"What about door-to-door salesmen, the Yellow Pages, phone orders, and that weird TV channel with the china figurines?"

"These methods all make people anxious, and anxious people don't spend half what they do if they're totally relaxed, like virtually in an Alpha brain state. No, what is needed is the domestication of space without the drawbacks— namely the cooping, the loss of anonymity— of home. What is needed are places able to combine only the positive features of home and space, where people can spend money in a state of tremendous relaxation, even euphoria."

"You mean shopping malls—"

"Right. The thing about malls—" Leon paused to look at her. "Why are you crying."

"I'm not crying, I'm *tear-ing*."

"I see. Why are you tear-ing."

But Rachel could only shake her head, face in a grimace of salt.

"As if I didn't know," Leon swinging around to find the waitress.

"Know what— Leon, please," Rachel blubbering now, a hand on the arm that supported his weight while he squeezed into his pants for his wallet. "Let's go and see Dr. Silver, together—"

Leon's head drew back and he went into a long blink. "What? Who?"

"Alex Silver, from your high school. He's a psychologist here in the Millpond."

Leon nodded, slowly, absorbing this. "You've already seen him."

Rachel shook her head.

"You took Wilkes."

Rachel continued to shake her head, adding a Why-would-you- think-that expression.

"OK. Tell me again," Leon methodically, "why I should go. Because you're still on Harry."

The waitress gave Leon the bill. "You guys know Harry too?" she said.

They both looked at her.

She laughed, tossing her head as she walked away.

"Leon, we need help as a couple."

"This is news to me. *You* need help. You go see Silver. Maybe he really is Harry—as you believed before you decided Harry was my father— and your problems will be over."

"Both of us, Leon. Please."

"Hey, Rachel. Listen," Leon here with the slow menace of the completely reasonable male. "If anybody's off the rails right now it's you, not me. You realize that, don't you. It happens all the time. I get myself together and you go all alienated and strange. I move on, outgrow it, whatever, and the next thing I know you're into some dippy variation on what for me is a dead horse. Remember when I got into music and you had to have a flute?"

"Leon, so we could play together!"

"A flute and electric guitar? Or when I fooled around on the market a little and you bought all those stupid term deposits and had to cash them early and lost the interest—"

"Because you wanted to buy a house in the Millpond!"

"Ah, and you didn't?"

"Leon, these aren't the same kinds of things at all!"

"What is going on with you anyway, Rachel," ignoring her. "Is this some kind of a game for you? Are we competing or something? Can't you take your own initiative once in a while? Don't you have your own goddam centre?" This last was a low, hard, milestone blow. It redefined the boundary of cruelty over which tacitly in their fights they did not go. Morally on shaky pins, Rachel had been rigid, wide open. She took it hard. Leon would have been a monster not to notice. The next voice to carry the pleading was his. "I mean, don't you think there just might not be enough energy around here for both of us? Do you really have to go all weak and weepy and mysterious and sneaky and fall to pieces every time I get a little enthusiastic, a little focussed on something?"

"*Sneaky?*"

"You heard me," Leon assuming an impassive face.

And Rachel bluffing. "And what exactly am I being sneaky about?"

"Isn't that your business?"

"Leon, what are you implying?"

"Aw hell," Leon cried with sudden passion. "Let's get out of here. I've listened to enough bullshit for one night."

Next morning, in the clear light just before dawn, it was evident to Rachel that Leon would surely suffer for her lunch with Nick Sirocco, and when he did he would be even more reluctant to go with her, to see Alex Silver. And if by a miracle he was not, she would be too busy worrying that he and Dr. Silver were ganging up on her, or that one of them was striking the other as a fool, to be able to get to the root of this Harry thing.

And so she decided to go and see Dr. Silver alone, and as soon as she had decided that, sleep returned, actually more like down-market worry, her mind gone weaving arabesques of anxiety around and through the various aspects of the stubborn disturbing fact that she did not know if she would be seeing Silver to check out if *he* was Harry or to tell him that Harry was her problem. The former? More direct? Like making an appointment to see your primary symptom? On the other hand, what could be worse karma than consulting a psychologist under false pretences? By the way: What false pretences? Doctor, my husband had this problem and now I think I've got it— Tell me, does this tune I'm going to try to hum for you here sound at all familiar . . . ? These and other arabesques of anxiety floated down out of upper darkness and settled like doilies upon every glass-mark of old fear on the coffee table of Rachel's soul. And when it was all over, when everything had been accomplished, when all the doilies had floated down and settled themselves, she lay in a perfect peace of exhaustion, until her alarm lifted her straight into the air.

Alex Silver was looking at his watch through heavy lids. "So that was when you came and saw me the first time? But wasn't Leon still around?"

"I kept putting it off. Until he disappeared."

"Huh." Silver made a big yawn. "What I can't understand," he said, stifling another, "is what a man of Leon's calibre would see in a yob like Sirocco."

"Success?"

"You think so?" Silver sighed. "By the way. As I mentioned earlier. That of all the psychologists you could have come to, you should come to me is not irrelevant here, is it? Aside from the mutual admiration society that was so secret neither Leon nor I knew the other belonged. I mean, there's another ticket for you that I could be Harry on."

"Which one is that?"

"You came to me because I'm the big expert around here, right? Interesting implications to this particular choice of solution to a problem like Harry, aren't there?"

"What kind of implications?"

"I mean, Freud said women have underdeveloped superegos. Guess what they've got instead."

"Husbands?"

"Rachel, let me tell you something about what it's like to be the big expert in a place like the Millpond. The fact is, any guy like me who's got the smarts and the charm and the, like, literally eighteen-hours-a-day energy has no great difficulty setting himself up as Mr. Big in a place like this. There is a real demand out there for answers. Look at SMILE. Look at PAGO. These groups fill a need. The problem is, promise answers, and right away you're into two syndromes.

"The first is show business. As you may know, I host my own show here in the Millpond, *Share That Dream.* Ever watch it?"

Reluctant, afraid Silver would ask her opinion of a show in which contestants dressed up like characters from their recent dreams, Rachel admitted that she had maybe caught it once or twice.

"Anyways, it gives me the exposure. TV made me. It's also made me over, I suppose, but hey, that's showbiz.

"The second is faddism. It *un*makes you. Expertdom dates. You catch their attention with some new angle, grab the spotlight, and before you know it your successor's arrived on the crest of the next wave. Clients tend to be followers, and followers just hate it when leaders change. Change looks like opportunism, moral confusion, betrayal. Once a man of science climbs up on that pedestal, he might as well have himself bronzed. They're not going to let him develop and evolve. Instead, he'll always be over-generalizing to satisfy them, always disclaiming because he knows he can never live up to such expectations— but that only makes them think he's even more wonderful. So wise and modest too! They just won't let him off that one-way road to the boneyard where they keep the spats and the hula hoops and the dead therapies."

"Gee, Alex. I'm sorry."

"So does the reality of my situation here make me sound like Harry to you? I mean honestly? And to think, Rachel, I'm putting myself through all this just because I hated so much not being the coolest guy in creation, like your husband, who I now learn has problems too. As of course, given my field, I should have known. Ironic, eh? But I guess what I'm trying to say, Rachel, is experts are just people. None of us are what anybody really wants when they go to an expert. And that's because nobody can exist beyond all accidents of culture and history. Your Harry can maybe, but not us. We just try to act like it, to keep our careers going. It's called being professional. But believe me, ninety percent of the time we feel like total frauds—"

As Alex Silver sat shaking his head and rueing his choice of career, Rachel noticed that her hour was up.

Silver noticed too. "Same time tomorrow?"

At 201 Dell that night, Rachel wandering like a horny ghost through the dark house, the phone rang.

Her mother. "No sign of What's-his-name, I suppose."

"No."

"By the way, I just got a call from Elmer."

"From who?"

"At the Agency."

"The private investigator? Are you still paying that crook?"

"None of your business. It happens he's hunting your father on his own time."

"Why?"

"Dedication."

"To what? Mother, it was thirty years ago. Anyway, *we* left *him*. Why can't you just drop it?"

"Because on the night breeze I can smell the prick's money."

"You don't know."

"Not yet."

"Mother, you're just getting your hopes up again."

"Hope energizes. Even at my age. But don't think I'm still interested. This is strictly monetary. Anyway, that's my news. Take it or leave it. *Adios*."

Rachel drove back to the Dream Centre that night worried about her mother. To be stalled for thirty years. "Are we stalled too, Cat?" She asked quietly of Puff while extending a long-handled bowl of warm milk towards her little fiberglass island in the big tank; Silver had gone for dinner at his own mother's. Puff's reply was a savage paw swipe that bounced the bowl off the wall and split it on the concrete floor.

"Goddam you, Cat!"

"What the fuck is this?" It was Babs, with Frankie. Not expected back for at least an hour.

Puff continued to spar a few seconds then crashed. When her face hit the water it jerked up. She sparred a few seconds more, dozed off, and did it again.

Rachel tried to explain. Found herself talking to a pair of dream-deprived paranoids convinced that there had been conferred here some special privilege.

"How could you!" cried Babs, startling Puff, who deked and nearly fell off her platform.

"I'm trying to help her—"

Babs had turned to Frankie. "She's probably not even dream-deprived."

"The hell I'm not."

"Then how could you stand by and let him—?"

"Babs, he's going to do it anyway—"

"That is the most—"

"OK! Everybody out!" It was Alex Silver, herding them. "Come on, come on! Cat's in a fragile state as it is. One person in here at a time. This ain't no zoo—" When he had the door closed behind them all, Silver said, "Babs, Frankie. Listen to me. Rachel found out by accident. So I asked her to help. This is not favouritism. If you find the whole thing too upsetting, quit now. But I want to say.

Neither is this idle curiosity, I have the necessary papers, she'll be a better cat for it, just as all of you will be—" Here Silver began to move around the floor like a hockey coach, shouting. "I'm telling you all to stay on and stick with it and do what you can to make Puff's life a little easier. She's got less than a week to go, and it would be such a damn, crying shame if she didn't get to set the world record for mammalian dream deprivation and become unimaginablyfamous. We're all in this together. That at least has been my understanding. But if any of you—"

Silver went on haranguing in this vein for several minutes, bellowing down objections, giving everybody headaches. Vaguely Rachel remembered something about the dream-deprived being easily conditioned by brow-beating. "I'm going to bed," she muttered.

"I told you before!" Silver screamed. "It won't help!"

"Alex, I'm staying on," Rachel said in a low voice. "I told *you* that before."

"Got it. Frankie? What about you?"

Frankie had been sitting on the edge of her bed having a smoke while Silver yelled. Now she looked at him sidewise and without moving her lips said, "I got no illusions."

"Exactly," Silver cried, as if he knew perfectly what this meant. "And you, Babs?"

Babs was leaning against the Hewlett Packard with her arms folded. "I'll see," she said. "But Dr. Silver, you should know. I think you're a real little bully."

"What the hell's that supposed to mean?" Silver shrieked.

"It means I'll see," said Babs.

"Fine." Silver threw up his hands and strode back to Puff. The door slammed behind him.

All that night Rachel's brain struggled to have a certain dream only to be beeped awake by the Hewlett Packard. It was an old dream from ten, twenty, maybe thirty years ago. By morning Rachel was either so frustrated or so steeped in the thing she woke up weeping. Immediately Alex Silver was crouched at her ear, earnest and whispering.

"I panicked, Rachel. I saw my whole career on the line. I was fighting for my life—"

"It's not you, Alex," Rachel mumbled, wiping her eyes with a corner of the sheet.

"Oh." He slipped a non-REM dream report clipboard into her hand. "Anyways, I apologize. Carry on."

But the dream was gone. It came back at a Millpond Indemnity claims meeting that morning but passed right on by. Later that morning Mr. Felpson, Rachel's supervisor, poked his head in her door to wonder if by any chance she had picked up a touch of that flu that was going around? She'd seemed a little feverish at the meeting this morning. Rachel, who had already noticed Marg from Road Accidents looking at her queerly, and earlier, in the Millpond Indemnity washroom, had had to wash out electrode glue she'd forgotten to at the Dream Centre, allowed as to how this might be the case. She did not quite feel right today, somehow. Would he mind too much if she went home early?

Oh no no no. Go right ahead. He only hoped to see her old self back bright and early Monday morning.

"How old," Rachel murmured.

"What was that?"

"A cold. Maybe it's a cold."

So Rachel, who was feeling pretty crazy, sort of on overload, went home.

But first in a delicatessen on the Village Green concourse near Timbers 'n Spokes, she bought an egg salad submarine, a jar of pickled herring, a quarter raspberry cheesecake, a litre of homogenized milk, and walked to her car stuffing her face and spilling egg salad and herring juice down the front of her blouse. What the hell, what's Martinizing for?

And then on the drive home she got lost and found herself passing a little plaza she had never seen before. What caught her eye was a shop called Joaxalot. She went in. Novelties. Rubber faces, party stuff, a magic section. The usual. Somewhat depressing. Tempted to punch out the beady-eyed, toupeed proprietor who watched her browse with a singularly unattractive blend of suspicion and concupiscence, she instead bought a small black water gun and dropped it into her purse.

A half hour later, back at 201 Dell, fingers still sticky with raspberry cheesecake, she didn't care, was into her pants with both hands, staggering. By the time a third orgasmic convulsion had finished arching her body a foot off the floor, she was sprawled on the living room shag, skirt bunched at her waist, tights at her knees, one high heel missing, breasts out the top of her bra, heart pounding, thinking, "Whew, this is real animal stuff." Naked then, drapes pulled, she got out the mops, the Spic 'n Span, and the vacuum cleaner. In forty minutes, mind going like a broken record— "Just lost my grip and can't do a thing with it"— she cleaned the entire house. She then had a shower, filled the water gun, jumped into sweats, and with the gun concealed in her hand, jogged over to Village Market Square for her evening session with Alex Silver, who wanted to hear about the repercussions for Leon of her lunch with Nick Sirocco. Fingering her water gun, Rachel told him the whole sad story.

The weekend after her lunch with Sirocco Rachel spent mostly wondering what Leon was up to, as he alternated between holing up in his basement den with a pot of coffee and two three-litre bottles of Pepsi on ice in a cooler "brainstorming" for his meeting with Sirocco on Monday and attending to Wilkes with born-again solicitude. He seemed to be renting him another bus and driver.

"Leon, no!"

"Rachel, I know exactly what I'm doing here. Believe me."

What was going on? Leon was the last person to be capable of two passions at once.

Sunday Cam Wilkes called to say that he could not express how much he appreciated everything Leon was doing for him, but he wondered if Rachel knew why.

"Wouldn't Leon just like to see you out of your basement, Cam?"

"No. It's more than that. It's as if— I know this sounds extreme— it's as if he wants me to sell my bus yard!"

Oops—

"Rachel? Hello? Hello? Operator?"

"Maybe he does, Cam—" Rachel said quietly, not feeling very well.

"Did you— tell him about my bus yard?"

"No, honest. I never said a word."

At that moment Leon appeared from the basement. "About what?" he mouthed on his way to the kitchen.

Rachel dropped her voice. "But I think I know what this is all—"

"Yes—?"

"Say it!" called Leon from inside the fridge.

"Anyway, I should go—"

Leon came into the living room with a drumstick. "Who is it?"

"Cam—"

"Yes, Rachel?" said Wilkes.

"Oh really?" said Leon, grabbing the phone from Rachel's hand. "Hi, Cam. How's it going? Listen. I just got a call from Hong Kong. I've got these three billionaire Chinese brothers on the hook who— Uh, Rachel. This is business. Could you please—"

"No. I was talking to him first."

"You were ready to hang up! Cam? Hold on one sec? I have to go upstairs. I'm getting absolutely no cooperation here—" Leon handed Rachel the phone. "What's up with you. When I lift it, *hang up*, OK?" As Leon took the stairs two at a time, Rachel told Wilkes she would explain later.

"Rachel!" called Leon, now on the line. "Time to hang up now!"

Rachel waited around for Leon to finish talking to Wilkes. When she heard him go downstairs she knocked on his door. A chair squeaked and a rapid burst of typing hit the Selectric. "Come in!"

"Leon, are you trying to get Cam to sell his bus yard?"

"I *am* lining up a buyer for him, yes. Why?"

"Would this buyer be Nick Sirocco?"

"It might be."

"But, Leon. This means you're cooperating with a Mafia front to take away something precious from a man who trusts you."

"A classically loaded statement, Rachel. How about this: Arranging a very generous sale price for a piece of junk property that belongs to a friend who not only doesn't need it but will benefit both financially and psychologically from being free and clear of the damn thing for good."

"Leon, you're not God. You can't start making Cam's decisions for him."

"I fed him, didn't I?"

"Leon, that's not funny. It's an evil, imperialistic thing to say."

"You want evil imperialism? A lone nobody with four acres, Rachel, sure isn't going to stop a project like Arcadia Centre."

"What does that mean?"

"I'm just trying to get myself in a position to steer him through this at maximum advantage to himself. That's all. That's all it means."

"And what if he won't sell?"

"Don't worry, Rachel. We don't have to think about that, and the reason we don't have to think about that is, Leon Boseman is here. Sirocco needs me. The big boys like to avoid bloodshed when they possibly can. It's only good business."

Slumped there in profile because he was too ashamed to look straight at her, Leon seemed thinner on top, tuftier inside the ears. He did not look like a mover and shaker taking a moment to defend the ethics of a particular move and shake. He looked like just another tired, aging, implicated little man.

"The further aspect of all this that you don't seem to realize, Rachel, is that at this point I am far more important in this deal than Sirocco. In the scheme of things I suspect our Nick is small fry. There are a lot bigger boys than Sirocco running Mortprop Investments, you can count on it. And I wouldn't be surprised if before too long somebody with my savvy in this deal wasn't dealing directly with Mr. Big. This is only the beginning. A foot in the door."

Rachel went back upstairs and called Cam Wilkes, to whom she explained the situation, adding that she had good reason to believe that Leon's connections with Mortprop Investments would soon be severed. Wilkes listened in silence. When she had finished, he said, "Thanks, Rachel. This is an awful lot to take in at one time. I hope you'll understand if I don't feel much like talking right now. But I have to say I'm terribly disappointed in Leon."

"Me too, Cam. Me too."

After work the next day Rachel nosed the Civic up to the garage door alongside the Subaru. Climbing out, she thought she had left her lights on, but it was the Subaru's. Strange. She switched them off. Leon could be pretty distracted sometimes.

The front door was standing open. He was just leaving—? "Leon!" By the front closet was a pile of random folds: Leon's coat. At first, in the gloom, she thought he was in it, shrunken. In the kitchen his good shoes had been kicked off and just left there, one of them in a corner, vertical. On the counter his Gucci tie was curled around a butter wrapper. "Leon!"

She found him downstairs in his little den beside the garage, reclined in his old leather La-Z-Boy. In a saucer on his chest was what remained of a pound of butter. She set the butter on the floor, out of reach. He did not object; the spoon she extricated from loose fingers, saying kindly, "You never wanted to sell real estate anyway." Kneeling, she laid a hand on his arm.

"Did too."

"You saw Sirocco today?"

"Secretary."

"His secretary? What did she say?"

"Help myself."

"Yourself—?"

"Coke."

"Ah."

"Machine in reception area. No coins required. Coke Classic, Diet, Tahiti Treat, iced tea." Pause. "Hate Coke."

"I know."

"Chose iced tea."

"The Think Drink."

"Check. Read magazines. *People, Newsweek, Housing Today, American Builder.* Even *Maclean's.*"

"A lot of magazines."

"Two hours of magazines."

"And you had an appointment?"

Leon's eyes closed, meaning *Yes.* "Finally see Moe."

"Moe?"

"Joke on me. Thought she said Moe Mortprop."

"Leon, *Mortprop*'s not somebody's name—?"

Leon raised a staying hand. "Thought: Second meeting and already to see Mr. Big. Mahogany panelling, heavy broadloom. Moe big guy. Neck thicker than head. Thought: Can't judge cover. First thing Moe said: Got five minutes. Thought: Tight schedule necessary to go-getter like Moe. Outlined efforts. Unfolded plans. Bared mind. Guaranteed willing seller in three weeks. Moe taking notes. Head of Moe lolled for look at watch."

"Had to go."

"Got it. Stood up. Stood up too, hand extended. Moe did not shake. Saw then, upside down, on pad, Moe's 'notes'. Doodle. Stick woman. On knees. Balloon bazooms. Cock in mouth. Big cock."

"I guess Moe was thinking about something else." When Leon did not reply, Rachel added, "Moe doesn't sound like a very nice person."

"Wasn't supposed to be nice person. Supposed to be Mr. Big."

"Did he say anything?"

"Quote: 'Don't call us, huh, Bozleman? We'll call you'."

"Oh, poor Leon!" Rachel cried.

"Poor Bozleman." Leon's right hand came up holding the remote TV tuner. The TV crackled and came on.

Rachel climbed the two flights of stairs to the bedroom, where she sat on the bed. After awhile she went over onto her side and continued like that for some time, staring into the darkness of an open closet.

It was the phone on the bedtable that winched her from many fathoms of sleep. "H'lo—"

"Rachel? I'm calling from a pay phone across the street from my house."

"Cam? Are you all right?"

"I'm fine. I'm in costume. It's my birthday."

"That's wonderful! Happy birthday!" Here Rachel noticed that she was fully dressed. "How nice of you to call and tell me. What time is it?"

"Five a.m."

"*Shit*, Cam! What's up?"

"Leon traced the original driver of the old Downtown 16 from Madison. His name's Big Phil, and he's coming out of retirement to drive me and the Girl on My Bus around the Millpond all day, not in our old bus, which of course is at my place, dismantled, but in one from the same company that Leon rented from before."

"Uh-huh—" Rachel had just noticed that the bed was still made on Leon's side and he was not in it.

"Big Phil's picking her up first, at Flume Fields. They're due by here at 6:07. Sleep's out of the question, so I'm waiting here. Anyway, the reason I called. Why don't you ride around with us for a bit before you go to work this morning— Get acquainted before tonight—"

"Tonight—?"

"Give her a chance to relax with you. Smooth out her day. It's a total marathon date for us. Going to the taping of the Alex Silver show tonight with you and Leon is definitely the highlight, but by then we'll be into the thirteenth hour of our date. By the way, it was Leon getting us the *Share That Dream* tickets that really started me wondering what he was up to."

Leon! Pretzled with a coronary in the light of a test pattern!

Doctor, he ate a pound of butter, and the next thing I knew—
"Listen, Cam. Leon hasn't said anything about this to me. And
right now I have to go and look for him. He hasn't come to bed—"

"OK, we'll be waiting! Tell you more then!"

"No, don't do—" But Wilkes had hung up.

Rachel went down to the den, which was dark, stepped in the
saucer, the last of the butter squelching between her toes. No Leon.
She checked the driveway. No Subaru. She went back to the den.
Felt the TV. Cold.

Rachel got dressed and called a cab to take her to Wilkes' bus
stop. The cabby, a squat, somnolent man with a partially-eaten
bologna-in-a-kaiser on the dash, had never heard of Hillock Rise,
and the print on his greasy Millpond street guide was so smudged,
the morning so early, the light from his dashboard so fitful, that
they ended up driving around for twenty minutes completely lost.
And then Rachel spotted one of the phosphorescent ribbons that
Leon had once tied on selected lamp posts to mark the way. With
difficulty they followed the few that kids had not torn down until,
up ahead, there blossomed the rear window of an idling bus.
"That's our baby," the cabby said.

Under the chill grey sky of pre-dawn, that rear window ema-
nated a homey warmth. As they pulled up behind, Rachel could see
Cam Wilkes in the rear seat of the bus with an arm around what
appeared to be, oh dear, a young girl. Rachel tumbled some balled
fives into the cabby's lap and scrambled out.

An expulsion of air, the rubber slap of bus doors, and she was
boarding the bus. The driver kept his face averted. She could not
tell if he was The Mucal Snuffler. "I don't know you, do I?" Rachel
said, glancing anxiously towards the rear seat.

His knuckles tightened on the wheel. "Never seen you before
in my life."

"The Downtown 16 from Madison?"

He gave a start, eyes all over the place. The doors whapped shut
behind her, and the bus started to move. Rachel nearly fell.

"It could have been the 19—" she admitted, grabbing a pole.

He jabbed a finger at the sign over the windshield: *Do Not
Attempt to Engage Driver in Conversation While Bus in Motion.*

"Rachel!" Cam Wilkes, in raincoat and dark glasses, was coming up the aisle. He was chewing gum and carrying a cane. When
he reached Rachel he tipped forward, confidential. "Rachel, she's

not lively like you and Leon. But she's coming out of it, a bit more every day. This date is a major step for her. I know you'll be understanding."

"Cam, she is— of age?"

"Past it, I'm afraid—"

And Wilkes turned and led Rachel down the aisle to meet the Girl on His Bus.

"Rachel," Cam Wilkes said proudly, "I'd like you to meet my very good friend *Jane!*"

Jane was a timid, frail woman with uplifted blue myopic eyes set wide in a small head covered with soft, thinning yellow hair, her narrow hands folded demurely in the lap of a pretty pink pinafore, shiny red shoes positioned side by side, soles flat.

Wilkes sat Rachel next to Jane, positioning himself sideways on the seat in front, twisted uncomfortably to talk. "OK Rachel," he cried. "Guess who Jane's in costume as!"

"As Jane, of Dick and Jane," said Rachel, with goosebumps.

"*Right!*" Wilkes cried. "And do you know why?"

"I've heard about you, from Cam," Jane told Rachel, her smile tremulous and vague and not exactly warm.

Wilkes reached back and placed a hand on Jane's. "Because not only is Jane the Girl on My Bus, Rachel. She is also *the* Jane of Dick and Jane! I've been in love with her from the moment I opened my first reader. You can imagine my astonishment when I realized the two were one and the same. No wonder I fell so hard!"

"I don't understand—" A TV series?

"Then I'll explain it to you," Jane said in a voice straight from the fridge. "Dick and Jane are the creation of a University of Chicago Professor of Education named Gray. William S. Gray. Gray believed in measurement, testability, facts. Graduated word repetition. One new word per page, each used a minimum of fifteen times, and so on. Numbers. The man was a goddam behaviourist. We happened to live next door. Chicago suburb. Late thirties. And that's all there is to Dick and Jane."

"And now," Rachel said stupidly, "you live here—"

"If by 'here' you mean over on Smutter Circle with my brother Dick, when, that is, I'm not medicated to the gills at Flume Fields, the answer is yes. I live here. So does Sally—"

"Why, I met Sally!" Rachel cried. "And that means—I met Dick too! He wears a fedora! This is incredible!"

"Hardly," muttered Jane. "And I suppose they told you what a nuisance I've been."

"Not nuisance. Sally's so worried—"

Jane nodded, grim. "And now you're going to try to talk me out of it."

"Absolutely!"

"Well, screw off."

"Cam!" cried Rachel, ignoring this. "You can't let them give Jane shock treatments!"

"We're stopping in for lunch at Smutter Circle today, Rachel. I'll be having a word with Dick. Jane says he's a mule, but that makes two of us."

Here Wilkes was interrupted by Big Phil, who shouted into his mirror, "OK, what's the big tête-à-tête back there? If my driving isn't good enough, why don't you just say so! I can take abuse!"

"Same old Big 'Paranoid' Phil!" Wilkes called amicably, and added, "Hey Big Phil! Grind us a pound!"

"It's the whispering!" Big Phil complained. "It's driving me crazy!"

"The reason Big Phil's on call with the bus company even though he's retired," Wilkes revealed in a low voice, "is he's saving up to move to the open prairies. No place out there for people to hide while they're talking behind his back— He thinks about the prairies all the time." To Big Phil, Wilkes called, "Hey Big Phil! You already are crazy! How about a franchise? PAGO WEST! Of course as a simple paranoid you yourself don't qualify for membership. On the other hand, you might contribute perspective!"

"Some day, Wilkes, you'll tell me what you're talking about and then we'll have a nice long chat!"

"Hey, Rachel," Wilkes said. "Aren't you going to ask me who I'm in costume as?"

Rachel had forgotten to notice that Wilkes was in costume. "As yourself?"

"Close. As a PAGO person! See? Sunglasses— The raincoat because I prefer rainy weather. Gum because chewing makes me feel more secure. And see? A cane— and I've even brought along a collapsible shopping cart, for that extra bit of psychological support. Get it, Rachel? I'm disguised as what I no longer am!"

"But why, again, are you both—"

"Leon really didn't tell you? We're all going to the Alex Silver Show tonight, *Share That Dream*. You dress up as something from a recent dream. Leon should have said something. You'll be needing to get your costume together."

"Cam, Leon didn't come to bed last night." She told him about Leon's rejection by Mortprop Investments and how devastated he had been.

"That explains why he forgot to tell you about tonight, Rachel," Wilkes replied. "He's disappointed, understandably. And yet perhaps it's all for the best."

"But what about you, Cam—?"

"Don't worry about me. I've dealt with those goons before. I'm used to keeping my eyes open."

Soon they were approaching Village Green, and it was time for Rachel to disembark. She said goodbye to Wilkes, Jane, and Big Phil. Wished them all a happy day on the bus. Wilkes she told to be tough with Dick.

As soon as Rachel got to work she called home. No answer. Of course he could have come in and fallen asleep. At 9:20, pretending to be a customer, she phoned Bi-Me Realty. Sorry, Mr. Boseman had not been in yet this morning. Repeatedly that day Rachel called home and Bi-Me. Nothing. She could of course have called Gretchen but did not want to find out that badly.

Back at 201 Dell after five, no sign anywhere of Leon, who if he had been home even just to pee would have left a trail.

Rachel was not exactly sure of the quickest route to Village TV. It was a clear, cold night, the kind that up on Village Drive North would have stars fastened like penlights to the misted black crepe doming the fields. Here in the Millpond the magic was handled by streetlights: crisping lines and shadows, Stretch-'n-Sealing surfaces, turning live grass to Astroturf, making shiny monoliths out of the cars on their licorice pallets of driveway.

Soon she had no idea where she was. On her left was a deserted playground like a detention compound. Chainlinks of refusal: No Bicycles. No Dogs. No Active Games. No Loitering. No Entry After 11 PM. In the sky above, a glow. At first she thought night tennis courts a few streets over, and then she realized it must be Hopperboy High Street, a shopping strip to the southeast. Reasonable working hypothesis, anyway. Except, next she passed Millpond Collegiate,

rising like a fortress across unfeatured darkness, yellow walls
floodlit against vandals. And then a building she had always
imagined being in some totally different part of the Millpond , the
A-frame Presbyterian church, with its floodlit cedar shakes, red
and amber glass-brick fronting, obligatory House of God façade:
impressionistic welding. Sunday's sermon, "The Church in a Rapidly Changing World (Part 14): Facing Some Implications of the
Millenium" by Dan Mauserhamlin (D.D.). After that, homes again,
architecturally uniform, varied occasionally by landscaping differ-
ences, incorrect black stable boys holding carriage lamps, etc.
Pickups now and again instead of cars in the driveways.

It wasn't until she had twice driven past the entrance to Village

Frankly lost, Rachel gave up her eyes to the passing windows.
For the first time she realized that the *picture* in *picture window* is
what the passer-by gets to see, not the resident. At night the thing
is one-way, especially when illuminated by proud floodlights.
Spoilsports had their drapes drawn, but most residents offered the
minimum of a teasing glimpse, and many wondrous sights did
Rachel see: sad gold chandeliers with hundreds of glass tear-drops,
grand pianos, a fat man in jockey shorts asleep in a beanbag chair,
brocaded sofas, framed weed arrangements, frazzled Leon
lookalikes doing paperwork at dining room tables. Through one
window she saw what appeared to be a white rabbit staked out on
an altar before a velvet painting of Elvis. These sights suggested
even greater treasures in the rooms beyond. Routine Millpond
homes revealed themselves to Rachel that night as honeycombs of
promise, of astonishing display. Tombs of the Pharoahs. Not much
from the outside, but inside . . . look out!

It wasn't until she had twice driven past the entrance to Village
Market Square that she recognized it and from there figured out
how to get to the Light Industrial Park, home of Village TV, whose
studios, situated near the mouth of Endosperm Circle, a loop of
mostly high-tech small businesses, had the appearance of a Frank
Lloyd Wright mink ranch. On taping nights for shows as popular
as *Share That Dream*, the cars overflowed the parking lot to both
sides of the street all the way around Endosperm Circle. Rachel was
forced to leave the Civic beyond the circle and hike the rest of the
way.

Inside the front door no one was around, just lots of fluorescence, desks, and partitions with posters of kittens tumbling out of
seaboots or saggy-eyed beagles captioned, "There oughta be a law

against Mondays." Finally, somewhere deep in a warren of low-ceilinged corridors, she came to a door with a green light over it.

As Rachel took that door the light flashed red, and she found herself in total darkness. She was pushed into a seat. She thought of a theatre where the ushers are too violent to be issued flashlights. And then the lights went up.

Amidst furious clapping, Rachel was blinded. Those kleigs. When she could see, a manic in safari jacket and headphones was eliciting applause from an excited audience in costume. Clapping, they raised eyes, masks, vizards to a pair of TV monitors located at the sides of the stage. Made a travelling flurry of eagerness and hope.

As Rachel scanned the audience for Leon, a disembodied voice announced that it was time to *Share That Dream!* with Your Host, Dr. Alex Silver! Theme music then, derivative game-show fanfare, and onto the stage bounded Silver in those scarlet glasses and a luminous purple suit. Enthusiastic applause.

"Hi everybody! Welcome to *Share That Dream!* The show that helps you, get in touch, with your unconscious mind! I'm Dr. Alex Silver, and I'm here to, find out, what makes *you*, tick!"

Here Silver left the stage and came running up an aisle. It was one of those moments Rachel avoided all theatre to be spared. She started from her seat, but the red light was on, and an usher stood guard with folded arms. And then she realized that between the last dozen rows of the audience and the first dozen was a low barrier. The wild, elaborate dream costumes were to be found in the front rows only; back here people were interested in the monitors all right but were ordinarily dressed, not so keen to share their dreams.

Silver was holding a microphone at the deep red lips of a guy in an evening gown who was quietly reporting his name and address.

"OK Derek Harmsby of Grappling Claw Crescent, Village-on-the-Millpond, did your dream involve *flying in the air*, because if it did *not*, I will give you twenty dollars—" Silver snapping a crisp twenty-dollar bill high in the air above his head—"and if it *did*, you may choose between this twenty dollar bill and The Mystery Box!"

Here Rachel noticed curtains parting on a pink box the size of a dishwasher, a big red question mark on the front.

Derek Harmsby studied his eyebrows. "Yes it did," he said,

and everybody cheered.

"Great, Derek! Now, the choice is yours: keep the twenty or take a chance on The Mystery Box. What will it be?"

Here repetitive suspense music while the audience cried, "Take The Box! Take The Box!"

But Derek's glances at The Box were anxious. "I'll keep the twenty," he said finally with a soft exhalation.

From the audience uncompromising groans of disappointment that turned to laughter when Silver did some comic business about tucking the twenty into Derek's bodice. Then Silver's face filled the monitors. "OK, Derek Harmsby of Grappling Claw Crescent, Village-on-the-Millpond. Let's see, what you missed, by not choosing, The Box!"

Here Silver's mother— a popular feature of the show apparently: whistles and cheers — came onstage looking somewhat boxlike herself in a sequined sack dress and matching silver heels to push aside the panel.

"For your mother, wife, or best girl, Derek," cried Silver, "you'd have won a complete beauty set of Elizabeth Arden Night Magic skin conditioner and perfume, a value of eighty-five dollars!"

Oohs and aahs from the audience, a few *We told yous*, Derek melting in genuine chagrin.

And then Silver was off again, to *Share That Dream* with a woman dressed in bonnet, little sun dress, and booties, who because she had had a dream about being *helpless and loved* won seventy-five dollars; a man dressed as a rat, who kept ten dollars because his dream involved no *dark passages* but if it had would have won a three-hundred-dollar garbage compactor; and a woman with a giant papier mâché change purse on her lap who, to moans of envy, won one of those Casiotone pianos with a memory, for a dream about leaving an inanimate object, excluding a hat, at the home of a friend of the opposite sex. Suddenly then, Silver was talking to a fellow in raincoat and dark glasses named Cam Wilkes, of Hillock Rise, Village-on-the-Millpond. When Wilkes said his name the audience broke into scattered applause. "Family and friends here, Mr. Wilkes?" asked Silver.

"No, Alex," Wilkes replied, twisting in his seat to see who they were. "This'll be PAGO folk." He half stood, Jane pulling at his sleeve, and cried, "*Oh, oh, oh!*" to further applause. "We're getting out more," he told Silver.

While this was taking place, Rachel craned to see who was sitting on either side of Wilkes and Jane. Next to Jane was a woman wearing the whiskers of a cat. Next to Wilkes was a Victorian-looking man in a trilby, with a full beard. Leon? As Harry? Rachel strained to see the monitor.

"OK, Mr. Wilkes. Does your dream involve *a matter of life or death*? Because if it does *not*, I will give you one hundred dollars, but if it *does*, you may choose between this one hundred dollar bill and going on to another question about your dream that *could* be worth much, much more to you than one hundred dollars!"

Silence in the studio.

"Yes, Alex. It does," Wilkes said quietly.

Cheering.

"OK, Cam Wilkes of Hillock Rise, Village-on-the-Millpond. Here is your second question. Did this matter of life and death take place outside, of the home? I will repeat the question." He did. "If your answer is *no*, you will win five, hundred dollars. If your answer is *yes*, you will win a choice between five, hundred dollars and the Mystery Prize behind Curtain Number 3!"

"Yes, Alex," Wilkes said without hesitation. "It took place outside of the home. My home."

Cheering.

"OK, Mr. Cam Wilkes of Hillock Rise, Village-on-the-Mill-pond, what will it be. This mint-condition five-hundred-dollar bill I hold in my hand or the Mystery Prize behind Curtain 3?"

Reiterative music. *The prize! The prize! Take the prize!*

"I'll take the Mystery Prize," Wilkes said, and the monitor showed a close-up of his hand squeezing Jane's.

Bursting through Mystery Curtain 3 came Silver's mother driving a pedal car in the shape of a Greyhound bus. Wilkes had just won a ninety-day bus tour of North America for two! The audience went crazy. They whistled and clapped and stamped their feet.

But now there was very little time left in the show, and even before the excitement died, Silver was holding his microphone under the face of that bearded guy in the trilby, who was not Leon, had dreamed *about his father*, and refused two-hundred-and-fifty dollars in favour of the Mystery Prize, an electric carving knife. Disappointment and perfunctory applause escalating to real end-of-show thanks-for-the-fun hand pounding.

"OK, folks," cried Alex Silver above the din, having leapt back onto the stage, "That's all our time for tonight! Hope you've had as much fun as we did. Don't forget, everybody: What can't be remembered can't be left behind!

"I'm Dr. Alex Silver. If you think the unconscious is not a whole lot of fun, just tune in next week, right here on Village TV, and watch your very own friends and neighbours *Share, That, Dream!*"

The manic in the safari jacket moved in sideways from the left, eliciting applause. Some kept their eyes on him, some on the monitors. A groundswell of waving hands pursued the panning camera.

And then the kleigs had been doused and the studio was emptying out. Cam Wilkes had spotted Rachel and waved. Still scanning for Leon, Rachel waved back. Wilkes came over, holding tight to Jane's hand.

"Congratulations, Cam," Rachel said.

"Thanks, Rachel. What a wonderful, appropriate prize! I can't believe it! I just can't believe it!"

"Cam, was Leon here tonight?"

"No Rachel! We thought he must be with you! Did you try his office?"

As they left the studios of Village TV, Cam said, "Listen, Rachel. I couldn't get anywhere with Dick this afternoon. They're going ahead."

"When?"

"End of the week—"

"But they *can't!*"

"I know—"

"Life is shock," Jane muttered.

Rachel and Wilkes looked at her together. "Too true, Sweetheart," Wilkes cried, "but has it done you any good?"

"I want more," Jane said quietly. "That's all. More. M-O-R-E. More. Got it?"

Rachel gave Wilkes and Jane a lift to The Buhrstone Restaurant in the Olde Mill, declining, when she saw true animosity flit like a bat across Jane's face as Cam issued the invitation, to join them for a late dinner.

Instead, Rachel drove home. She was glad she did, because who should be there but the missing Leon.

"He came back!?" cried Alex Silver, starting in surprise and nearly knocking over that giant antherium.

"Briefly. Only very briefly."

"So there's more." Silver seemed disappointed. "I was kind of hoping we could finish before the weekend."

"Well I'm sorry, Alex. Have I been going too slow?"

"What can we do. If there's more there's more. Tomorrow's Saturday. Let's say 11 a.m. Here."

Rachel sighed.

"Hey Rachel? I have to ask you. What did you really think of the show? Ever since we started taping I've had this fantasy that one day somebody'd walk in off Endosperm Circle who wasn't already a fan. What was your honest reaction?"

"My honest reaction?" Rachel fingered the water gun in her pocket. "Alex, please believe me when I say that in my opinion a show like *Share That Dream* suggests that there is no hope for Western science, culture, or intelligence. I experienced deep humiliation on behalf of everyone involved."

"Sure," cried Silver, "but didn't you love it?"

FIVE

No matter how fast Rachel moves, how much she takes in, she is still behind. Just that little bit late. To notice. Act. Has been scooped by an intimation neglected till this moment. Careless Rachel. Keeps failing to make it, can't ever seem to learn. Wants, accordingly, out. This is dream deprivation, this also— as it happens— is Harry. Habitual remorse in snapbrim, three-piece, thick shoes. He is the semblance of the main version, the official line, the better one. Like a promise, like regret, like the enemy himself, mostly he is built out of air. Oh yeah, and fear. Gee, it wasn't good enough, was it? What if I don't even rate a mention? *What if they can't see me?* Scared laughter. Ballooning shadow of the thing itself, with dustclouds. Harry is a light trick, a throwback. The friend of a friend. Somebody's cousin's brother-in-law, the one who turned the family business around in six months, who shot the kingsnake in his sleeping bag, who beat cancer. Harry is innocent of doubt, mercy, presence, fails to comprehend these virtues. The bastard has no mind, knows nothing appropriate to be on one—

Unless, unless . . . he does understand, everything, can know or love at will, anybody he puts his mind to, it's easy for him, and this is the real reason he keeps his mind empty at all times, receptive, not jerky and jam-packed like Rachel's—is a terrific guy, really, asks only to be looked at in the right way—

And what way would that be, this 'right way'? Wouldn't also be Harry's way, by any chance? I mean, is this *love and learn*?

Could be. What do you think?

Think? Are you kidding? Got eight hours straight REM I can have? Then I'll show you *think!*

At the Dream Centre a harrowing morning. Babs' fulsome concern for Rachel in her marital squalor, a concern already modulated by dream deprivation, had switched to outright bitchy needling after the Puff confrontation. And then, twice in one hour, she asked what Leon was up to these days, and Rachel offered to beat her senseless. After that, Rachel was outside of Babs' field of acknowledgement. A big relief on both sides. All Babs' energy was needed for a Grand Guignol struggle shaping up with Frankie for attention from the increasingly snappish and moody Alex Silver.

Babs (plaintive): "Dr. Silver, could you help me with my electrodes, pretty-please? They're not very well made, are they?"

Frankie (sneering): "They'd work just fine if she'd stop fiddling with them all the time."

Silver (with clenched fists): "Would you two back off for just five minutes? You're like a couple of two-year-olds—"

Babs (writhing coyly): "Yes, Bully-wully—"

Frankie (sniffing in Rachel's direction): "And I suppose *she's* not?"

Mind you, Rachel's version could have been a serious warpage of what was really going on at the Dream Centre. Her understanding, it seemed, had fallen into about the same condition as her powers of speech. Simple sentences were turning to rubble in her mouth. Probably just as well, because the merest gesture— Silver repeatedly pushing his big red glasses up his nose as he pored over his data, Babs' brazen cleavage-thrusting, Frankie's disaffected little sniff— were triggering massive rockslides of animosity in Rachel's head. Who knows what ugliness she might have screamed into the yatter of those three by the time it was sounding like shortwave chatter on some bad frequency over a cheap amplifier with a serious feedback problem?

As if this wasn't enough, Puff was going through a difficult run of dunkings. She would claw her way back onto the belt, doze, shiver, scramble, and it would happen again. Poor Puff. Then again, when Rachel tried to be right there for her, the cat made as if to rip the good intentions off Rachel's face. The thing was, Puff could take one look at this woman and know perfectly well that if she weren't empathizing so hard she'd be loathing every particle of Puff's feline being, even now could hardly restrain herself from

grabbing Puff by the chestskin and giving her a good rousing now
LOOK here cat LOWER those hackles DON'T spit at me when I am
talking to you TAKE your claws out of my arm, the inevitable next
step being Puff's whiskers pressed for the count by a leather glove
against the bottom of that tank. Rachel could only hope that before
this particular scenario unfolded, one of them would be allowed to
dream . . .

Unable to handle the atmosphere around the Dream Centre,
Rachel drove over to 201 Dell as soon as she had fed Puff— or
rather, left her cowering in a corner of her chickenwire cage too
busy fighting off predators to make it over to her dish. Silver said
he'd put her back in her tank when she had finished. "See you at
eleven, Rachel?"

"Eleven."

At 201 Dell the first thing Rachel noticed was that Leon had
been through to pick up clean socks and underwear. On her un-
slept-in bed he had left a one-word note— "Copycat"— that she
stared at more or less uncomprehending as she continued her drift
through the empty house, shedding shoes, skirt, blouse, bra (rubbing a damp indented line along the underside of each breast
where the fabric was stitched—pencil test? hell, she'd flunk the
flashlight test), stepping out of underpants, knowing that this
would banish the sadness, rage, lust, fear for all of twenty minutes— the lust, to be accurate, maybe twice that long . . . Still . . . an
old imperative it seemed, simple, its own time and structure, a
small respite, a private amusement, at a desperate time, to trans-
form the world from sullen environ of refractory mementoes to a
shopper's choice of voluptuary delight: mirrors turning to windows on an outrageous stranger, knobs to cocks, open flames to
scary crotch magnets, shower heads to vibrators; sofa, chairs, rugs
to possible hasty venues for the panting collapse.

Off to one side thinking . . . *This* time I refuse to rush, absolutely
refuse, will do it properly, my poor pleasure centres deprived long
enough, I am tired of telling myself, 'It's only me', like not caring
what you eat just because you're eating alone, talk about *self-
abuse*... And so it was, some time later, Rachel found herself in
Leon's little den, of all places, stretched out in his La-Z-Boy, of all
things, the chair tilted all the way back, vague fingers working a
breast, a leg over each chair arm, stroking slowly, ass already

slippery against the leather, lubricious sensation broadcasting from the radio of crotch . . . this whole delicious white-on-black lewd sprawl here vivid in her mind (legs wide, fingers working, hips finding their own eager rhythm, nipple risen hard now under the rub of palm, free breast tossing), until, until, until, until, until—

Ahh, ahh, aahh, *aaaahhhh*!

Ahh.

Ah.

And Rachel found herself back in Leon's messy dope-stale den, sunk indifferent in an ugly mechanical chair with a wet rear end, sticky fingers, shivering— it was *cold* down here next to the damn garage. And yet she did not on that account feel sad, or even sordid. The down-car plunge to tacky was just too rapid to cause her to feel anything other than like laughing out loud. Which she did.

The tears were freak.

But as she heaved the old chair vertical and got up to hunt through the chaos of Leon's desk for some Kleenex so she could mop up and get out of here, put on dropped clothes, switch on some lights, climb back on the rails, lay renewed claim to what little sanity remained, she did find herself wondering who exactly that sprawl had been for, anyway, what being of the air. This, she knew, had been no fantasy exhibitionism but fantasy voyeurism. So under whose authority could that image claim to be so absolute? Through whose eyes could watching it so arouse her? Familiar eyes or a stranger's? Hostile eyes or sympathetic? The eyes of the maker of that scene or the eyes of its consumer? A lover's or a beloved's? Exactly whose knowledge had she just strapped on, anyway?

Her own? Or Harry's?

And then Rachel was upstairs in the bedroom, modestly holding a towel around her with one hand while tugging at the handle of her underwear drawer, when that Harry dream from the night before last came back, all of it, at once, as memory.

She has just boarded an old train. Out the window snow passes horizontal, bone-white trees like silhouettes in negative; an occasional rainbow or shark, colours staggering, sometimes a word such as *Bleet* in Stone-henge lettering against distant hills, short crowds of gold kids eating white Popsicles, slowly waving. *Weird train*, she thinks. I'm all alone? Vague memory from the platform: her mother weaving forward through the cars, heading for the engine. Anxious, Rachel looks around. Worn plush. The aisle's rubber matting trodden through to lino. Looks around some more. In the back of the seat in front of her is a handle, a rivetted baroque metal dangling thing. A dresser drawer handle. A deep sad drawer, in shadow. In the dream, this drawer is meant to be a suitcase, for the trip, but who is it kidding. A wooden fragrance of musty containment. On tiptoes— shrinking now— little Rachel peers inside.

It is his drawer. Green-lensed sunglasses with tortoise-shell rims. Rare, monogrammed tie clips and cufflinks in a leather case. A dozen straight-nib pens held by a bright green string. Ace playing cards, in blue. (An intricate design, exact nature not available to memory.) Architect's drawings in a tight roll. A pocket watch, steam locomotive on the back. A stack of silver dollars. Silk handkerchiefs in auburns and wines . . .

Repository of wonder. A whole drawerful of the thing itself, of things to set the standard for all such things. Things half a child's belief.

The phone rang. "Your voice is funny," her mother said. "You're not on drugs, are you?"

"I was sleeping."

"Sleep and drugs are no way to handle this, Rachel. You've just got to comb your hair, fix your face, put on a new skirt, and get out there and wrestle another son of a bitch to the mat. Maybe this time you'll have learned from experience." Suddenly her mother was talking about money. "I happened to buy some stocks that did all right, not fifty thousand all right, more like thirty-five as a matter of fact, but what's fifteen thousand nowadays? Another nickel and dime investment. If I will the money to you, the government takes half. It's my life. I'm the one who put in the time. I'm only telling you because I never see you anymore since Whozits dragged you out to that subdivision in the middle of nowhere where nobody knows anybody, and the old traditions, like family and keeping in touch, are dead."

"Mother, why are you talking about large sums of money?"

"Elmer found four hundred and thirty-seven Stanley Jardines."

"Where?"

"Phonebooks of Europe and North America."

"And—?"

"He says he can do it for two per city plus expenses."

"Two *what*? How many cities?"

"Thousand. Twenty-three. And then there's the long distance. He says he can probably come in under fifty."

"Mother, you're not—"

"I'll tell myself I've gone to Reno with fifty, that's all. Maybe I lose it, maybe I hit the jackpot. Who wants to go to Reno? I'm happier sitting here with six months of reasonable hope."

"Mother, do you still keep dad's drawer in the big dresser?"

"I never look in there. I'm a hoarder, that's all. Get off my back."

"What's in it?"

"You know perfectly well what's in it."

"Mother, I haven't looked in that drawer for twenty-five years!"

"Well it happens I'm in bed, so it's right here. If the phone cord stretches that far I'll tell you what's in it." Her mother then, like a clerk recording the contents of the prisoner's pockets, went through the drawer. By the time Rachel was begging her to stop she had named quite a few of the paragon items from that dream plus many others more mundane that the dreamer, a selective child, had overlooked: A pencil stub with collapsed metal tip. Three rusty paperclips clinging to splayed scissors. An eraser dusky and moistureless with time. Scattered, linty Aspirin. Loose change, mostly nickels and pennies. Assorted keys. Petrified Wrigley's Spearmint. Petrified Smith Brothers Cough Drops. Petrified Sheik condoms. Cheque book. Matches in a box . . .

"Junk," her mother said. She was weeping. "What is it you want? Oh, here's his dog tag. I'll send it to you."

"It's OK—"

"Why are you making me do this?"

After talking to her mother, Rachel got dressed and drove over to Village Market Square for her final session with Alex Silver. She found him roaming his office like a caged panda.

"Rachel, those two are driving me crazy!" The sun was hitting him from behind, making a wild blond aureole for his face.

"As crazy as you're driving us?" Rachel replied, breathless. "What's in it for them, anyway?"

"For me to answer that question would be unprofessional."

"Oh, right, I—"

"Babs is working on her problems around authority figures, Frankie on how to come to terms with a world full of assholes."

"Should have guessed. Alex, I remembered that dream."

"What dream?" But Silver wasn't interested. "Rachel, we're after the one you haven't properly had yet!" He was staring at his watch. "Oh God there's no time. Already we've blown ten minutes. Why don't the bunch upstairs give us all a break and take the wings off the chariot once in a while—"

"Pardon?"

"So tell me what happened when Leon came back that once. That'll bring us up to speed. And then you go beyond. That's our plan. Stick to it. Don't mind me." Silver was strapping himself into a pair of brackets on his office ceiling. "Helps me concentrate," and he proceeded to hang upside down while Rachel concluded her story.

When Rachel got back home from *Share That Dream* Leon was sitting at the kitchen table with a coffee and a cigarette, the first cigarette she had ever seen him smoke. He was using the fingertips of his right hand to compress and lift ashes from the arborite surface of the table, then holding that hand out over the floor and brushing his thumb against the appropriate fingers.

"Leon, where have you been?"

Leon's other hand came up to remove a shred of tobacco from his tongue. This he examined. As he did so, something in Rachel's not-so-unconscious rolled over. Plain tips.

"Your mother called," Leon said. "I hung up."

"Where have you been?"

Leon was wearing his red plaid shirt, his quilted vest, and a peaked cap that said Prime Northern Turkey. "Rachel, sit down. I have something to say."

Rachel sat down across the table.

"We're practically middle-aged," Leon began. "We've got a nice little house here. Deck, garden, yard. We get along fairly well. Not great but fairly well. We've both played the field. We know the score. It's not as if we were born yesterday. More to the point, we understand that life doesn't last forever."

Leon stubbed out his cigarette and took the package from his shirt pocket.

Player's Plain. The cunt.

The phone rang.

He looked at her. "Aren't you going to answer the phone?"

"Tell me first what you're going to say."

"It can wait."

Rachel went to the phone. "Mother? I'll call you back. Soon. As soon as I can . . . You must have had the wrong number. I just got in. That's right . . . An hour . . . I'm fine . . . No. Mother? I'll call you . . . Out. Mother? I'm hanging up now . . . Yes. Soon. Goodbye."

"OK," said Rachel, resuming her seat. "Say it now."

Leon's fingers went for more ash.

Rachel got up to find him his favourite ashtray, set in a miniature Firestone tire.

"What I want to say is—"

The phone rang.

"The phone's ringing," Leon pointed out.

"Let it ring. I'm waiting."

"What if it's important."

"You answer it. I'm tired of always being the one."

"On second thought—"

They listened to it ring. "Leon? Maybe you should. It's been more than fifteen."

Leon stood up. "If they hang up when I lift the receiver I'm going to smash it." Slowly he left the kitchen. "Hello? Oh, uh, hi— Actually, no. That's right. OK. Right. Me too. Bye." Leon returned.

"Who was that?"

"Nobody," lowering himself into his seat. "Wrong number—"

"You say hi to wrong numbers?"

"Rachel, there's something I want to say."

"So I understand."

The phone rang.

"My turn?"

Leon nodded.

It was Cam Wilkes, drunk. He and Jane, still on their marathon date, had progressed from The Buhrstone to the Reservoir Bar, upstairs at the Olde Mill.

"Rachel? We found a way around our problem! We're getting married!"

"Cam, that's wonderful! What a good idea! Of course! Congratulations!"

"Rachel, this moment is the Mount Everest of my happiness!"

"Cam, I wish you the very best, and I'm so relieved Jane's going to be spared shock."

"She'll never miss it! I'll be all the shock she needs!"

"I'm sure you will, Cam. Thanks for telling me right away."

"Rachel, do you believe in developmental leaps for adults?"

"Why not?"

"*Yippee!*"

Rachel returned to the kitchen table.

"What'd Wilkes want?" Leon asked. "Calling to say he's sold his bus yard to Mortprop through another realtor?"

"No. He's getting married," and Rachel told Leon about Jane.

Before she had finished, a certain smugness had entered Leon's features, the kind a person might be inclined to punch off. Several moments of reflection had no appreciable effect on that look. "Isn't it funny," Leon said, "how there's always a woman right there to step in when a void opens up in a man's life. Boy, they sure do have a nose."

"What are you talking about?"

"All I'm saying is, he wanted you. You were taken. So for awhile there we had a classic case of desire without an object. As is the guy's wont under stress, he goes even deeper into retreat. And before you know it a woman has sniffed him out. Women are like some kind of primitive life form, able to scent musk at ten miles. Men bumble around in the clouds with this vague idea that women are aloof and unattainable, and yet it happens all the time. They know everything, they're all-cunning, they're a bunch of predatory animals. You know what I say to myself every time I go into a public washroom for a leak? *They can't get me in here!*"

"Is this what you sat me down to tell me?"

"Rachel, let's have a kid."

"A *what*?"

"Why are you acting surprised? The whole idea when we moved out here—"

"Leon, where were you last night?"

"There's so much bullshit in the world, Rachel. The only justification for leaving the house is a family in it. The best reasons are the ones made out of flesh. Memories, ideas, goals, role models are fragile things, insubstantial as dreams. But a kid is something real. And it's alive. Growing, every day. I know this sounds corny, but a kid is a stake in the future, a future that otherwise is fast-diminishing for both of us. Anyway, isn't this what women are all about, when you get right down to facts? You need some facts in your life, Rachel. You can't go on at Millpond Indemnity, betting people they'll live and them betting you they'll die. It's not a healthy dynamic. And think of your body. It's only got so many years left. I mean, the biological clock is really ticking away. Especially lately—"

"Leon, where were you last night?"

"Maybe I'm just getting old, but just now the thought of actually having my own son chokes me right up. Think of it, Rachel. My own son!" Tears stood in Leon's eyes.

"How about your own daughter?"

He shrugged. "Sure, daughter. I can live with daughter. We could always try again."

Rachel nodded, watching him. "I'd have trouble with guys with acne and a mickey of Kahlua in their windbreakers showing up at the door to take her to the drive-in," Leon continued. "But I could ask for references, or something. So what do you say?"

"I'm not saying anything until you tell me where you were last night."

"Driving around. Thinking. This past twenty-four hours has been a major watershed in my life, Rachel. Getting dumped by Mortprop was the best thing that could have happened to me. It's turned me back to my old dream of a family. If you want to know the truth, I'm sure that for me this is what Harry has been all about from the beginning. What Wilkes' need for you stirred in me was not memories of my father, or Alex Silver, but the anticipation of my own unborn son, who I'll be like a brother to. None of this hierarchical authority stuff. I'm talking about forging allegiances against the powers of darkness. A family is where you dig your primary trenches. Otherwise the Siroccos and the women get you. They eat you up, they lay waste to your soul."

Leon reflected awhile. "There's something else. You and I . . . we've been . . . drifting apart lately, Rachel. I don't know. I've been feeling so undirected, basically, so lost. Just clutching at straws. And when I get that way, I get scared and when I'm scared I know I can be a pretty distant kind of a guy. You don't have to tell me it's been hard on you. But a kid, Rachel! A kid would give me a reason for going out there again and smashing my head against the wall for twenty-five more years. A kid would yoke us. Bringing up a kid would be a project we'd work on as a team. You'd handle the daily stuff and I'd be there for those crucial moments of inspiration. And it would be so *easy* for me! That's what I'm saying! I'd love it! My kid and I would inspire each other! We'd move mountains! So what do you say, Rachel? Why don't we go upstairs and start right now on our little dynasty? Rip off our clothes and do what we came to the Millpond to do in the first place? A set-up like the Millpond only doesn't make any sense at all when you leave out kids. Come on. What do you say?"

"What do I say? *What do I say?*"

"Why are you getting excited?"

"Leon, where were you last night?"

Leon stood up. "OK. If that's all it is. Your veins are sticking out because there's a few hours in my life you don't happen to have track of— More convoluted maternalism. You're not God, Rachel! You're just a frustrated mother—"

Here Rachel threw that ashtray— it bounced off the top of Leon's head— then came around the table to strangle him. Leon's chair went over backwards, and they hit the floor, Rachel on top, beating him with her fists. This went on for some time, Leon's head inside a helmet of forearms. When fatigue rendered further pummeling ineffective, Rachel slumped against the cupboards to weep. Leon got up, tucked in his shirt, and staggered from the house.

Leon did not come home that night. At work next day panic gave a little fillip to Rachel's clerical style. Home again to a waiting 201 Dell Drive, she did not have the resolve to turn on a light, did not want to be too blatantly confronted by the fact of Leon's renewed absence in the form of her own undisturbed chaos from the morning— bed unmade, taps dripping, scummy coffee on the kitchen counter . . .

Maybe if she had something to eat. In the brightly lit fridge a rancid half of lemon, hard-skinned; cream cheese cracked and yellow; a zucchini broken out in white fur. On the other hand, why eat if you're not hungry?

Instead she called Alex Silver, got his answering machine.

"Alex here. I'm not in right now, but if you'd like to leave a message, please do so when you hear the beep. The tape runs three minutes, so there's no reason to freeze. Three minutes is a heck of a long time, even for an incredibly complex state of mind. Got a watch with a timer function? Great. See for yourself."

Pause.

"If you're thinking you can't do it, consider this: It's only a machine. It has no expectations and therefore no feelings to be hurt as a result of your failure to respond to its 'invitation' to leave a message. Hang up now, and there is no reason in the world to feel guilty. None whatsoever. Any *click* you leave behind will fall into precision sequence with dozens of others just like it, a domino in a falling row.

"If, however, you hang up at some point *into* the three minutes, then a little bit of guilt *may* be appropriate, because when I play back my machine I must listen to anywhere up to three minutes of pointless silence as you waste exactly as much of my time as you have wasted of your own.

"So. If you don't want to feel guilty— and remember, guilt is just another way we have of feeling bad about ourselves— *hang up now*. Otherwise, when you hear the beep, you will have exactly three minutes."

Beeeeep.

Rachel waited about a minute and hung up. She called back feeling guilty and for punishment had to listen to the message all over again.

Beeeeep.

"Um, Dr. Silver, this is Rachel Boseman. I really need to—"

"Hello, hello?"

"Dr. Silver?"

Alex Silver explained that when he worked late at the office he sometimes used his machine to screen his mother's calls. Rachel asked if she—

"Rachel," said Alex, still hanging from the ceiling. "You don't have to tell me the rest. It was a conversation with *me*! I remember! We had a few sessions, and I brought you into the study. In other words, we are now here. We've arrived! We're up to speed!"

Alex unbuckled and swung down. He seemed distraught. His face was red with all the blood in it. He stumbled over to Rachel, breathing hard. His glasses lay on the floor behind him. His eyes were naked, scary. "Know what I still want to know from all this?"

he asked.

"No, Alex," said Rachel, interested. "What?"

"What Leon ever really saw in Nick Sirocco. It can't just be success! Already a guy like Leon lives and breathes success! Oh sure, he'll have setbacks, but that just makes him more human!"

Rachel considered this. Then she said, "That's all you want to know?"

"I mean, with you I can understand it. Weak superego. Frustration, lust, and so on. But Leon? A man of Leon's stature?"

Already Rachel was on her feet, water gun drawn, shouting. "That does it, Alex! This whole thing stinks, and I know exactly why! It's all the alienated male bullshit in the air around here! Keep your goddam heroes and your goddam giant antherium! Look after your own goddam cat! And your own goddam conscience too, if you've got one! I'm going back to my own life—!"

While Rachel shouted, Silver went to his knees, his face contorted like a snakehandler's. "That's just it, Rachel! Unless you find Harry, your life is *nothing but* alienated male bullshit! All our lives—!"

Suddenly Rachel felt very weary. She lowered her gun. Sighed. "Now you're just being dramatic," she said quietly. "Alex, don't count on seeing me back here or at the Dream Centre ever again. I'm really pissed off. I mean I'm finished here. You'll just have to excuse me. Goodbye. I've got some shopping to do."

"*Harry*, Rachel!" Silver called as she passed out through his reception area. "What about Harry! Moving on won't mean a thing unless you find him! Remember Leon! Remember Cam Wilkes! Remember your mother! Remember me—eee!"

The electronic door of the Mortprop Mall SuperSpend knew Rachel was coming. Just as she leaned into it it swung wide open. She staggered forward and on through the turnstile into the hangar-sized chamber of bright, orange-walled fluorescence. The air smelled of apples, clove-scented floor cleaner, cold shopping carts fresh from the lot. One of these she wrestled off the end of a fifty-metre telescope of the damn things and headed out around the checkouts, not wanting to think about the minimum of five fully-loaded carts that waited at each, discouraged shoppers leafing through *People* magazines they had snuck from the racks by the registers. Not wanting to think, either, about being in the hands of that maniac Silver for the past two weeks. Slipping the water gun into the pocket of her sweats, Rachel headed for the produce section. One of her mother's main rules: *Never go food shopping when you're hungry.* Rachel was ravenous, the produce dazzling. It had been waxed and buffed. Rachel could see her face in apples, peppers, eggplants. There were mirrors and spotlights. She needed sunglasses. Better pick up some of this fabulous food! Her eye fell on perfect pears, even perfecter cukes. *Hmm.* So smooth, so thick . . . Tore off a piece of plastic bagging, couldn't get it open. Which end? *Why doesn't the fucker part?* A man stepped forward from nowhere to show her how to do it. (Solution: from the *corner* of the end indicated.) But he was not Harry.

Rachel worked both sides of the produce aisle at once, for maximum activity. Move fast. Keep your mind occupied, in this womanly pursuit. Decided paying three bucks for a block of tofu would force her to find some way, this time, to make the stuff edible. Bean sprouts looked a little yellow on the bottom. Later, guys. Broccoli fights cancer: inta da cart wit' yuh. They used to inject tomatoes with red dye. Still do? Parsnip, yuck, though didn't she once have it baked, and it was terrific? Or was that only in a dream? Why did every apple have a little gouge in it? They pick them with litter sticks? *Hmm.* Oranges poorly dyed this week, except these mini, green incredibly coarse, seedy, sour ones from Swaziland, not dyed at all, should be.

She moved on to pickles. The little devils were looking terrific, especially the sweet baby gherkins. Grabbed a litre. Next fell in love all over again with that plastic Ketchup bottle, life imitating art and doing it so well! Mayonnaise, mmm-*mm.* Could chugalug a whole jar right now.

Down by the cheese section a tired woman in calico and bonnet under a patio umbrella was staring out over a dozen toothpicks stuck into small cubes of mottled white and orange, some kind of 'cheese product'. On her face was a smile like an arrested tic. A sign at the front of the table said *New Product! Rennettes!* "Thanks," Rachel taking one as she passed.

"Cows' assholes," she thought the woman replied. Chewing more slowly, Rachel glanced back. The woman was inserting one into that smile. Must be all right then . . . couldn't have heard right . . .

In the meat section a kid in a white apron was transferring packaged cuts from a metal trolley to the display cooler. He had spotty skin, a thickness between the eyes. His hands were bloody. He was whistling *Harry's Theme*.

Rachel accosted him. "What's that tune?"

He listened. "*Moon River*?"

"*Moon River*!?"

"Sure. Listen." But he meant the Muzak.

"No, I mean, what were you whistling?"

"*Me*? Gee, Ma'm, I don't know. Just some tune."

"Do it again!"

He looked around, embarrassed, as if she had asked for a feel. "I don't even remember what it—"

"This is important! Try!"

But it was hopeless.

"What's your name?"

A possibly hostile question, however. His face assumed an expression of mingled alarm and defiance.

"I'm not going to report you!" Rachel cried, exasperated. "It's just, I've got a bad memory for—" She paused, observing his face. "Never mind. Yours I'll probably—"

"Rick," he said, blushing.

Rachel told Rick to be sure and come find her if he happened to remember the tune before she left the store. Heading down the soap aisle she thought, so it's come to aural hallucinations now, has it. A little test: What was that on the Muzak at this moment? Could she tell? *Harry's Theme*, or *Bei Mir Bist Du Schön*?

Rachel had made her way through the check-out jam at the top end of Soap and was just heading into Women's Needs, moving at quite a clip actually, looking back over her shoulder wondering if that guy with the big nose in the horned rims and bushy moustache reading a *National Enquirer* with the headline "Bride Gives Birth at Altar: Lost Ring Found Under Baby's Tongue" could be Harry, in disguise, when she broadsided another cart into interlocking pyramids of *Shake 'n Bake* and *Light Days*. "Excuse me. I—"

Rachel opened her eyes to see the man opening his. It was Dick, saying cheerfully, "All hands safe and accounted for," as he reached into his cart to remove boxes of *Shake 'n Bake* and *Light Days*. "How are things on your side?" He was exactly as Rachel remembered him from in front of the Café Smile, except that his arm was out of its cast. He wore an identical brown suit and hat.

"I'm really sorry—"

Here Rachel noticed four white knuckles against the arm of his suit jacket. He noticed them too, turned, and Rachel saw that it was Jane, standing amidst fallen boxes, hissing. *"It's her,"* as,

"Hi, Jane!" Rachel cried, too late. "How's Cam?"

"You ought to know the answer to that one, *Mrs. Boseman.*"

"Who'd you say, Jane?" asked Dick, peering into Rachel's face.

"Oh really?" said Rachel to Jane. "Why?"

Here the three of them had to squeeze over to let other carts by and to make room for the assistant shelf manager, a lean, haunted fellow, to get at his fallen display.

Receiving no reply from Jane, Rachel extended her hand to Dick. "Rachel Boseman. We met outside the Café Smile last—"

"Sure, I remember," with the amiable nod of the total amnesiac. "Café Smile, eh? You don't by any chance know Sally—"

"*De-eck,*" from Jane through clenched jaws.

"Yes, I—" Rachel began.

"Whups. Nearly forgot. This is my sister—"

"*De-eck—*"

"Yes, dear?"

Jane was pointing down the aisle with her chin. Her eyes were circles of pale blue hatred.

"Right, then," Dick said. "I think Sis would like to get on with, ah—" He tipped his hat. "Nice to have 'bumped into you', Rachel. Must do it again—"

Rachel watched them go. What was that about? In the next aisle she encountered them again. Jane would not meet her eyes, so to Dick she said, "Where's Cam Wilkes?"

Jane's face came round from the Coco Puffs slowly, an expression upon it of terror and disbelief. "You haven't seen him?"

Rachel shook her head.

"This Wilkes character is best forgotten," observed Dick, examining a box of Froot Loops. "Nothing but a hairbrain and a Romeo."

In installments from Jane as they met in subsequent aisles, by the freezers, and finally in adjacent check-out lines, Dick leafing through a *Reader's Digest* with a feature article entitled, "How to Get the Maximum Out of Your Stress," Rachel learned that Jane had not seen Wilkes in five days, not since two after he had proposed. With downcast eyes Jane apologized for assuming that Rachel had stolen him back.

Back?

Rachel asked Jane if Wilkes had said anything about Mortprop Investments.

"If Cam's in trouble," Jane said. "Just tell me. *Please!*"

"Ma'm? Excuse me?" It was Rick from Meats.

Rachel grabbed the front of his jacket. "*Yes!?*"

"I don't know what it's called. But—" He held up his hands. On each the tips of two fingers were pressed against the thumb. "I just went to my level, and right away I remembered where I heard it. At The Buhrstone. They use a different Muzak channel than SuperSpend."

"Can you whistle it now?"

Eyes closed, fingers and thumbs together, Rick tried, faltered. Hung his head. "I can *hear* it but I can't—"

"I know what you mean. The Buhrstone, eh?"

Rick nodded. "I'm pretty positive—"

When Rick went back to Meats, Jane told Rachel that the night Cam proposed he had asked the rhetorical question, What did he need with a bus yard now? "Do you think his price could have been too high?" Jane asked Rachel.

"What price is that?" Dick wondered, looking up from his *Reader's Digest*.

They left the store followed by two check out kids pushing carts filled with groceries. When Dick realized that Rachel was watching for a cab he offered her a lift. With Dick and Jane! Who could refuse? They came to a lustreless soup-green '49 Dodge in immaculate condition. There Dick discovered that Spot, left to guard the car, had locked himself in.

"Darn mutt's always doing this!" Dick cried proudly, above the clamour of barking.

Fortunately, one of the check out kids carried a shim. Jaw clenched, his big moment, he went into a crouch at the car door. It yielded in seconds. Relieved applause all round. Big uncontrollable grin from the kid. Spot bounded out, yapping.

Rachel sat between Dick and Jane in the front seat, Spot in the back, all the groceries in the trunk. Spacious trunks in these old buggies. "What a great car," Rachel said as they pulled out of the Mortprop Mall onto Mortprop Boulevard, the hot wet sound of spaniel panting in her ear.

"This was Father's last car," Dick replied. "Remember those

fun outings, Jane? Me up front with Father? Spot on the running board? Mother, you, Sally, Puff and the toys in the back? We'd visit that farm, those sweet, white-haired old folks—"

"Sometimes Dick confuses our childhood with the books," Jane whispered. "Our real grandparents lived in Trenton. They were alcoholics. It's like he's always talking about the community here in the Millpond, how it's so nice to be a part of it. But it's a big lie. We're strangers here. Everybody's strangers."

"Or we'd go to that green lake, where Father would row us kids around in the 'big blue boat', and then we'd all have a picnic on the grass and watch the planes fly over— Remember what Sally used to call planes, Jane?"

"No Dick. I don't."

"'Red and yellow somethings'. Or 'blue and silver somethings'. Sally's always been wild. Always wanting to 'go up and away'. Jane, remember that time we were all standing by the steam shovel hole and the little minx dropped Tim? She was always dropping that bear! Pushing everybody to the limit. Remember what happened? 'Oh, Sally', Father said. 'I can not jump down. I can not help you.' I always think of those as the ten words that shook my life. I still wake up sweating—"

"Didn't Tim fall into the steamshovel scoop?" Rachel said.

"How did you know that!" Dick cried. "Out of sheer respect to Father the operator raised that scoop on its big rivetted brown arm and swung it over to the fence where we were all standing, and Father just reached over and plucked Tim— It was one of those moments you never, ever forget."

Jane's hands were twisting in her lap. No one said anything for a minute or more. Rachel was thinking about Cam Wilkes. In the back seat Spot seemed torn between licking Rachel's ear and circling to lie down.

"A backdoor Johnny like this Wilkes," said Dick, gearing for a turn, "can't compare with a man like that. He's best forgotten. By now he'll be long gone. A shifty look about him, up to no good."

Jane's hands twisted more violently in her lap.

"I don't think Cam's shifty at all—" said Rachel, fingering her water gun.

"You know, girls, the problem with the world today," Dick said after a short pause, "is women don't understand men. Don't understand the first darn thing about them."

"And men understand women, I suppose?" Rachel said.

"Of course. Most of us knew our mothers. But how many girls get so close to their fathers?"

"And boys do get close to their fathers?" Rachel said.

This question surprised Dick. "Close! You bet! Father was always right there for us—"

"Dick," Jane said. "Father worked. He was away more than ten hours a day. He left at eight and got home after six. Sometimes seven. He was a goddam stranger."

"Jane! Of course he worked. To support his family. But he always made time for us. Every weekend we did things together, Dad and I. Planting potatoes, polishing up the car, juggling. I'd hang around his shop. Oh he was quite a guy all right, quite a guy . . . " Dick fell into glazed reminiscence. It was something like the look Leon once had for Harry.

Rachel took the opportunity to say, "I'll do what I can to find Cam, Jane. Promise."

Jane's small, red-knuckled hands continued to twist in her lap. She seemed to address the glove compartment when she said, "You've never really believed that I was the Girl on His Bus, have you, Rachel."

"Well, I—"

"But I was! I remember it all, every minute of those years I could ride a bus by myself, every giddy, terrifying minute. And yes, I remember the wonderful man with the trumpet case who used to stare at me every day. How could I not notice? I loved being stared at by him. I lived for the day, and yes I dreaded the day, that he would speak to me and I would have to reply. What if he found out how empty I was? What if he wanted someone with courage and self-esteem and a mind of her own? What if he noticed right away what a nothing I was inside and became appalled and sickened and walked away in disgust? Could I blame him? And where would I be then? Cast down from the slopes of the only love I had ever dared to live for, back down into the valley of the shadow—" Jane buried her face in her hands and sobbed.

"You remember him playing for you—?" Rachel asked.

In reply Jane closed her eyes and sank into her seat, humming, quietly at first but with increasing passion and volume, until her voice filled the car and Spot began a muted howl of respectful accompaniment. It was the *Melody for the Girl on My Bus*, a.k.a.

Harry's Theme. Tears rose in Rachel's eyes.

When Jane had finished there was nothing but the hum of the engine. Then, in a quiet voice, she said, "Yes, he played for me, and I was too terrified even to look at him. I kept walking. *I walked away.* I knew as I did it I was walking straight back into the darkness of my own fear and inadequacy, but at that moment I believed I had no choice. How could I be worthy of one who made such music? He would find out about me, what I was really like, and he would despise me, and that would be worse, much worse, than this fairytale courting, this tremendous hope—"

"Wow, Jane," Rachel said, wiping away tears. "Your side of the story is as sad as Cam's. We've just got to find him—"

Here Dick came out of his reverie. "You know the reason I never married, Rachel? I always knew in my heart I could never have a family as wonderful as ours. I could never be to a son of my own what Father was to me. I knew I just didn't have that kind of authenticity. It got diluted in me, somehow. Mother's influence, I guess, her genes—"

"*Dick!*" Jane cried. "How can you say something like that?"

"Oh, she was virtuous enough, I suppose, but how much trouble can you get into when your whole life is routine maintenance? Mother was the kind of woman, Rachel, when you entered a room either she'd be vacuuming or you'd sit on her. Why I remember one time—"

"Dick, would you, please, shut, up." As Jane said these words, her brother was pulling into the driveway of 201 Dell.

Depositing the last of Rachel's groceries on her kitchen counter, Dick apologized for Jane's behaviour. "It's Wilkes," he explained. "Before she met up with that Lothario she was such a soft-spoken, giving little thing. Now she's like her sister. Wild. He's been a bad influence. Even tried to interfere with her medical treatment."

"I just hope he's alive," Rachel replied darkly.

This struck Dick, who shuddered. "He *is* the type, isn't he? Two of a kind that pair."

A few minutes later, back fingering her water gun, Rachel watched from the window the immaculate old Dodge back down the driveway. In the front seat she could see Dick and Jane arguing. The Dodge stopped and Jane ran towards the house. Rachel got the door open just in time. Jane threw herself into the hall and turned to slam the door with both hands. She crouched before Rachel wild-eyed and breathless. "If Dick asks, I went to the bathroom. Rachel, it's not just Cam who's missing! So's my cat!"

"You think Cam took your cat!?"

"No, no! Puff's been gone for— What's the matter?"

"*Puff*!?" Of course. Puff.

"The Sixth. What's wrong?"

"How long has Puff been gone, Jane?"

"Fifty-five days. Forty-eight more than Cam. Why are you nodding your head? What do you know? *Tell me!*" Jane's crouch had become one of supplication, with a wringing of hands. "*You've got to tell me!*"

"Jane, it's OK. Try to be calm." Rachel made pacifying gestures. "Do you have any clues?"

"I know it was Dick. I saw him on the phone, with the Classifieds under his arm. Later I found where he'd torn out an ad under *Wanted*. Rachel, he's given Puff away! That's why I ended up in Flume Fields again. I couldn't handle it. Our whole lives he's hated Puff. Our whole lives it's been Spot this, Spot that. Dick cared about as much for Puff as he cared for Tim or Raggedy—"

"Jane, I'll do everything I can to get Puff back—"

Jane seized Rachel's arms in strong thin fingers. "I'm begging you, Rachel. Don't go to Dick. He won't admit to a damn thing. And he'll make me pay, for years and years—"

"I won't go to Dick," Rachel said in a soothing voice while trying to loosen Jane's grip.

"Then you do know she's still alive?"

"Ginger and white? Heart face?"

"Oh yes! That's her! Thank God! Did he give her to somebody you—"

"Lent her. I'll need a couple of days—" Except, this would mean going back to the Dream Centre, wouldn't it, not quitting the study— "But right now you'd better get back to Dick. He'll he wondering what you're up to."

"You're right," Jane said, wiping her eyes. "I'll have to tell him I had a Number 2, but he'll know it's the third today, and he won't let me forget it."

"I'll do my best to get Puff and Cam back to you, Jane. Honest. You go now."

"I will, Rachel. Thanks." Jane pecked Rachel on the cheek and slipped out the door.

Weird, Rachel thought as she watched the immaculate soup-green Dodge pull away down Dell Drive. Inside, both Dick's hands were on the wheel, his eyes straight ahead, his face immobile, while Jane sat shrunken on the seat beside him, her head turned aside. In the back seat Spot had thrust his muzzle out the window to pant into the wind. "Cam Wilkes," Rachel said. "Where are you? You're needed here."

Rachel put away the groceries that she didn't eat and headed over to Wilkes' house in the Civic. Puff she would have to see to later. She got lost but nothing too drastic. The little bungalow seemed shabby and neglected in the grey afternoon. Snow bottomed the front lawn pit, weeds poking through. In the picture window a strip of aluminum foil hung down, unstuck. Rachel knocked. No answer. She found the key under the mat and went in.

Same place, dustier. "Cam!" From the kitchen Rachel stepped into the dining area and from there into the living room, saw the phone on a low table with drawers and continued to a room she had never entered before. It seemed to be a bedroom. Had he moved up from the basement? A narrow bed, neatly made; closet, orderly and unrevealing; above the dresser a framed photograph of the Downtown 16 from Madison. Rachel could see plants in the bus windows, next to the grille the outline of a silver propane tank against a darker background of corrugated metal.

She returned to the kitchen. Stood at the door to the basement and called to Wilkes. No answer. She switched on the light and went down. This was a first. She found a rumpus room with imitation pine panelling, big old sofa, braid rug, cot, music stand, TV. Not bad really. And all those weeks she had pictured him squatting on concrete. This was actively homey. Funny how people were always saner than you thought. Also, of course, crazier. But right now she wouldn't mind holing up down here herself. Hibernate, perchance to dream. Perchance, hell. There was also a laundry room with a little washroom, and a gas furnace exactly the same model as hers and Leon's.

She looked everywhere, even checked behind that furnace: Wilkes was not here.

It took Rachel half an hour to get out of the Millpond, but once she had done that and was headed east on the 303 she got lucky, looped around on the 37 intersection, came west into the setting sun on the south service road, and there it was. She pulled up to the padlocked chainlink gates and got out to take a look.

Wilkes' bus yard was just as he had described it, although late on a November afternoon with the wind and powdered snow making shifting patterns across the heaving, pot-holed asphalt, it was even less inviting than Rachel had first imagined— and yet here it was so close to the chartered tracts and comfortable freeholds of the Millpond. One of the four-metre gateposts canted in such a way that she could squeeze through. Hugging herself— should have worn a thicker coat—she headed for the battered metal shed. A sheet of roof metal the wind was flapping seemed to beckon. All about, at various angles, as if they had been blown there, were buses, ten or twelve of them, discarded hulks.

Don't ask Rachel what she was doing here. Looking for a clue, she might suppose. But inside the shed were only huddles of blown refuse; crushed and fallen metal shelving; a pit for grease monkeys, brimmed with garbage; a filthy foam mattress kept from blowing away by a cement block; a vandalized tap; remains of half a dozen hobo fires, the inside walls and ceiling black from smoke. A sooty pissoir. But what did they burn? Shredded truck tires harvested in summer along the 303? Stolen Millpond sod for make-believe peat? Bus seats? Asphalt?

Rachel left the terrible shed and walked from bus to bus. By the third she found that she could see all she needed by standing on the front or rear bumper, the setting sun more or less at her back, her eyes following its shafts down the inside of the vehicle. Ransacked interiors. At the rear window of the eleventh and last bus a cadaverous face rose exactly with hers, like the face from the jail roof, like her own sad haggardness reflected, like a devastated Harry, and Rachel jumped down screaming. Two ravaged old mugs rose then in that window, side by side, like characters for a Muppet remake of *Night of the Living Dead*. Rachel backed away, the right side of her brain furiously studying those faces— Had Cam found a friend? But no. Just a couple of wasted people living in a bus. Rachel turned and walked away fast. Looking back, she saw one hand waving, another toasting her with a can of varnish thinner: a double-headed person, toasting and waving. Twin skulls split in toothless grinning.

It wasn't until Rachel was back at the Civic that she noticed a vast sign high above the ditch that ran between the fence and the service road. It was mounted on raw timbers with big mounds of oyster-coloured clay around their bases. She climbed back through the gate and crossed to the other side of the service road to read the monster credits:

Opening soon on this site
ARCADIA CENTRE of VILLAGE-ON-THE-MILLPOND
World's Largest Shopping and Residential Mall

Now Renting
784,876 sq. metres of retail space
243,753 sq. metres of residential space
The finest in condominium living
Enquire Today.
Dial REALITY. A Mortprop Investments Project
Architect: Stanley A. Jardine
Construction by Mortprop Construction
Mortprop: The Folks Who Put the "I" Back in REALTY
Stanley A. Jardine.
Holy shit.

Rachel sat with the engine going and the heat turned all the way up. Was this what they called serendipity? Felt a lot like shock. All she could think was, *Harry.* And after that, all she could think was, If Jardine's here and he's working with Sirocco, maybe he knows where Cam is.

She drove to the nearest phone she knew, inside the main doors of the old Mortprop Mall. There she called Mortprop Investments. The woman who answered, very much like a receptionist with her coat on to leave, denied the existence of Stanley A. Jardine. When Rachel told her he was designing Arcadia Centre, there was a pissed-off pause. The woman went to ask. She came back. "Mr. Jardine's the architect, but he's not here."

"I was told he was."

"I'm sorry. Mr. Jardine is in Paris. That's where his office is."

Rachel called her mother. "Any news from Elmer?"

"He thinks he might have found your father. Beyond that he won't say. I'm worried sick. Elmer usually calls at least every other day."

"How long has it been?"

"Two days."

"You're being neurotic. Tell me what he finds, OK?"

"Your voice still sounds funny. Are you dieting?"

"No!" and hung up.

Now what. Dieting, hmm? Now she wanted to walk into the Mortprop Mall Surf 'n Turf over there and eat a steak, two lobsters, four or five baked potatoes with sour cream, carrots, beans, pie, cheese, ice cream—

This Rachel did. And it was all great, just great, except maybe a half cup too much cornstarch in that raisin pie, and the green beans didn't really need to be canned, did they? But the best part was, while she ate she did not have to think. And afterwards all she could think was *sleep*. So she drove back to the Dream Centre to do exactly that and wake up even more out of control in the morning.

But first at 2:23 the Hewlett Packard audio-oscillator climbed from fifty to ninety dB's without waking Rachel. And the hand that had to shake her out of REM onset— Rachel crawling across a Plexiglas desk like one of those *trompe l'oeil* checkerboard surfaces that infants are placed on to see if they are crazy enough to trust their mothers more than to fear gravity— did not seem to belong to Alex Silver. But Rachel's eyes would not open.

Sometime later the hand had to wake her again.

This time she mumbled, "Where's Alex?" Did not quite catch the response.

Not long after six a.m. somebody started rustling print-outs. Later the same person sharpened a pencil and crossed the room to check on everybody's electrodes. Rachel, a little irrationally, considering that whoever it was could glance at the spindle and read exactly how awake she was, kept her eyes shut. The footsteps went on to Babs, then Frankie. Five minutes later they returned along with wafts of coffee. "Wake up, everybody. Time for another day of escalating psychosis." The voice moved in close to Rachel, whispering, "I know you're awake under there, Rachel. Thanks for coming back."

That's when she drew the water gun free of the bedclothes and got him in the ear, twice.

"Hey—!"

Maniacal laughter from Rachel.

"Cooperation and Interpersonal Aggression Quotients are gonna hear about this," promised Silver, grim. He wiped at his ear with his sleeve.

"Who woke me in the night?"

"Harry?"

"Seriously. A trainee?"

"No, no trainee. Me. The Hewlett Packard wasn't waking you up, so I did it myself. What did he look like?"

"Couldn't open my eyes."

"A dream, right? I'll make a note."

Babs went by for the bathroom, still breathing hard from sleep. The Gorgon Look. Frankie sat on the edge of her bed, scratching her narrow shanks.

At his desk Silver made harried jottings, glancing over constantly. He was back. "Hey, Rachel, listen. Maybe you should stay around here for the rest of the study."

"What are you talking about? I can't stay around here!"

"Why not? Take off work. And anyway. The point is, you don't dream and *he* comes to *you*."

"OK, but I have to find Cam Wilkes."

"The PAGO Wilkes? Why? Where'd he go?"

Babs came back from the bathroom.

"Took you long enough—" Frankie growled as she passed.

"Run, Frankie, run," Babs replied. "Run, run, run."

Rachel did not want to talk with those two around. Silver noticed and suggested Sunday brunch at Chez Pond, the freshwater vegetarian restaurant below his office at Village Market Square. A glare from Babs. To which Silver returned a mad scientist laugh. If breakfast went OK, he said, turning to Rachel, she could do what she liked the rest of the day. As long as she promised not to leave the Millpond or curl up somewhere unauthorized and go to sleep. He also made her promise to surrender her car keys the first time she hallucinated Harry on the road, to call as soon as everything became too much, and otherwise to be back at the Dream Centre by nine p.m. From here on in better take this one day at a time.

"Alex, why are you giving me orders?"

"Harry may be your responsibility now, Rachel, but as long as you're dream-deprived, your safety is mine."

"How's Puff?"

Silver winced. Spread his hand horizontal and waggled it to mean *so-so*.

Chez Pond had a mud-brown floor, a blue ceiling of water lilies viewed from below, and pondweed wallpaper. Diners were intended to feel they were eating at the bottom of a millpond.

But why?

Rachel could also not imagine where Silver was. She was *starving*. Fidgety, she looked around and understood that he had been right: She was no longer fit to be out. Here at Chez Pond her brain was now and then giving over all pretense to any sort of experiential flow, opting instead for successive frozen shots crystallizing out of a ground of wedgelike streaks and blurs. An incoherent slide show instead of the usual movie. Strobe Brain, except that the flashes succeeded each other on just about every principle except chronology. A face, for example, would flash a survey of its physiognomic type— e.g., "Swine"— not a guy shovelling down breakfast.

And then Silver did arrive, stout, harried, in a cotton suit, a lavender pocket handkerchief. "Sorry I'm late. 'Unavoidably delayed', as they say. Tell you about it sometime—" A local celebrity, Silver had also been obliged to sign autographs for Chez Pond diners before actually sitting down to join Rachel, who immediately focussed on what seemed to be a fan of white powder around his nose. Not—!? Her sanity had been in the hands of a celebrity *coke addict*?

Slipping his crimson frames into his jacket pocket with that lavender hankie— "Never should wear the old trademark in public, but I love it"— Silver reached for the menu. He had not yet shaved, was grizzled, somewhat wild-eyed, smelled powerfully of . . . lavender. Of course. Rachel gaped. Those wild eyes were all pupil. Even as they studied a menu they were all pupil. He removed his jacket. His shirt was white, collarless. That white stuff powdered more than his nose. It was all over his face. It was even in his hair!

The waitress was waiting.

"Think I'll have the Water Lily Popovers," Silver said and looked at Rachel over his menu. "They dry and grind the roots for the flour right here on the premises—" He looked at her more closely. "How are you doing?"

Flour! It was flour! The man was *dusted* with the stuff! What was happening?

"Um, fine," Rachel said. "I'll have everything under 'Breakfast', please: The Pondweed Cereal and the Fillet o' Mock-Chub, with a side order of Popovers. A large Willow Juice."

"One Pond and a Mock!" the waitress shouted. "Side o' Lily, big Willow to start!"

"Hungry, eh," Alex said. "We should come here on a Thursday sometime. "They do cattail crepes on Thursdays. You could tell your grandchildren."

Rachel just smiled. Even dream-deprived she was too discreet to bring up the business of the flour. Equally embarrassing for both of them if her brain happened to be extrapolating from a coke clod stuck to a nostril hair. Like him smelling so strongly of lavender just because of the colour of his handkerchief. This is what schizophrenics must have to put up with, day in and day out. What a grind. *Grind*, hmm. Talk about the powder of suggest— I mean flour of—

Looking around, possibly wild-eyed, Rachel understood in a flash of insight that the coke/flour, like this whole brunch here, was an integral part of the experiment. This Chez Pond situation was a test of her rapport with the reality principle, in fact the test Silver required her to pass if breakfast was going to qualify as having gone "OK" and she was not to be forcibly confined to quarters. No way could these be run-of-the-Millpond diners. One man in here this morning seemed to be suffering from Tourrette's syndrome — convulsing and swearing; a woman was talking with animation to a man who made no acknowledgement, simply stared stonily at his plate; that young fellow over there seemed to be nodding out over a bowl of something phosphorus green (must be the Algae-Style Muskrat Milk). Clearly these people were hired, crazy, or both. Or were they?

Fortunately Rachel's brain was working at maximum speed, so she had plenty of time to scrutinize Silver's face for clues. Less fortunately this only made things worse. The closer she examined it the less sure she could be whose face exactly that was. It was like staring into a fanned deck of the day's snaps from a Photomat booth.

He was holding up his thumbs. "They say millers have gold thumbs."

"Pardon?"

"You said I looked like a miller."

"I did?"

"Right. And *I* said, millers have gold thumbs." He looked at his thumbs. "Would you be satisfied with short, fat thumbs?"

Rachel smiled nervously.

"Hey," Silver added. "Bet you didn't know a 'miller's thumb' was a kind of freshwater fish. Sort of appropriate— or do I mean inappropriate— in here—"

Rachel felt that she was in trouble.

"Listen, Rachel. You're sure you're up to being out? So far you're testing a lot more sensitive than Frankie and—" he ruffled his hair; a cloud of white powder filled the air . . . a smell of lavender— "well, than Frankie, anyway—"

"Oh yes, I'm fine, fine," a shaky smile. He did look like a miller. A fat little miller with giant pupils and heavy thumbs. All dusted with some poor cheated farmer's flour. With a wretched cat's bleached braindust.

"So tell me about Wilkes."

Rapidly, breathlessly, to the best of her crippled ability, Rachel did this. Silver kept nodding. She also told him about the Arcadia Centre architect's being one Stanley Jardine. As she finished, their orders came. Silver seemed to eat thoughtfully, occasionally drumming his fingers on the table in an irritating way. Rachel felt that she herself was eating too fast, exactly how much too fast she could not be sure. The food was simply awful. Really bitter and impossible to chew.

"Weird food, eh?" commented Silver.

Rachel just smiled and went on eating.

"You know," he said, looking sadly around Chez Pond, "that's the trouble with conceptual living. The quality of the experience does tend to suffer. Man cannot live by thought alone. But he'll try." Silver sighed. "He sure as hell will try."

Not by *bread* alone, Rachel amended. He *is* a miller. So what does he mill? Problems? Cats? Lives? What do the Gods mill? Destinies? Hailstones? Buckwheat? In her pocket Rachel fingered the watergun. Flour and water. What's that?

Glue.

"You know how I got into dreams?" Silver asked. "Fletcherism. Know what that is?"

Rachel shook her head.

"Chew therapy, first promulgated a hundred years ago by Horace Fletcher. Slow and lengthy chewing. As soon as calves are weaned and start grazing, their dreaming goes way down. No ruminant dreams much. Of course, ruminants don't have very challenging lives. Human adolescents do have challenging lives, and that's why they chew gum, to handle the emotional material their dreaming can't keep up with. Compulsive eaters, bulimics, etc. don't just care about food, they also need to chew. Dreams connect with chewing via speech— 'jawing'— muscular adjustment patterns, body image, ego.

"Eventually I said, OK, so it's all true, but there's no future in it. Sure chewing calms people, helps them order their lives. But where's the grabby general theory? With no grabby general theory there's no sustained market. Also it's base. I felt like Freud listening to all these women describe how their fathers and uncles and friends of the family molested them when they were children. Super depressed. Where can you go from there? Career suicide, that's where. You don't attack the family and its friends! Chew therapy? So it works as well as anything else. But what about *me*? I'm a psychologist, not a vet. You don't attack people's *humanness*! Freud saved his neck by dreaming up psychoanalysis, and it took him a long way. I'm saving mine by being the cutting edge of dream deprivation for therapy. You see, Rachel. I finally figured out that the only way around the Doomed Expert bind is long-term commitment to an experimental position. That way you can stress the commitment or the experiment, depending on how the larger situation evolves. So suddenly I'm doing clinical work. And Rachel, believe me, the feelgood stuff you can spin off this is a PR dream. I mean, I can write three bestsellers without even touching the material I've got already on you, Babs, and Frankie."

"What about Cam Wilkes?"

"Right. Wilkes." Silver's mouth did an embarrassed smile. "Self-absorbed little prick, aren't I?"

Rachel nodded, belching softly.

"So you're absolutely sure he wanted to sell the bus yard?"

"That's what Jane said."

"OK. First thing Monday morning, the property registry. You do a title search. See if— when— it's changed hands. Next— Next I don't know. Even if you weren't dream-deprived I wouldn't advise tangling with the Mortprop boys. You could end up in a ditch on Village Drive North. Maybe next you should contact the police. No— you're too crazy; they'd notice. How about Jane calling the police? But she doesn't understand the Mortprop thing, does she? Rachel, you know what? Give me an hour for my paperwork and I'll take you back to the lab— I'm going back anyway, I'm there for the day, Puff needs me— and you can sleep and dream until you're sane. When you wake up, call his home, check with Jane that he hasn't shown up yet, and then call the police. I mean, please don't feel bad about dropping out of the study. I've already got plenty of—"

"What about Harry?"

"Ah, yes. But he's not Wilkes, I thought."

"If I sleep now I'll never find him."

"As a man of science and as a friend, I'd say your safety comes first."

"Then what about Stanley Jardine?"

"Stanley can wait. That one I'm sure of. They haven't even broken the ground yet. If he is already here he'll be here for awhile. Or be back and forth from wherever—"

"Paris."

"For a long time." Silver looked at his watch. "Listen. Gotta get upstairs. And get this talcum off of me. That's what it is, you know. Talcum. I told Babs the real reason she was doing the study. To find a man. That this was the limit of *her* dreams. I also told her I wasn't him. A submissive woman I don't need. She got a little incensed. Attacked me with a box of the stuff. Talcum. Lavender. Smell it? Almost choked me to death. You wondered? You thought flour, right? Miller?"

Rachel nodded, sheepish.

"Rachel, you'll meet me in an hour, or call? Tell me where to pick you up? You'll think of me, too? You do something insane and I could get hit with a malpractice suit that'll have me back giving government aptitude tests in remand centres."

Rachel nodded, disguising her lie in a blush of silence.

"Great. See ya."

On her way out, Rachel visited the washroom. Wallpaper of diving loons. Filled her water gun.

Loons.

The rest of the day Rachel spent back at 201 Dell, eating her way through the rest of yesterday's enormous grocery shop when her hands were not too busy between her legs to get the food to her mouth. She did not answer the phone. Just let it ring. If Harry was watching, he was hard to make out amongst the sweep and flow of so much eating and coming.

That night Rachel boomeranged back late to the Dream Centre, wired her own head, and left early Monday before anybody was up, test forms completed in a neat pile.

By eight a.m., after two Super Specials at the twenty-four Pancake Corral in Hopperboy High Street, she proceeded to the township registry office, which had recently, it happened, moved to sub-basement quarters in Village Green. Terrified of being seen by an early Millpond Indemnity person— in half an hour she would phone in sick— she snuck onto a down elevator. Took a number. Vinyl seats, foamboard fluorescence. An endless wait, with others there even earlier. Fortunately the pale, crooked-toothed young woman behind the counter, though she seemed to understand only slightly better than this madwoman what was required, had the tolerance and kind heart of an anxious green-horn, and with her help Rachel was able to ascertain that Wilkes had sold the four-acre bus yard to Mortprop Investments on Tuesday of last week for a half million, the realtor being one Leon Boseman of Bi-Me Village Realty.

Except that that was not Leon's signature, was it? Was nothing like. A fact apt to throw Cam's into doubt.

What happened next happened so fast Rachel must have blacked out the interim. Probably ran into Mr. Felpson and just cancelled the whole experience. One moment she was leaning across a government counter listening to that greenhorn young woman explain the signatures, the next she was opening fire with her water gun across a white desk, soaking the face and cleavage of a screaming blonde, thinking *Where am I and what am I doing?* And then Nick Sirocco was trying, and failing— got squirted himself— to grab the water gun, gave up to grip Rachel's elbow, vice style, and walk her into an office like the wheelhouse of a large liner, cutting through suburban seas.

"*Sit.*" Rachel got pushed towards a leather chair. Her adrena-line at full throttle, she did not so much sit as crouch, however, studying Sirocco, his back. Dark tube-cut suit. Very stylish, very expensive. A monogrammed silk handkerchief out to mop the back of his gunned neck.

Click. He is across his desk, seated, looking at her. Not a good man. "What's the matter with you?" he said. "You look like hell."

"Where's Cam Wilkes?"

"How should I know?"

"You got a signature for his bus yard."

"Yeah, we gave him a good deal. Maybe he went on a holiday. What are you on?"

"Holiday where?"

Sirocco came around the desk. "A real dingbat, aren't you, coming in here soaking my girl."

"Where is Cam Wilkes."

"Listen. I got a question for you. Did you ever hear of a guy by the name of Stanley Jardine?"

"What about him?"

Sirocco laughed. A mean laugh, from the throat. "'What about him'. You tell me."

"He's your architect—"

"Very good. Our flake architect. Who won't look at the facts of what I am trying to do here. An architect who can't understand the words 'super-regional mall'. You're a woman. You shop. You tell me. Four stretch dumbells in an octagon. Is this hard to understand?"

"You're talking to me because I shop?"

Sirocco had been pacing. Now he stopped. "Look. We check people out. Don't get smart with me—"

"Where's Wilkes?"

"I want you to talk to Jardine. I want you to tell him my concerns about your face—"

"Take me to Cam Wilkes and I'll talk to Jardine."

"You don't get it yet, do you? This is not a deal. This is me telling you what you are going to do."

Rachel jumped up. "Here's a better idea. I kick you so hard you get to use your nuts for a brain."

Tactless, tactless. Sirocco lunged, swung. No open-handed womanslap either— But how could he take into account Rachel's reflexes after eight days without dreaming? Her head snapped back, its own intelligence, and her face felt the wind from that ugly Sirocco fist. A real sweetheart, this guy. Lost her balance exactly as he recovered his. There came another swing, but Rachel was already falling, and it fanned the top of her head. A crablike scramble then, backwards across the floor, trying to squeeze into her pocket for the water gun, her only weapon, while Sirocco came stumbling to lift her by her jacket against the wall and smash her—

once, twice— thumbs on her throat, no air, this was it, no air, not such a handsome face when intent on strangulation this Adonis, *no air*—

The door opened. A blue-jawed character, hesitating.

"Moe, get the fuck outta—" Sirocco paused long enough to say. That must have been how Rachel got him with her water gun, in the eyes. And during the pause that gave him, jerked her knee nutsward, hard, whispering, "Moe, please stay," as she deked past slow Moe, out the door, and into a big blur of corridors, office doors, doors to whole clusters of offices, all *Mortprop* somewhere in the name. Elevators stalled at distant floors. *Come on, come on!* Rachel took a Fire Exit, concrete stairs, to fool her pursuers went up, not down, bounding, three at a time, to a red door with a bar, gave it a good slam. To find herself panting like a hounded muskrat in the cold still air on the roof of Village Green, Tower B. A blue sky. Crushed stones. Chilly out here. Low perimeter wall. Evergreen shrubbery in aluminum boxes. She could always throw herself over. Wary, Rachel circled the brick cubicle that she had burst out of, came back to its door. Now closed. Handleless. Oh dear. Put her ear to it. Footsteps, climbing. Next she was scaling wall-bolted rungs to flatten herself against the cold tar roof of that cubicle. Below, all of the Millpond and more, much more. Open fields and distant, smogged-in city. A savage slam on the door and two— no, three— of them were crunching around on the roof. "Hey, Rico. Watch the door," somebody said, meaning the door whose top edge Rachel could have reached out and touched.

Fortunately Rico's idea of watching the door was to lean against it while trying to drag a cement block over with his foot. Rachel landed right next to him already throwing herself sideways through that open door, twisting and writhing in the air to keep on descending without actually being stopped by stair, landing, or wall. What's a broken ankle or wrist at a time like this? Rico, who had flunked high school physics, let go of the door to plunge after, thereby locking the other two on the roof. Shouts. Heavy pounding. Lighter than Rico by about a hundred pounds and ten times faster in the head, Rachel took the twenty-six flights to burst into the Tower B lobby, all mirrors and burnished marble, getting to see dozens of herself at full tilt, heads turning— *Who was that woman?*— "Sprint jogging, folks, coming to your neighbourhood soon!" out the big revolving door— *"Hey, excuse me!"* waving her arms the

way arms wave at disappearing cabs, running right into the
hornblast of another one. She got in.

"You likely get killed that way," said the cabby, a guy in a
knitted cap.

From the back seat Rachel gave him a big hug and told him to
Drive, Rastaman. Drive.

Next Rachel was stumbling down a narrow alley between a
seven-foot Permawood fence and the white-brick rear wall of a
building where green garbage bags clustered like supplicants
around steel doors. There she discovered a parking stall with a *Dr.
Alex Silver* plaque bolted to the white brick. Also his Morgan.
Rachel ran her hand along the pneumatic bulge of the silver thing,
made blinders with her hands to peer inside. An AAA guide to
Southern California. A deerstalker in red corduroy. On the back
seat a warped fungus-green book by Horace Fletcher, entitled
Chew Your Way to Mental Hygiene.

So here she was in the alley behind Village Market Square. Alex
Silver being the person she felt most reluctant to see just now, she
had been drawn to him as a bobby pin to a magnet. Now what.

Straightening, Rachel became aware of an idling engine. A
stretch limo with black windows, chrome boomerang on the trunk,
had slunk up alongside the fence maybe ten feet away. Electrically
the driver's window came down, maybe four fingers. She saw eyes.
A flicked cigarette butt bounced in front of her, rolled against her
shoe.

"Asshole," she said. But already she was shaking, stepping
through one of those steel doors.

Next Rachel found herself standing in front of another desk,
this time looking down at an old woman in an orange blouse and
mud-yellow cardigan, buffing her nails. Rachel asked her if Dr.
Silver had any cancellations this morning. Even a minute or two
between clients would really be appreciated.

"I know he wants to see me."

"Oh, he *wants* to see you?"

"I had brunch with him yesterday! And he said—"

"So you had brunch with him yesterday. Sunday brunch. I
suppose this gives you special privileges? Will this solve your
problems? Why don't you get him to take you to a movie. With
dinner after. Marry him maybe. Have him set you up in your own

little split level. Like a queen. Then you will be cured, I suppose. All the craziness will go away."

"Listen, Mrs. Silver. I'm dream-deprived—"

"You think I'm not dream-deprived? I have news. I had my dreams deprived a long time ago, by the biggest dream-depriver of them all. Adolf Hitler. He made a science out of it. That's what he took away when he didn't take your life."

"Your son," patiently, "said, to call—"

"Am I talking into a phone? Do I hallucinate you standing here? I know. This is a hologram. Ma Bell has done it again."

"Mind if I use your washroom?"

"Go ahead. Only, wash the sink after you. Have consideration. And flush. Don't be a pig. Flush the toilet. And please, *please*. No Tampons."

Rachel's face in the washroom mirror was wilder than she had dared to fear. It came at her in blazing snapshots, none the same. An unspecifiable period of baffled scrutiny, and Rachel dropped her mad red eyes from the mirror to fill her water gun. The water seemed unusually cold.

Then she went out and fired it into the startled face of Mrs. Silver. When the gun was quite empty, she left.

Rachel found pay phones by the cab rank outside and tried Wilkes' house. No answer. She looked up Dick on Smutter Circle and called.

"Howdy, Rachel. Nice of you—"

"Dick, could I speak to Jane, please."

"I'm afraid Jane's not in. Are you all right, Rachel? You're sounding a little—"

"Yeah. Will she be back soon?"

"You bet. Shouldn't be gone too long. You're doing all right, yourself?"

"I'm fine. Should I call back?"

"That's a terrific idea."

"When?"

Sound of meditative pipe-sucking. "Why don't we say a week Thursday."

"*Pardon?*"

"By then we should have a better idea." Sound of interior barking. "Excuse me, Rachel. It's Spot— I'm afraid I— There's somebody at the door."

"Dick, where is she? Cam didn't come back, did he? She's not
on her honeymoon?"

"Wilkes? That's it. Wilkes' doing— A week Thursday?"

"Right."

"We should know better then."

"Goodbye Dick."

"Bye, Rachel. Thanks for the call."

Rachel took a cab to Flume Fields, a massive beige-brick
addendum to the Millpond General, designed by the same architect who had done Millpond Collegiate, a specialist in the Correc-
tional Look. When she asked at the front desk for Jane, the woman
located the name in her book and said, "You want the D Wing. D
for Depression. Straight to the end, hang a left, a right, another left.
Big cheery room."

Rachel found Jane in a ward that must have contained fifty
exhausted and defeated women of every age. They lay staring in
their beds or stood about singly, like caryatids stooped under
enormous weights. Jane was sitting on the side of her bed dressed
in a pink nightgown. Her head was bowed and her hands lay
upturned in her lap.

"Jane!" Rachel cried.

Slowly Jane raised her head. A gradual, antidepressant smile
seeped into her lower face. Stopped just short of the eyes. "Rachel—
Did you find—"

Rachel shook her head. "Puff I'll resc— pick up when I can.
Cam I'm still working on. Why are you here?"

Jane sighed and bowed her head.

"Jane?"

"So tired—"

"Are they going to—"

Jane nodded.

"When?"

Another big sigh. "—afternoon."

"Let's go."

"So tired— Want it—"

"Come on."

As they left the ward a nurse stopped and looked sharply at
Rachel, who said, "Just going for a little walk—"

"All right, I suppose. But be back in ten minutes. We have to have our shot."

"Right."

Before they reached the front lobby, Rachel put her jacket over Jane's shoulders. They then walked past the desk, out the front door, and got into a cab. "Where to, Ladies?"

Good question. "Jane, where does Sally live?"

With some effort Jane remembered that Sally had moved to Bolting Reel Manor. The tower and apartment numbers she did not know. Rachel thought, Isn't that where Gretchen lives? Still another last place in the Millpond I want to be right now? Please oh please, Unconscious Mind, no more bobby-pin-to-magnet stuff for Rachel Boseman. She told the cabby to try Tower One. In one oiled movement he flipped the meter, checked his side mirror, and pulled away. Rachel spent the trip like a new boyfriend, not knowing what to say, giving reassuring squeezes to Jane's strengthless little hand.

Bolting Reel Manor, Towers One to Three, was a sound buffer for singles, designed to absorb the steady roar of the 303. They got the right tower, Two, on the second try, Sally's name in Dymotape on the massive mock-marble plaque, like a memorial to the war dead. Number 1403. So, however, was G. *Molstad* on the fourteenth floor. No thirteenth. Gretchen Number 1423. Remember that. Do not press the wrong one. Rachel pressed Number 1403. It was a long wait, or seemed to be. Rachel was ravenous. "Who is it?" Sally's voice, indistinct. The connection?

"Rachel and Jane!" Rachel shouted.

A pause. "C'mon up," Sally said and buzzed them in. Across the giant terrazzo lobby was a waiting elevator big enough to move the contents of an entire bachelor apartment in one trip. "Have you seen Sally in her new place?" Rachel attempting normal conversation as the elevator deposited her stomach on the floor.

Jane shook her head. "Dick didn't think I—" She sighed.

They left the elevator and moved along the deep red shag of the corridor. A muffled experience. A humming tunnel of indirect light. The sound of clanking metal grew near and receded. A buckle flying around in a clothes drier. And here it was. Number 1423. Rachel pressed the doorbell.

The door was opened by Gretchen Molstad. Instamatically the moment was caught by Rachel's brain, never to fade. Wrong apartment. 1403. Fuck. Gretchen was wearing leather slippers, black socks with calf garters, jockey shorts, a vest-style undershirt, and a tweed driving cap pulled down low over her eyes. She was smoking an Old Port cigar. In her right hand she held a hairbrush the size of a small paddle.

It was a moment of shared confusion.

Gretchen spoke first. "Er— hi—" She looked to Jane, whose eyes were fixed upon the carpet, then back to Rachel, who was taking in those calf-garters. "This—?" indicating her outfit with a dismissive flick of her hand. "This is just—" She stepped towards them, pulling the door shut behind her, then put her arms around their shoulders and walked them down the hall a short way, remarking, "I thought you people were the Pizza Hut kid."

"Gretchen," Rachel said. "What are you doing?"

"What does it look like. I know you'll be assuming this is what I always wear around the house, but believe me. You caught me at an exploratory moment, that's all, a moment likely to be experienced, sooner or later, by any curious and sexually courageous adult."

"You sound familiar."

"You noticed. We're staking out the true parameters of our sexualities. Guess who's winning." Gretchen turned her head and looked at Jane from two inches. "Who are you?"

"This is Jane," Rachel said. The three of them had reached a mirror at the end of the corridor, in which Rachel was dismayed to see her hair limp, make-up a ruin, expression desolate, coat misbuttoned. She looked like the valedictorian at Bag Lady U.

"Jane!" Gretchen cried, pumping Jane's hand. "*The* Jane! You've been a persuasive case for us all!"

"We came to see Sally—" Rachel said.

"Right. A Freudian slip. I told Sally about 1403 when I heard the people were moving out. Speaking of slip, like to come in and have a word with Krafft-'Bozo'-Ebing?"

"No thanks. Sally's expecting us—"

They had looped at the mirror and now were back at Gretchen's door. "Jane, fabulous to meet you. Rachel, has he ever done anything in a simple way?"

"No. Have you?"

"Too-shay." Gretchen dropped her voice. "Listen, Rachel. I have this feeling he's all yours."

Rachel dropped hers. "Hey Gretchen. I don't want to spoil you guys' day or anything. But that might not be in the, uh—"

"Cards."

"Right."

"You're not serious."

"You mean you're not, how can I be?"

"Sort of."

"The thing is, it's Harry. He'll never find him this way."

"Hey, Rachel—I'm not sure he's, looking for Harry. Anymore."

"That's it! That's what I'm saying!"

"You're not being arbitrary here? Unrealistic?"

"Not at all."

Gretchen lifted her arms off their shoulders and stepped back into the doorway. "Rachel, you look terrible. Just awful. Are you sleeping?"

"Sleeping, yes."

"Rachel, think about this. Probably you're just angry and hurt."

"Could be."

Rachel took Jane's hand, and they went to find 1403.

Even Jane agreed that it took Sally a long time to come to the door. When she did it was on the chain. "Um. Wait a sec— Shit—" Fumbling. The apartment behind Sally was dark. She was wearing a terry-cloth bathrobe and carrying a teddy bear like a brown rag. Her feet were bare. Her hair was dishevelled and she was squinting at the light from the corridor. "Thought I imagined you."

"We got delayed—"

Sally hugged her impassive sister. "Hello, Janey. You look like bleached dogshit— Rachel, what's wrong—? Listen, I've been having a little apartment warming here, come in, come in. Join me—"

Sally's drapes were pulled and the lights off, probably so she would not have to look at the wall-to-wall chaos of random furniture and unpacked cardboard boxes. Switching on a floor lamp while shielding her eyes, she offered her guests a drink.

Both declined. Jane sat stiffly on the edge of the first chair she came to. Rachel sank into the chesterfield next to a flagon of vodka. The spot was still warm.

"What's happened?" Sally said. She had tucked her bear into the pocket of her gown.

Rachel told her about Wilkes' disappearance, and Flume Fields.

"Dammit Jane, you should have called me—"

Jane did not reply.

"Sally, she can't go back to Dick. And she can't go back to Flume Fields—"

"Right. Coffee?"

"I want shock," Jane said in a small voice.

"Coffee, Jane?" Sally stood over her.

"No, thank you."

Rachel did not need caffeine. "We'll find him," she told Jane, who nodded, eyes on the floor.

"So what happened to Wilkes?" Sally called from the kitchenette. "He seemed so taken by you, Janey."

Forgetting Jane for a moment, Rachel told Sally about Cam's bus yard, Mortprop Investments, and her visit that morning to Nick Sirocco.

"Are you crazy?" Sally coming back into the living room.

"Yes." And Rachel also told her about the dream deprivation experiment.

"Like Babs and Frankie—"

"You heard?"

"Babs got barred from the Café Smile yesterday. Friday she goosed José, and he complained. Sexual harassment, right? She opted for putting her case to the board, but I guess the primer study got to her. Went in with these big boxes of talcum inside her coat. Remember that one where I climb onto Mother's dressing table and get powder all over Spot and Puff and Tim here, and Dick comes in and throws up his hands in amazement?"

Rachel nodded. She did remember. Perfectly.

"Well," Sally said. "The board threw up their hands too. But it wasn't amazement."

"Yesterday she got Alex Silver—"

"Good. He should pay for this. But anyway, Wilkes. You are in no shape to do anything about Wilkes, Rachel. Call the police. No, I'll call the police. I'll have eight coffees and then I'll call the police."

Jane got up and went to the bathroom.

"The police won't do anything," Rachel said, watching Jane go.

"Why? Because they're too slow or because they're on the take?"

"Yes."

"So what do we do?"

They sat for a while not speaking. Rachel was far too wrecked to think. When the kettle whistled she heard *Harry's Theme*. Sally left to make coffee. "You're sure?" she called.

"No thanks, really—You know," Rachel said, "if I had a couple of grenades I could just walk back into Sirocco's office—"

"It wouldn't find you Wilkes. If that's what his fate was. What I'm thinking, if it wasn't for my poor sister I'd say we should just forget it. It's hopeless. If people don't want to think about where the money comes from, they also don't like to be reminded. I mean, there is not going to be a whole lot of public outrage about this. 'Oh, he got mixed up with the Mob. What else do you expect.' Can you hear them?"

Rachel nodded. "But I can't just—"

"No. On the other hand maybe we're being too dramatic." Sally was leaning against the kitchenette doorway to sip her coffee. "Maybe he realized what he was getting into. I know I'd have second thoughts about— Is that the *bath* I've been hearing—? *How long has she been in there?*"

"*Oh Jesus—*"

Sally ran to the bathroom door. "*Jane!*" pounding. No answer. It took Sally a dozen body blows to splinter the frame. They found Jane curled in two inches of incredibly red water. Sally snatched up the wastebasket, rooted through it, threw down an amber bottle. "*Shit!*" She started ripping strips off a towel. "Rachel, call an ambulance. *Oh Janey, Janey,* you little airhead—"

SIX

The thing about Harry, Rachel reflected from her crouch at the bottom of a Dream Centre closet in the *Keep Out* room, you find him, you find him. You don't, well— He'll be some kind of error, that's all. A figment of an imagination that doesn't happen to be yours. Agent for nothing but the distance between you and not being imposed on by somebody else's fantasy, ever again. What if there really is only one of each real thing, and the rest, half phantoms, are Harry's work? Or what if Harry is unmeetable, and yet this unmeetability fails to make him unreal, and this failure is one of those irreducibles that whole societies get built on? Or what if when Rachel comes calling he has happened to step out for a few minutes, to the cleaners, the shoestore, to bowl a few lanes? Gone fishing? What then? Leave a note? *Sorry I missed you.* Smash windows? Blow up the place? Come back like a philosopher, arguing he doesn't exist?

After Rachel had left Sally and Jane at the Millpond General, another memory gap suggesting experiences too damaging for recall, and then she was back at the Dream Centre, Silver's giant leather gloves on, trying to free Puff from her terrible treadmill. It wasn't easy, Puff failing to appreciate the gift of sanity from a fellow traveller on the treadmill of terminal psychosis. Here was Rachel sustaining extensive loss of blood from the upper arms in a selfless attempt to restore to this fur spitfire the precious freedom to dream—a freedom enjoyed by all the world's creatures save fish (and on down), certain reptiles, alcoholics, drug addicts, insomniacs, and the dream-deprived for experimental reasons— and you would think she was attempting to send her to her long last home. Puff hissed and clawed, was too crazy, too fierce. Rachel gave up, retired to this Dream Centre closet here, fingering her water gun.

Empty.

Renewed spitting and snarling as Rachel emerged to fill the weapon from Puff's tank before returning to her crouch among Silver's sneakers. No paternal footwear for this sometime Harry. To pass the hours, Rachel tried to account for and justify being here, wound up blaming it on the horrors outside.

A universal complaint. Just ask PAGO.

Still, things were pretty bad out there.

In Sally's bathtub Jane had been conscious at first— a lot of listless begging for death— but slipped beyond speech some time before the arrival of the ambulance, which had raced to the wrong tower of Bolting Reel Manor. Sally rode in the back with Jane and a medic, Rachel up front with the driver. At a stoplight she punched him in the side of the head. "Hey, *ouch*!"

"Stop cracking your gum!"

And so back to the Millpond General. This time, Emergency. Where Jane, chameleonic against the white of her stretcher, was wheeled off while Sally answered demographic questions for her sister's file. And then for an hour—two?— Sally slumped next to the Coke machine drinking that contraption dry as Rachel paced the walls and ceiling. They hardly spoke. Once Sally went away to call Dick. "What did he say?"

"You don't want me to answer that."

Finally a nurse in a smock sprayed pink with vomit said they could see Jane and pointed back down the corridor.

They found her in a dark room, strapped to a high white bed. Her wrists had been bandaged. Enunciating with drugged deliberation, she spoke of an abiding desire to witness their slow deaths in certain states of unspeakable anguish: boiling oil, fire ants, razor barrage, etc.

"She's furious," Sally said with satisfaction on their way back to the waiting area. "Always a good sign." She told Rachel to go home and sleep, made her swear on an old *Psychology Today* to stay away from Mortprop Investments. She herself would hang around the hospital to make sure that Dick didn't show up and have Jane transferred to Flume Fields, also that she herself didn't just go home and drink.

Rachel must have then taken a cab to the Dream Centre.

Where, from here inside the closet, she now heard a familiar voice, calling her name. *But whose?*

With caution Rachel kneed open the door, and honestly, she had no idea who she was looking up at. It was the experience of recognition without the content. Familiarity minus comprehension. To be safe, she drew and fired.

"Rachel!" he cried, reeling back.

Rachel lunged forward to fire on the tumble, heard an elbow crack on the concrete floor, not as deft as she'd hoped, one foot tangled in a lab coat, right hip feeling as though Gravity had crushed it personally, but her right hand was free and she was firing with that, opened a wet spot on his shirt and another on his pants below the knee before he fell over a chair and from there went sprawling backwards across Silver's bed.

It should of course have been Alex Silver but did not seem to be, a fact that confused and alarmed her.

"Rachel, what are you—" He knew her. A good omen, or the worst? She squirted him up a nostril. He sneezed. She hauled him off the bed to his feet, but he was lighter than anticipated, continued over her leg and down hard, an interminable delay between the whump on his kidneys and the crack the back of his head made against that concrete floor. Head raised, eyeblinks coming faster, all movements otherwise slowed down as if for a good long cry. Already Rachel had a handful of shirt front, buttons bouncing along the floor like ivory popcorn, to drag him across the room towards Puff's tank, where Puff was not on her treadmill but sitting soaked on her island, licking herself. Must have fallen in.

All right. By means of a headlock Rachel got the interloper right up next to the tank. Grabbed him by the back of the neck and pushed his head into the fetid water of Puff's undreamable nightmare. His hands went clawing for the sides. "*Let go!*" Rachel screamed. Reluctant, he did, got pushed under again, inhaled water, came up choking.

Here Rachel had to wonder who it was she thought she was drowning. Silver? Considering Puff, it seemed only fair. Leon? Considering herself, ditto. Harry? Except, shouldn't she first find out who he is?

Puff, meanwhile, no fool, recovering from an initial startled freeze, leapt onto the man's back, and from there made a longstretch fearless catleap to freedom, a blur for the door to the main lab.

"Stop that cat!" and then she remembered that the outside door would be shut.

Grill the bastard. Gripping the back of the neck and holding the face just over the water, Rachel shouted her first question. Oddly, it came out, "*Why aren't you here?*" Startled, Rachel ran these words past again. From the assaultive point of view, an error. Her grip dissolved. She sagged against the side of the tank, weeping. Warily the man drew his head from the water and turned dripping to comfort her.

Who knows how long Rachel sobbed against the bony chest, the protuberant belly. She might even have subsided into forbidden dreaming had she not thought to murmur, "Who are you."

"Cam Wilkes," he replied with surprise.

That woke her up.

"Cam, where have you been!?"

"Out west with Big Phil," Wilkes replied immediately. "I went along to help him set up PAGO WEST. We took the bus. He drove. All that space— such high clouds— I was sweating. It was like going outside for good. But Phil seemed to feel right at home. 'No blind spots', he kept saying. 'No hidden cover'. He was rapturous."

"But what about Jane!?"

"She's not home— I was just over there. Dick sicked Spot on me— and now this. What's going on?"

"Cam, why did you leave Jane?"

Wilkes bowed his head. Rachel had torn his shirt to the navel. The entire upper half of his body was soaked. "Dreams are general things, Rachel, anonymous and safe. But 'Real folks got warts', as the saying goes, 'and them warts got hairs'— How is she?"

But Rachel was already heading for Silver's phone, to reach Sally at the Millpond General. The switchboard put her on indefinite hold, and when she called back it cut her off. Trying again, she noticed poor Puff backed into the corner behind the Hewlett Packard, snarling and clawing at invisible enemies. When she looked around, Wilkes was gone. "Cam!"

Wilkes appeared from the corridor to the outside door.

"Where were you—" Rachel started to say as Sally came on the line. Then she told Sally the news.

"What's his excuse?" was Sally's initial question.

"Cold feet."

"They're all the same. And this one's the love of a lifetime."

"I know. But anyway."

"Yeah, right. Anyway. As soon as she's conscious again I'll break it gently. Does he have an official version?"

"Just a sec— Cam, what do you want Sally to tell Jane?"

"No no, let me—" He was reaching for the phone. At that same moment Puff ducked clear of her demons long enough to make the bolt of her life, towards the outside door. Both Wilkes and Rachel froze to watch her go. "I propped open the door," Wilkes explained. "Thought that poor cat might like to go out—"

"*Aw geez*—" and Rachel made a dash for the door, in time to see, at the threshold, like a cartoon cat, Puff stop dead— *eeeeerk!* Then walk out regally, twitching her tail. When Rachel got there Puff was nowhere in sight, unless that flash of ginger behind a warehouse two blocks away was her. Dammit.

Back at the phone Cam was saying into the receiver, "But Sally, I really would like to tell Jane myself—" As Rachel took the receiver out of his hand, he said, "Is that where Jane is, Rachel? At Sally's?"

"Not exactly— Uh, Sally? I think we'd better come by."

After she had hung up, Rachel sat Cam down on the edge of her bed and handed him her towel. Then she said, "Cam, you've been irresponsible. To Jane, and to me."

"To Jane, sure. You don't have to tell me. But to you, Rachel?" He had stopped towelling himself. "Why?"

"Cam, did you sell your bus yard to Mortprop Investments?"

He nodded. "Just before I left. The instant Jane accepted me I knew it was part of my past, a dead part. They made me a generous offer, and the thought that 8% of the cash amount would go to Leon, for all his trouble, seemed appropriate—"

"Cam, I don't think they bought it through Leon."

"Oh. They just said that, then, to win me over. I wondered why he wasn't there. Never mind, Rachel. I'll raise hell—"

"Who were you dealing with?"

"Rachel, don't worry! I've got the money. It's real! Jane and I will be able to live very nicely, thank you. No more scraping by on the ChemLawn inheritance—"

"Cam. I know how much they paid you. It isn't half what you told me they offered you six years ago."

"You're forgetting the condo. It's worth twice that."

"Condo?"

"Arcadia Centre's more than retail, remember. They gave us a condo in Arcadia Centre. Arcadia Centre, Rachel. Think of it. Stan has a vision—"

"Stan? Jardine?"

"The architect. He's also honorary head of PAGO International, though he's always been too modest to acknowledge the honour. All his work is agoraphobia-aware. Context-sensitive. Framing Not Disclaiming. Space for People, People for Space. Monolithism Go Home. These are his watchwords. He's very postmodern. He *understands*, Rachel. He's like one of us. He's done dozens of malls and public buildings all over the world. No architect has done more to combat the horrors of going out. It's not that the old compound-style malls are necessarily so bad, but there's never any doubt that you're *inside*. They're a little too much like home to be exactly therapeutic. The thing about steel and glazing, on the other hand, it's there and it's not there. Kind of an architectural white lie. Jardine allows us to pretend we're outside, and that really builds our morale. In fact, one eminent critic has called his work a 'decompression chamber to the literal outdoors'.

"It was funny. Sirocco took me to see 'the architect' for Arcadia Centre, to convince me to sell. (I was playing up my gut reluctance, to put the squeeze on him for his best price. But also I was expecting the usual kind of mall and a little depressed by that.) Well, you can imagine my amazement to find myself shaking hands with *the* Stanley Jardine. Of course, I happened to mention a few things about my PAGO work in the Millpond, and he seemed very pleased, in his gruff, understated way. If it wasn't for Stan Jardine I might have held on to my bus yard like a sentimental fool—"

"Sentimental dead fool."

Wilkes laughed happily. "But after talking to Stan I was ready to hand it over gratis— Just kidding. But tell me. How's Jane? Did she miss me?"

"Cam, I think I'd like to meet this Stanley Jardine sometime—"

"How about right now? Knowing, as I do, the particular psychic landscape of the Millpond, I've already offered my services as a consultant. Stan works on the principle that agoraphobiacs' problems are everybody's, writ large. Hell is other people. That line of thinking. Also, I sensed some friction with Sirocco, so I'm sure he'll welcome in-put from a sympathetic quarter." Wilkes consulted his watch. "Ten to five. He should still be in his office. He's working flat out to finish the plans."

"I promised Sally I wouldn't go to Mortprop today, Cam. Sirocco's after me—"

"To buy a condo?"

"I don't think so."

"Well anyway, Stan's not at Mortprop. He's got his own office in Village Market Square. When he's not in Paris. His own stretch limo and driver out back. I know you'll be as impressed with him as I was—"

Outside, to Rachel's joy, they found Puff curled magically asleep on the warm hood of the *ComputerGrafix* guy's car. Rachel lifted the dead-weight, whisker-twitching, paw-flexing creature and slipped it inside her jacket. "After we talk to Stan, we'll see Jane, right?" Wilkes asked anxiously as they waited for their cab.

"Right."

After a few minutes Cam said, "Rachel, are you all right? You look terrible."

"I know."

In Village Market Square a light shone from the Fred Hogg Dance Studio above Chez Pond, now closed for the day. Next to Chez Pond was Market Square Video, a blaze of light, and above that, the Tease 'n Please Hairstyling Salon, also in full swing. The office of Stanley A. Jardine, Architect, was on the third floor, along the hall from S. Thurm, Dental Surgeon, and down one floor from Alex Silver, Ph.D., Psychologist. So while Rachel had been talking to Silver about Harry, Stanley Jardine was eight feet below. Isn't life ironical?

The door said *Walk In.* They did. Darkness. Wilkes switched on a light. Shadowless cathode illumination. The receptionist's chair was empty. "Doesn't have one," Wilkes whispered, making elaborate tip-toe motions towards an inner door that stood ajar. Rachel's mental state had temporarily improved while she focussed on trying to drown Wilkes and subsequently on trying to grasp his story. But now that she was about to meet Stanley Jardine, shades of Strobe Brain were back to afflict her. So was a tickle of extrasensory terror that splayed out from her sphincter to oochie-koochie down the backs of her legs and up, up, up into the pit of her stomach and from there still upwards into her heart, throat, mouth (dried it right out), brain (emptied it . . .).

Holding tight to Puff, who was purring now, Rachel followed close behind Wilkes. Lightly— he was nervous— Wilkes knocked on the open door.

"Come in."

The office was dark except for the pool of lamplight on a drafting board.

"Stan?" Wilkes said, abashed.

The figure turned, pushing the lamp aside with a slow hand. "Turn on the goddam light—"

His face was shadowed. Wilkes touched the light switch, Rachel— hugging Puff— touched the water gun in her pocket. For an instant then she thought he had turned back to his work as if he would talk to them that way, like the inimitable Mr. X in an old serial, but as the fluorescence came on, she saw that he was placing his palms on that drafting board, elbows lifting, to swing round in his seat, and then she was looking at him.

Stanley Jardine lowered his body from the stool carefully, as if warily, and moved toward Wilkes and Rachel. He was wearing a giant cream-white jacket with sparse stripes and baggy cream-white pants. He had recognized Wilkes and now as he came closer he studied Rachel, who studied him right back, every stroboscopic flash. Under normal brain conditions Rachel would probably have been able to tell right away if this was the man from the jailhouse roof. As it was, the face from that photograph got recursively interleaved in fraction-of-a-second flashes with what she could only assume was the face of the man in front of her— with him and with all the other possible and impossible Harrys she had been stumbling into over the past few months . . . So it took a while. But it was him all right.

Wilkes, meanwhile, was failing to come through with introductions. And then Stanley Jardine was extending a thousand hands. Rachel looked down. *Hand*, make that. She reached for it, missed. Her jacket had fallen open, and now he saw Puff. Quickly, as if it were a bare breast, Rachel covered the creature. "She's asleep."

"A cat—"

Rachel remembered about him and cats. "You hate cats, don't you, Harry?" *Harry*? Did she say *Harry*?

Stanley Jardine just looked at her.

And then Wilkes was introducing them, stressing the *Stanley*, saying how interested Rachel was in hearing about Arcadia Centre. But first he himself had a question about the 8% from the sale of his bus yard that was supposed to have gone to Leon Boseman of Bi-Me Village Realty—

"Talk to Sirocco," Jardine said. "Sit down. I want you both out of here in ten minutes."

They sat in chrome chairs around the table where he ate his catered food. His heavy forearm bulldozed aside a week of card-board and aluminum foil. From Rachel's chair she could look out across the back lane into darkened backyards of colonial bunga-lows in brick and handsplit shingle as Stanley Jardine searched for something among the cardboard boxes, luggage, folders, and rolls of blueprints stacked along one wall. Photographs of his own, to show her? No. Bourbon. He set out three shot glasses and filled them. "Drink."

They drank.

"What do you want," Jardine said.

"Jane had a cat, too," Wilkes began conversationally. "Puff VI. I'm afraid she's missing."

"Will they build it the way you want it?" Rachel asked Stanley Jardine, her tongue lolling disastrously.

"If we find her we'll be needing chicken wire for the sofa legs," Wilkes said.

Jardine looked at Rachel. "You're a goddam reporter."

"Puff thinks she's a rake," Wilkes chuckled. "Not Rachel, Stan," he added. "She's just interested— Stan, could you tell us something about how you see Arcadia Centre in the postmodern world? As future tenants, Jane and I—"

Jardine turned to Rachel. "You're a future tenant too."

"No—"

"No inside stories. You can write on the place when it opens. Not before."

"I'm not a writer."

"So why are you here. Nobody takes a healthy interest in a complex that doesn't exist yet."

"I just tagged along with Cam. He's the fanatic."

"Where'd you find her, Wilkes? What is she? Your sister? A hooker? She's on the nod, for Christ's sake."

"Say, Stan," said Wilkes in a loud, bright voice, pretending he had not heard this. "I've been thinking. How about deer mice in Mill Court? You know— sneaking the grain? They're such cute little devils!" Wilkes turned to Rachel, explanatory. "Mill Court'll be one of the theme squares, so shoppers will know what sector they're in."

Jardine looked at Wilkes.

"That way, Stan," Wilkes continued, "Puff and the other condo cats could mouse."

"No mice," Jardine said.

"Prairie dogs?"

"What will Arcadia Centre be like, Harr-*uh*—?" Rachel jerking out of a doze.

"Flying squirrels might be a big draw," Wilkes suggested, "or— bats! Swooping around the gaslights in the Victorian Arcade!"

Stanley Jardine stood up. "You people should level with me."

"Cam," Rachel said. "Would you mind giving me a minute with— Mr. Jardine?"

Surprised, Wilkes went to find them a cab.

Stanley Jardine sat back down and poured a drink for Rachel and himself.

Rachel continued to stroke Puff inside her jacket, probably wearing a bald spot on the little skull.

"Drink," said Stanley Jardine.

They drank. Rachel's eyes watered. She lifted out Puff and placed her on the floor beside her chair. "Lorna Gillese," she said. This was her mother's maiden name.

Stanley Jardine's face showed no change of expression, only of identity, maybe two hundred a second. The one that recurred most often looked as though somebody had taken their thumb and— A pause of two, maybe three decades, during which his eyes remained on his glass. "You're on junk."

"No—!"

"What do you want?"

"Nothing," fingering her water gun. "See you." She swallowed.

They both had their forearms on the table and their glass cupped in their fingers.

"She need money?"

"No. Maybe. I don't know."

"You need money."

"*No.*"

"What do you want?"

I want Harry, you monster, and if I can't have Harry I want him cancelled, and I want the cancellation retroactive from this fucking second.

"Listen to me," said Stanley Jardine. "I'm an architect. I design buildings. I know two kinds of people. The ones who help me. The ones who try to stop me. Everybody else is the public."

"Makes me the public."

"You don't know how lucky you are."

"And Lorna Gillese?"

"Tried to stop me."

"By being Lorna Gillese."

Stanley Jardine stood up. "If you or her need money, talk to my lawyers."

Rachel also stood up. Un-dream-deprived, she was the last person not to go peacefully. Dream-deprived, she said, "You're my father. This isn't good enough."

"Get out of here."

He said it with weariness, the way at the end of a trying day you would say it to a foolish dog who is happy to see you and wants to play. Already he was moving back to his drafting board, Rachel following helplessly. What for?

"Rachel?" The voice of Cam Wilkes, doggy to Rachel's ear. "I got us a cab—" He was pulling her arm.

"Let go, Cam— give me a minute—"

"Rachel, I think Mr. Jardine wants to get back to work—"

"I'll be right down—"

"Nick Sirocco's on his way up— If you'd rather not—"

Rachel snatched up the comatose Puff and took a last look toward Stanley Jardine at his drafting board.

"Shop there," he said, not turning. "Spend time. It's a way of life. It'll help you."

In the cab Rachel said, "Millpond General," and Wilkes cried, "Rachel! Are you all right?"

She told him about Jane. This information left Cam even more shaken and trembling than herself. When they arrived at the hospital she told the cabby to hold on, then helped Wilkes into the Emergency waiting area, where Sally said,

"You're an asshole, Cam Wilkes."

"I know. I'll never leave her again."

"She's awake," Sally told Rachel. "I can take him in. You go home and sleep. Did you find him yet?"

"Ask me when I've slept on it— Cam? Give Jane this?" In his arms she placed the unconscious Puff. "And this—?" The water gun.

"Hey Rachel. Remember what I told you." Sally aimed an imaginary buffalo gun at the ceiling. Squeezed the trigger. Absorbed the recoil.

Rachel nodded. Mumbled, "Thanks but— use my bare brains—"

"Your bare what?"

"Umm—" losing it. Really need to thleep— sink— theep— slink— What brains?

Outside, slumped in the back of the cab, she told the cabby, a sweet-faced balding woman, to drive around. And then Sally was knocking on the window. "Can I come too?"

"Where?"

"Small drink at the Reservoir?"

Another gap, and they were pulling up at the lights of the Olde Mill. Rachel looked at her watch. Could not make out the time. The Reservoir Bar was upstairs, but as they passed The Buhrstone, Rachel happened to glance in, and there, at a small table moving along the old mill mural, his back to her, was Harry.

Rachel recognized him right away. Something about a thickness through the head and shoulders, the nondescript hair, the posture. Something inevitable about the posture—

"How about down here—" she said to Sally.

"Wouldn't we have to eat—?"

"There's somebody I—"

Sally was gone. Just disappeared.

Rachel should have been able to see his face by now, the floor had come around. But he must have switched chairs, it was the back of his head she was still getting. Anyway, she knew. If this was to be one of those moments of surprise disappointment— the person turns, and it is as if your old friend has had the most *radical* surgery— Rachel would be very . . . surprised.

Next she was sitting down across the table from him, had

ordered cattail crepes— *cattail crepes?* at *The Buhrstone?*— struggling to see him and not succeeding. There was too much smoke in here, or too much glare from the lamp over the table, which was too low, too bright. It was like a dream, the way her eyes would refuse to focus properly, or even to open, as if the lids had been Crazy Glue'd, like when her brain did not have the dreampower to come up with the information it needed to show her what the dreamscript was calling for next . . .

Oblivious to Rachel or her problem, Harry was already talking, a singer with earphones on, Martian and strange, no human ear to correct the sound. So Rachel's mad brain pitched right in to knead and shape the flow into some kind of recognizable pattern, redeem it— failed— meanwhile struggling to do everything she could against that glare-, that smoke-, that blindspot, to pry open her eyes, her stuck lids— failed.

Had time passed? Suddenly she was startled as a dozer is startled by the sudden scrape of his chair— He was getting to his feet! Here Babs— *Babs*!?— was coming with their cappuccinos, and Harry was standing up and just walking away!

"Hey, hey, wait a minute! Hey! Babs is—" Rachel stumbling after him down a staff hallway past the kitchen and out the back door, pop cases piled high, dark shadows against the white wall under incandescent lane lights, fresh paving, a sheet of newspaper floating by, a litre carton of half and half, end over end in slow motion, and Rachel is following him through a gate cut in Permawood into a backyard of perfect grass now luminous in moonlight, scattered with boards and these have been kicked aside to leave slats of yellow.

The boardwalk has finished. The fences are fresh-built and high, there are stars out tonight, diamonds the size of fists, a hubcap moon, he is walking down the dark grass to the water where hired swans swim whitely back and forth along the shore, occasionally beaking in under their feathers. Little waves lap like tongues at a margin of crushed stones. *Now, there's a big swan* ! but no, it is only the white splash that Harry has made, delayed.

"Harry!" Rachel is squatting on the grass bank to stare across the black water, hearing the steady spill of the waterwheel, waiting for him to surface. It is not such a big pond, the millpond. A storm sewer, basically. Still . . . night breezes and cat's-paws dance and play across it. There's lots of time for a look at the stars. Except that the Olde Mill lights, the pansy garden floodlights, and the streetlights that ring the pond have made a sort of low white ceiling that the fine dark promise of the water can't penetrate. He will break the surface and shout to her in the breathless happy way that swimmers have. He will tell her it's not so bad once you get in. How long does she wait? A white rabbit almost slams into her chest, veers. This pond. Had some livestock watering hole, hooves squelching grey muck, been the inspiration for this unconvincing body of water that was no millpond because there was no millstream and because that was not a mill? It did not matter to anybody. Harry does not surface, does not shout. She puts her hand in the water. Liquid ice. She puts her hand on his clothes. They are shadow. She stands up, looks again to the surface of the water.

And that must be when it happens. The surface is jet glass. There is a kind of roiling, and a glimpse of something rising like a glimpse in a green-black mirror with the angle wrong. Already its red eyes are on her. The surface explodes white. The creature bursts high into the air, straining to breathe, white-faced, those eyes on Rachel.

It swims to the bank and climbs out, its fingers strong and cold on Rachel's forearm.

It is Rachel herself.

"Come on. Want to show you something—"

But Rachel is scared, resisting. Gone whiny. "It's *free*-zing—"

"Forget that. Move," and pulls her immediately into the icy water.

Pulls her down and down, for a long time. Rachel's problem is not the cold, or breathing, it is keeping her eyes open. She really should not be napping, she knows, ought to wake herself up right now, what will Harry think, if she really must sleep should at least first make it back to the Dream Centre . . .

There is nothing down here except darkness. Murk. Jade night. Brown fingerlings. Garbage in bags.

"Look!"

"What?"

"*Look!*"

There he is, on the bottom. A felt hat, striped tie, dark suit (rolled newspaper in the pocket), oxfords. Grey eyes. Square jaw. Just standing around. Watching the weeds sway. Picking his teeth with a double fishhook. Stirring up mudclouds. Leaning on a rock.

Snatching fish with a surprisingly quick hand, letting them go.

"It's him," Rachel whispers.

"It's him all right," the other replies.

And now he has seen them, and his eyes beam directly at Rachel, flood her with presence.

"How do you feel?" the other asks.

"Absolute," Rachel breathes.

"You mean like *absolved*?"

"Uh-huh. Un—unqualified."

"That's what I thought. Let's check it out."

The grip on her wrist tightens. They move closer, fast.

"Where are we going?"

"*In.*"

Turns out Harry is farther away than Rachel first figured, consequently bigger. Fifteen, maybe twenty storeys. That double fishhook is a half-ton anchor. Strangely, however, up close, gaps and fissures yawn in his movements. It's a lot like Rachel's old Strobe Brain problem, with the difference that the strobe seems to be Harry himself.

They are getting awfully close.

"You take the left, I'll take the right—" She means *eye*.

"What—?"

"Aim for the *pupil-ll*!"

Now, if Harry were a literal giant hanging around on the millpond bottom, next would come the dual splat into vitreous jelly. But here the issue is not flesh and bone, is it, and eye parts resolve into Muzak and Night. Oh, and Falling. Eye- and mouthlight above, fast diminishing. Darkness below. There is nothing to stop them. Like Alice doubled, Rachel falls. The other has grabbed her again, tenacious, got her in a headlock, actually. Either Harry is deep or they are falling slowly.

Soon the darkness pales. There are four surfaces. One is earth-hued terrazzo; opposite is dun acoustic, occasional circles of sunken light.

"Where are we?"

"What exactly does it look like?"

The third and fourth walls are composed of, hmm, a bank, a shoe repair, a doctor's office, an income tax place, a locksmith, a laundromat, a cinema. These are all on end.

In a flash three surfaces balloon to glass— clouds in a blue sky beyond— and contoured stucco. Familiar shop names. Behind them that terrazzo has spread out. It is littered with dead bees. People at right angles walk the terrazzo, defying gravity. The effect is of sudden, skylit space, an illuminated bubble, with people to shuffle the vertical. Curved soffits. Potted vegetation. Kiosks and kiosks: knick-knack, magazine, candy bar and gum. Rachel's eyes are on a K-Mart, open on the mall: three levels of retail colour stood on end, like a stretch triptych. Behind them a tunnel goes off horizontal, lined top and bottom with shops. Twisting in her headlock, she glimpses a shoe store, a video place, a stereo store, another shoe store— Promise of more light down that way.

Still falling, they enter a second passage, wider and brighter than the first. This has light cutting sideways. Falling is now made problematic by potted trees. They are nearly creamed by a eucalyptus. Rachel is anxious.

Flanking walls stagger in and out. Split vertical to create an up-ended mezzanine. Fuse.

They continue to fall. They pass through a fountain, are slapped by exotic plants.

Another, dimmer passage goes by, carved horizontal—a book-store; a shoe store; a cigar store; a nuthouse; a card store that sells scented candles, scented pens, pens shaped like strawberry ice cream cones, lollipops, penises; another shoe store—

And then it happens.

"Look!"

All four surfaces zoom outwards, on one side split to steel webbed with translucent sheeting. On the other, terrazzo goes mesa-ing to benches, fountains, distant trees, a skating rink, an amphitheatre containing a symphony orchestra playing light classical arrangements of *Harry's Theme*— Perfect sunlight slants in past three floors, on end, of exotic and name shops of every description; past bridging ramps; past escalators and stairs; glazed wall-climber elevators. It illuminates generous planting, hot air balloons moving horizontal on giant blower nozzles, a free-standing brightly coloured space-frame parasol structure containing impressionistic sculpture. It shines on horizontal dancers performing Balanchine ballets, horizontal mimes doing Man in Telephone Booth, horizontal actors enacting scenes from *Death of a Salesman*. It also shines on daycares, live sharks in brass-trimmed tanks, small horizontal crowds gathered around kitchen gadget demonstrations, horizontal clean-cut kids with razors on sticks scraping up gum—

Quick as they ballooned the walls collapse inwards. Terrazzo in pastels. More travertine. Oblique shops fronts. Lesser names.

Rachel's double looks around, releases Rachel's head, pushes her to arm's length. "This is goodbye—"

"Where are you going!?"

"To sleep."

"But you can't do that! You'll spoil the whole experiment!"

"Experiment's finished. We saw him. We went in through the eyes. What else do you want."

Dream at this point becomes a little confused. Rachel has reached out to prevent her less tractable self from spoiling the experiment, grasps air— Shudders.

A slight snore.

Huh?

Bumpff, and she is passing through a double set of glass doors, a small exit through a sloping dome wall, near where a line of delivery trucks waits for access to an unloading bay; passes into a parking lot overlooked by high lamps and flags and logos on pylons and a blue sky full of coloured balloons; skims the tops of the cars parked there. Seconds later also skims the tops of the cars passing on Highway 303. After that it is mostly small towns and countryside: farmland, forest— skimming pine trees— rock, scrub, and pretty soon Rachel is cruising over slate-grey seas in the white land where the sun has slowed to a crawl and the icefloes pitch and bark.

Meanwhile the other sleeps and dreams that she gets a job in one of the dozen shoe stores in the mall here. The smell of new leather is what brings her around. As her head jerks up, a customer enters wearing a beige suit and loafers. He is a handsome, greying fellow of distinction. A man whose judgments have been fully endorsed by success. A man who knows exactly who he is, what he wants, and how to get it. His motto: *I see, I take.* In this case a pair of shoes. Briefly his eyes pause at a spot slightly over Rachel's head as if a signboard there reads *Clerk (female),* then continue to scan the store. Perhaps he wants the store.

Rachel's eyes follow the pink razor edge of his haircut, the way it traces his ear. She is fascinated to see the skin there so pink and smooth against the fine grey hairs and to see it bulging a little at the collar, which is too tight, and she wonders what a slip of a straight razor could accomplish along there. She appraises the confidence emanating from his upper body: the upward square of the jaw, the element of preen in the pivot of the torso, the way he keeps his elbows in tight to his body as if one false move and his arms could fall off. She notices his heavy right hand, the clean square nails. The other is in his pocket, rattling change. She also notices that he is built on a larger scale than herself. Harry is not just thick he is tall. Finally her eyes rest on those loafers. They are very, very brown.

She indicates a seat. He tugs his pants at the knees and sits down, still looking to his left and right. His pants have cuffs.

"What's your size?" Rachel wants to know.

"Twelve and a half, thirteen."

Rachel mutters something in reply to this. It sounds like, "Why don't you just strap on gangplanks."

"What was that?"

She is eyeing his foot sceptically. "Better slip these off."

She straddles the footstool and reaches for one of those metal foot-measuring devices that cup the ball of the foot with a sliding metal bracket.

He has taken off his right shoe.

"Left," Rachel says, fanning a hand in front of her face as if something smells very bad. "An animal die in here?" she mutters, looking around.

"What did you say?"

"Left foot's bigger. Left shoe off."

"It's not bigger."

"Just take your left shoe off."

She measures his left foot, shakes her head—"Weirdest goddam feet I ever saw"— and disappears into the back. As if he suspects he has not heard right, he watches her go. She returns with numerous grey boxes. Straddles the stool.

"OK. Most people have normal feet, if you know what I mean. This is a shoestore, not some orthopedic clinic. Anyway, you're in luck."

The shoe is a brogue.

"The holes go all the way through," Harry says, looking down.

"Holes that don't are imitations. Haven't you ever heard the old Gaelic expression 'Fishy as a brogue has holes'?"

"I want to see something else."

The next is a normal oxford style but completely transparent. Harry glances down, sees his sock foot, assumes the shoe is not yet on.

Rachel tugs his pantleg. "So what do you say. You won't know you're wearing it. Neither will anybody else. Visually very striking, especially without socks."

"I always wear socks."

"What do you do, wring them out at lunchtime?"

"Pardon?"

"*Pièce de résistance.*" She removes the clear shoes and slips giant rubber feet over his socks. Cinches and fastens them tight.

Harry looks down, incredulous.

Rachel backs away. "Before you say anything, walk over to the mirror. Footwear always looks strange from above."

Harry stands, knocking over the footstool. He lumbers to the mirror, where the feet look even bigger. "I can't wear these," he says.

"You're wearing them," Rachel replies.

Two kids run over and start jumping up and down on them as if they are inflatable furniture.

"Take them off!" Harry shouts at Rachel.

"Off? You haven't tried the boots!" Rachel wrestles the lid from a box the size of a small crypt. Inside are strange, giant boots in blue patent leather with pointed toes and enormous silver buckles. "Fabulous," she murmurs. "With these babies and a little practice you'll be kicking the eyes out of boa constrictors."

"I'm not wearing these," Harry says.

"Hold your horses. I just got them out of the box."

"Take them off." He is feeling for the ankle strap.

"What are we talking about? The feet or the boots?"

"The feet!"

"We've done the feet. There is no point at all doing the feet unless we also do the boots. Even if you never wear them. Just *trying them on* you'll be miles ahead of quitting now. Wouldn't want to be a quitter. Nobody'd like you. There." She has got the big silver buckles done up. "How do they feel? Comfortable?"

"Comfort is not the point, is it?"

"Believe me. Comfort, in shoes, is always the point. And don't try to tell me they're not fashionable after coming in here wearing these things." She lifts a loafer between thumb and forefinger as if it is a turd.

"Loafers are classic!"

"Not as classic as togas."

This dream goes on for quite a while. Some time towards the end of it, Harry may be seen paying a fortune for the rubber feet and buckled boots and leaving the store a satisfied customer.

Rachel smiles.

Harry had second thoughts, but they were too late. Already Rachel was waking at the Dream Centre with her head wired and Alex Silver pumping her hand.

"Congratulations," Silver said. "Twelve hours straight sleep at 58% REM. Must be some kind of a world record for humans. Puff's got you beat in the mammalian class, though: 63%. And cats aren't big dreamers."

"Sorry, Alex—"

"Hey, you had to stop— start— sometime. Babs and Frankie didn't even bother to sign back in. How are you feeling?"

"Groggy— How'd I—"

"Sally. You were dead weight. So was Puff. By the way, you find Harry?"

"You bet—" Rachel already rolling over and on her way back to sleep.

When she awoke again Silver was there to give her a phone message from Leon, to call home. Beaming in a manic kind of way, he took her hands in his. "He came to see me, Rachel!"

"Harry!?"

"Not Harry. Leon. I had a cancellation. He just walked in!" Silver whacked his forehead. "Whew!" He laughed happily. "Surprised? Was I surprised?"

"I can imagine. Did you talk about old times?"

"*I* sure did. But you know—" Silver went pensive. "Leon was very quiet. That surprised me. It was almost as if he was shy with me, as if—I don't know. I just didn't expect him to be so—reserved, or something. Rachel, try to understand. Back at Willmott High your husband was easily the coolest guy in the universe! He was, like, Sal Mineo and George Maharis rolled into one, if those names mean anything to you. He was my idol for— Who am I kidding.

He's still my idol." Silver came forward to grip the edge of Rachel's mattress with feverish intensity. "Please don't tell him I told you. And Rachel? Did I mention he wants you to call home? I did? When you see him, maybe you could, you know, find out what it was like for him. I mean, that we could talk like that—"

"I'll try, Alex." Rachel washed her face and went to the phone to call Leon while Alex Silver bounced on his bed like a kid too excited to sleep.

But first she called her mother.

"Hi, it's me."

"Why? What's the matter? Whozits show up?"

"Yup, everything's great. I thought you might be worried about me, so I'm calling. You're OK?"

"Why should I be worried about you? You were better off. Where was he?"

"Staying with a friend. How's Elmer doing?"

"What sex?"

"Male."

"Get him tested. Elmer's fine. Did I tell you he found your father? The bastard's designing some big mall out near you. I was right. He's worth millions. I couldn't care less. We're getting married."

"*Who?*"

"Me and Elmer. Who do you think?"

"Why?"

"Listen, if you can marry Leon Boseman I can marry Goofy."

"But what about—"

"Your father? I don't know. The hunt was all. Once we closed in for the kill I lost interest. Who needs money when you've got love. Elmer's sweet. It's like a baseball bat. You can come to the wedding. This could be the last time you see me. We're moving to Florida."

Rachel hung up feeling so calm. She called Leon.

"Rachel? It's me, Leon—"

"I know. My mother's marrying Elmer."

"Is that right. Guess what I did today. I found Alex Silver in the phone book. I didn't feel like calling, so I went over. His mother was there. She told me she doesn't work in his office on the day they tape *Share That Dream*. I told her how in high school what a big admirer I was of her son. She said he had no admirers. We talked about the good old days. Hers were all in Poland. To get rid of me, she called Alex at his office. He had a cancellation. I drove over."

"So? You drove over—?"

"I don't know. I guess in the back of my mind I was trying to make a connection. Or check out an old one. He's always been kind of a touchstone for me. Maybe 'touchstone' isn't exactly the word ... Anyway, he kept saying how wonderful it was to see me and how well he remembered me and how much he used to admire me—"

"Oh Leon. That must have been so gratifying for you—"

"Gratifying? Are you serious? What a sleazebag! I was nobody, Rachel! Who's he trying to kid? This guy I admired so much has turned into just another one of these I'm-OK-You-Think-You're-Not-But-I-Know-Better types that people go to to be told they're God's answer to all their own stupid problems. To think I ever admired a guy who'd become a shameless opportunist like that. The creep came on so strong with all these sentimental Willmott High memories, I just went quiet. I think he must have assumed I was so impressed to see him again I was speechless. I was impressed all right. By what an asshole he is. But not for long. Suddenly he's got his hand on my elbow and he's quick-marching me to the door!"

"He probably had a client waiting—"

"So? She could wait five minutes, couldn't she? I admit she looked depressed, but I didn't see any razor blade at her wrist."

"Leon, I'm sure Alex really was happy to see you. You probably were a big deal at Willmott High. You can't blame him for his personality."

"Rachel, what are you saying? We're talking about a guy who wears glasses with bright red frames! I'm amazed he didn't charge for the visit! There's probably a bill in the mail!"

"Leon, is this what you wanted to tell me? How disappointed you were in Alex Silver?"

"No. Listen. I think we should talk."

"OK. Let's have breakfast."

"Breakfast? What kind of life are you living? It's five o'clock!"

"In the afternoon?"

"Geez—"

"Is there any food in the house?"

"Somebody cleaned us out. You have company or something?

It's depressing here. I'll meet you at The Buhrstone in half an hour."

As Rachel hung up, Alex Silver came back into the room frantic. When he saw Rachel he started to rave. "I just figured out why Leon was so quiet! Oh, what a fool I was! So thrilled to see him I never dreamt!"

"Dreamt what, Alex?"

"That he came to me for *help*! He did, didn't he? Oh God, the quiet one should have been me— What a fool—"

"Alex, sit down."

Something authoritative in Rachel's tone, probably. Immediately Silver sat on the edge of her bed. But when Rachel then folded her arms and studied him, he jumped up and crossed to the nearest wall. There he leaned his entire weight against his forehead.

"Alex," Rachel said. "One question. Have you been dream-depriving yourself too?"

Silver pushed off from the wall and turned. Rachel's question might have been an icepick stuck between his eyes. He blinked repeatedly. Then he said, "What is it? What are you going to say?"

"Sit down."

Silver did this.

I just talked to Leon," Rachel told him. "His impressions seeing you again weren't exactly— favourable."

"Oh," crestfallen. "Anyways, I can take it. You people are all hopeless neurotics. I can discount anything you say."

"Alex, what about my question."

"I'm fine, fine. Talk! Talk!"

Rachel talked. Told him exactly what Leon had said. Pulled no punches. When she had finished there was a brief silence, and then Alex, head bowed, said, "I can't believe Leon would say those things about me. What kind of an idol is that to have?"

"But Alex. People always say harder things about other people than other people can ever imagine. As a therapist you must understand that. And the only reason you found out at all in this case is I think it might help you. Under normal circumstances—"

"But Rachel," turning. "It's all true! Not in any absolute sense, but what is? From a recognizable, not-totally-off-the-wall point of view, I am a shameless opportunist! Who else would conceive and host a show like *Share That Dream*? Look what I've been doing to Puff! Leon, in his wisdom, has put his foot, I mean thumb—"

"You are dream-deprived, aren't you Alex. Why?"

"To find Leon of course." Silver seemed amazed to need to say this. And then he was moving again. "But *I'm* not important right now. What is— The bond between me and Leon, like Double Bubble, it'll stretch to a filament, but it'll never—"

Here Rachel lunged, caught Silver's shirtfront in both hands, and lifted him clear off the ground. "Alex Silver," she shouted at his face, "when you make three women and a cat crazy, somebody has to be in charge!"

She lowered him then, and Silver stood blinking. "OK, I nominate you—"

"Elected!" She grabbed him and threw him onto the bed so violently his glasses few off. Whimpering, "What are you going to—" he bounced a few times then tried to scramble away.

"*Get comfortable!*" Rachel screamed, throwing him back down. He eyed her in terror.

"*Now! And close your eyes!*"

"You won't hurt me—?"

"*Close those fuckers!*"

Silver did so.

"I said, *Get comfortable!*"

"Like this?" Silver made buttock-shifting settling-in movements. "Now what?" he wondered, yawning.

"Fold your hands across your stomach."

"You won't stab me?"

"I won't stab you."

"Like this—?"

"Uh-huh. How do you feel?"

"Terrific. Widescreen eyelid feature. *Willmott High Days*—"

By the time Rachel had got the electrodes attached to Silver's head, he was snoring gently.

The Buhrstone was spinning as ever, the miller and his sad family looking down, the Muzak playing. Leon was sitting where Harry had, but he wasn't him. The waitress was snapping a fresh checked tablecloth. It billowed and floated down. Leon was haggard, smoking, like a man who has been an increasingly reluctant participant in morale-sapping acts. Rachel noted there were now filters on his cigarettes.

"Where have you been all week?" he demanded when she sat down. "You're a wreck."

"I'm also starving." Soon she was tucking into a four-egg sour cream omelet with capers and red peppers, three toasted bagels with bacon on the side.

"Have you been eating like this all week?" Leon asked when she ordered cream cheese and more bagels.

She nodded.

"You haven't gained any weight. This could mean a tapeworm. I'm serious."

She told him about the Dream Centre.

"Maybe we could sue—" Leon suggested, half-hearted.

"Why?"

He shrugged. "Anyway, no use beating around the bush. We've both had our fun, and now I want you back."

"But you were the one—"

"Listen. I've decided you're right. Real estate is not it. A person like me needs to be doing something one hundred percent creative at all times. Otherwise I get too restless. I've decided to go back to writing. And I know what my first book is going to be. Hell, I've even mapped out the chapters. Are you ready? *The Cosmic Game of Real Estate*."

"Leon—"

"Not just another handbook. Not just the usual con-man tips. Genuine inner stuff to make people feel good about selling houses and therefore do it much more effectively. Here are some possible chapter titles: 'The Zen of Timing'. 'How to Package and Sell Positive Emotion'. 'Interiorizing the Interior'—"

"Leon—"

"Of course, once I got the 'Cosmic Game' format down, I could do it for anything. I'm thinking of money here, Rachel, you'll be happy to know. Bestsellers. A string of bestsellers. Culminating in *The Cosmic Game of Writing Bestsellers*. Why not?"

"Leon, I think—"

"But you know what this will be a stepping stone to? A publishing house called True Books that will only publish books that are completely clear, completely objective, and completely true. No biases, no axes to grind, no soapboxing, no hidden agendas, no warring schools, no fancy writing, no artificial word limits. Just the truth. Period. No more of this relativity-uncertainty stuff. It's a fad anyway. People are fed up with quarks. They want something they can get their teeth into. And where there's an unsatisfied need, that's where the ones with vision make their fortune. I've been thinking I'll call it Limpid House. 'Books for folks who only mess with the truth'."

"Leon, first things first—"

"I know. I'm just as sick of the Millpond as you are. 201 Dell is driving me crazy. What I wouldn't do for a proper rec room like a normal homeowner. Instead I'm bouncing between that freezing rat hole of a den and that living room. By the way. This morning I figured out what's wrong with our living room. It's only got light at one end, those French doors! We're hemmed in! If we could just smash a hole in that useless long blank wall—"

"Leon, we live in a townhouse. We'd be into the Barringers' living room."

"That's what I'm saying— I wish we had the kind of living room that nobody used. You know, a real showcase. That's a kind of lifestyle that despite all our education, despite the fact that we've been out in the work force almost twenty years, despite our high critical intelligence, we're not even close to. I'm saying I'm ready for a major push. Right over the top. Make it or destroy ourselves trying. That's how I'm feeling right now—"

"Leon, could you shut up for a minute, please?"

"What?"

"I don't want to live with you any more. Anywhere."

Briefly Leon resembled a man who has just received an unexpected jab to the nose. He blanched. Next his mouth twisted for sarcasm, but it quivered out of shape. "It's Sirocco, isn't it," he said, breathing with difficulty. "Now that Wilkes is taken. I wasn't born yesterday."

"Leon, I found Harry."

"*Harry*? Don't tell me you're still on Harry—Rachel, listen. This is Leon you're finding right here, and he loves you better than he loves anybody!"

"Then it shouldn't take him a week shacked up with Gretchen Molstad to realize it."

"But what if it did take something like that? And a lot of hard thought in between?"

"In between what?"

"Give me a break."

"You're a good talker, Leon. You don't need love, you need to be heard. Don't you realize how many starving ears there are out there?"

Here, on the subject of ears, an interesting thing happened. Over The Buhrstone sound system were coming the strains of a familiar tune.

"*Leon!*"

"What."

"Listen! That's the *Melody for the Girl on My Bus*! No—It's a little different. Hear it? This goes da-da-*da*-da— The *Melody* goes—"

"So you don't love me."

"*Now* I know where we heard it! In our bedroom our first spring in the Millpond, when we used to leave the windows open and make love all night— Remember how we'd hear the Olde Mill music on the night breezes? It was our song!" Rachel was sobbing.

"What's the matter with you," Leon said.

Here the waitress, a woman with an expression that was equal parts jaded and sympathetic, came by.

"Excuse me," said Rachel, blowing her nose on a serviette. "This is really, really important. Do you know what that tune is?"

"*This* tune?" The waitress listened. "Nope. More coffee here?"

"So you're telling me you don't love me," Leon said.

The waitress looked at him. "Yup. More coffee." She filled their cups and went away.

Rachel and Leon sat and talked for another hour, Leon pushing for the limpid truth and behaving in a hurt and hostile way when he got it. For Rachel a Buhrstone hour under even the most benign circumstances was an eternity; she was getting dizzy. When Leon had finally worked himself into a rage and stormed out, she sat for a few minutes, then stood up, gripping the table.

The waitress came over. "You told him you don't love him."

Rachel nodded.

"That's a hard one," the waitress said. "Especially when they leave you the bill. Tell you what. It's on the house." She held out a piece of paper with numbers on it. "You said it was important, so I asked the manager. He says call Muzak. This here is their number," pointing. "This here's the time it came on—"

At a phone by the front doors of the Olde Mill, Rachel called Muzak, asked about that tune. The man went away to his program schedule and came back. "It's a traditional, called *I Climbed the Rocky Mountains (But I Can't Get Over You)*."

"Oh really? Thanks—"

"Thank *you*. We try real hard here at Muzak, and it's nice to know somebody out there is actually listening."

EPILOGUE

A little more than three years later, on one of those raw spring days that provoke nostalgia for the soft snows of February, Rachel Jardine, formerly Boseman, her baby-sitter sick, took a day off work and with one travelling companion, her daughter Clare Elizabeth, aged three months, made her first excursion to the newly opened Arcadia Centre, in order to visit her friends Cam and Jane Wilkes in their condominium home. Clare's father John, a lecturer in Geography, was working that day and anyway, though curious as most people about Arcadia Centre, had a horror of the suburbs.

It was the structure itself, breaking the horizon just south of the 303, like a harvest moon ribbed silver, that told Rachel long before the overhead signs that Exit 37 was the one she wanted. And even after all she had read and heard, she was impressed. It was not the usual brick compound but a sort of grand Victorian arcade in the round. An intricately arched dome of steel and retractable plastic. A bowl inverted upon a wheel with a green hub, eight broad shopping-street spokes, and a three-storey rim of retail and condo development. Like a covered baseball stadium with a park instead of a field. Shops and condos instead of stands.

Got to hand it to you, Stanley.

As these things go . . .

Clare Elizabeth appreciated the PeopleMover, the gondola-type monorail that carried them from their underground parking level to the Centre itself, and on, if they had wanted, all the way to the Olde Mill. Rachel liked the spacious sunniness of the place, the

way her eye kept being drawn to the green of the park, the way
when she happened to push Clare's stroller up one of those spokes
it ended just like that and the heavy greenery and the white and
yellow and crimson blooming began.

She knelt to loosen Clare's clothes . . .

"Rachel! Rachel!"

Rachel raised her eyes from Clare's face. High above her, above
the highest level of shops, were condominiums where white
shutterlike windows stood open on the scene below. From one of
these windows two distant, tiny people were leaning out, side by
side, a middle-aged couple with pale hair. Waving. Calling. In
mouse voices.

"Rachel! Rachel! Welcome to Arcadia Centre! Welcome!"

Rachel and Clare had a genteel tea with the Wilkeses in their
new home. Cam wore a blue blazer with buttons that rattled
tinnily, grey flannels, and sheepskin slippers. Jane wore a cream
rayon crepe blouse and pink slacks. She had the plastic off the
furniture by the time Rachel and Clare arrived at the door. Selected
bus parts remained polythene-draped in a sort of viewing area off
the front hall. There was chicken wire stapled to the legs of the
chesterfield. Puff VI lay orange and dozing under the dining room
table. The condo, which was large and airy, had the neat, sanitized
look upon it of Jane's small hand. In addition were occasional
Wilkesian touches, such as those bus parts, his trumpet and music
stand, a framed letter of thanks for his role in bringing Arcadia
Centre into the life of PAGO (now a loose-knit bunch who called
themselves The Mall Rats), and an extensive collection of the Dick
and Jane readers— the fruits of his recent hobby: attending Board
of Education used textbook sales. "See how in the fifties the clarity
of the line goes, Rachel? See how vague and blurred Jane looks in
1951 compared to 1940? See how she's been redone, exactly the
same pose and story but softer? What on earth do you think it
means? Do you think it might have something to do with World
War II?"

For a long while they stood at the glassless window looking out
over the green glory of Arcadia Centre as Puff VI rubbed purring
against Rachel's leg and Cam spoke sadly of the tragic death of
Stanley Jardine just as construction was nearing completion. Rachel
had noticed a small item in the newspaper about an unspecified

accident. She had sighed and gone to warm Clare's Pablum. According to Cam, who had hung around Arcadia Centre throughout construction and was acquainted with many of the workers on a first-name basis, there was said to be a body in cement somewhere under the marble of Xanadu Place, a spoke in the northwest sector.

"It's the kind of accident a hard hat is no protection against," Cam commented.

"So's a push from behind."

He nodded sadly. "The Mall Rats are having a tile engraved over the approximate spot. The sort of thing you see in Westminster Abbey. We owe him everything."

They stepped away from the window, and the rest of the visit passed mostly with the Wilkeses, proud godparents, fussing over little Clare. The TV remained on. Curious, Rachel studied the Wilkeses carefully and decided that they were exactly as happy as they appeared to be. Cam's salacious doting, though tedious to the observer, did not seem to bother Jane at all. Rachel managed these observations shortly before she, like Clare, fell into a profound sleep while Cam was showing his new ordering of re-developed slides from the ninety-day bus tour the Wilkeses had won two years earlier on *Share That Dream*— "And here's an amusing one of Jane in front of that remarkable gift shop shaped exactly like an oven mitt—"

Jane: "Tea cosy."

"— just outside of, um—"

Jane: "Akron."

"Rachel? *Rachel?*"

The bi-weekly taping of *Share That Dream* had continued to be a highpoint in the life of the Wilkeses. This Friday, for example, Cam was going as a bus driver and Jane as a windshield wiper. Once they had even taken Dick, who went in shorts and high-lace sneakers and won a car polishing kit with a real chamois. He wept, remembering Father. Both Cam and Jane agreed that the show had lost something since the departure of Alex Silver and his mother, now in L.A.

About Dick the Wilkeses were in mild disagreement. Cam maintained that he had not changed at all, Jane that he had mellowed. They checked on him daily to make sure he had not stepped on a rake or brained himself with a window sash.

"Cam," said Rachel, tearing her eyes from the TV. "Do you ever see Leon around?"

"As a matter of fact I ran into him just the other day. He's got a terrific new job selling computers at CompuTec, right here in the Centre. It was too bad that faster-than-light computer company he invested in after he made all that money selling my bus yard was so far ahead of its time. He's been through a rough patch these past few years, but I think he's beginning to see the light at the end of the tunnel. Still, just between you and me, I don't think that Molstad woman makes the best sort of companion. She's far too— What's the word, Jane?"

"Needy."

After Rachel had left the Wilkeses, who wrung from her a promise to bring John next time—they thought the world of John— she drove back to the city through the Millpond. First she headed for Smutter Circle, where she got to see Dick, pipe in teeth, knees slightly flexed to examine his shrubbery in preparation for the warmer months ahead, Spot with his dewlaps flat on the grass between his paws, tail going, the house and yard perfect in a way that suggested importation from a rarer, purer, altogether simpler planet, but then Spot bounding high, as for an invisible ball, the leash somehow pulling tight around Dick's knees, Dick's arms flying into the air, his mouth going *Oh, oh, oh!* as he fell.

Rachel did not stop, passed on to 201 Dell Drive, where Leon and Gretchen had their less-than-perfect home. From Sally— who had moved back to the city about the same time as Rachel and become a good friend with a trying habit of passing out before going home—Rachel had heard that Gretchen and Leon were both in therapy with Silver's successor in the Millpond, a practitioner of Implosion Therapy. Individually or as a couple? Willing or unwilling? A good sign or a bad? Who knew? Who except Rachel cared, and then in such a distant, sad way?

There— slowing down now— was the rusted-out old Subaru in the driveway, all the plants gone from the kitchen bay window, that would be Gretchen's killer thumb, weeds in the front lawn, Leon must be off the Millpond, or perhaps more generally demoralized. But of course, really, Rachel had no idea what life was like inside that now weathered-looking rose-coloured townhouse-type two-and-a-half in Contractor Modern. Probably, like life in the

Wilkes condo, pretty ordinary and pretty strange. Like most life, anywhere.

The unfamiliar effect of 201 Dell Drive, its otherness, caused Rachel to realize that the routes the cracks in the foundations were busy tracing had a genuine complexity; so did the paint bubbles and missed bits, dents in the aluminum, lime stains on the brick; and the subtle angles that doors and windows were tilting on, the way two baseboards no longer quite met in their corner; that chalk oatmeal the drywall was here and there dissolving to . . . And she noticed that people had been building weird additions, the trees were filling out and getting so tall already, some houses were looking quite a bit more lived in than others, some more spiffy, on some streets the landscaping and home improvement competitions had veered off in remarkable directions.

I am as imperfect, as particular, as anything else, the Millpond seemed to be saying, and if I am not, then I aspire to be. If I have been a disappointment to you, then remember that all along Time has been erasing my promise. And anyway, hasn't Arcadia Centre been pinned to me unashamed, like a glorious boutonniere? Stanley Jardine understood that I could be the thing itself, can't you?

Sure, Millpond, sure. Just remember it took Time, and the thing about Time, he works with a scythe.

Hey, same to you, sister!

Fifteen minutes later Rachel was heading back to the city on the 303. It was not being free of the Millpond that made her feel this way: half drunk. It was the Millpond reminding her that Harry really had made the return trip to the dump where the phantoms go, and that right now there genuinely was nothing else to do but sing *I Climbed the Rocky Mountains (But I Can't Get Over You)* into the rearview for Clare Elizabeth, who slumped in her carseat and drooled on her hand and saw light and colours and heard the wind and the engine and her mother's song and smelled and felt the warmth of her mother's love and had no thought, no thought at all, of Harry.